Manitoba J Heppingstal

GOD KNOWS
Or Sorbo Grundy

novum pocket

All rights of distribution, including via film, radio, and television, photomechanical reproduction, audio storage media, electronic data storage media, and the reprinting of portions of text, are reserved.

Printed in the European Union on environmentally friendly, chlorine- and acid-free paper.

© 2019 novum publishing

ISBN 978-3-99010-873-4
Cover photo:
Robert309 | Dreamstime.com
Cover design, layout & typesetting:
novum publishing

www.novum-publishing.co.uk

The whole or any part of this work may not be used in any form without the prior written consent of the author.

With the exception of God, all living characters in this book are entirely fictitious and products of the author's imagination.

Copyright©ManitobaJulyHeppingstal2018

CHAPTER 1

Thursday 1ˢᵗ May 2014 – 10.00

"May Day, Kate. May Day. Unfortunately not Mayday, but May Day."

"Finally lost it, Charles? I've seen it coming for quite some time, come to think of it."

"No, it really is May Day – May 1ˢᵗ. And we've had nothing like a Mayday call in the two years we've been doing this job, more's the pity. But isn't it wonderful fun being in a helicopter all day and scoping everything with the video camera. Just why I trained as a doctor for all those years. I guess we could always pretend we were helping Google Earth check their satellite pictures, but somehow I honestly don't think that would wash. Anyway I'd rather be up here than down there at the moment – just take a look at the M26. Five-mile tailbacks in either direction, and we can see the cows all over the carriageway, but the poor drivers can't, and they're going to be stuck there for hours. And there's not a Portaloo in sight – well there wouldn't be on a Motorway I suppose. I wonder what on earth they do if they're really desperate. No, just open fields and I can't see a tree for miles either."

"Charles, they're bulls, not cows. Even a bozo like you should know the difference from only a thousand feet. That's three hundred metres to you. Andy works in feet, but you've probably never heard of them. No, me neither, but I've read about it. Something called decimalisation, but you'd only have been in short pants then, and I wasn't even born."

"OK, bulls then, if you must be so picky. They all look the same to me, but I suppose it might make a bit of a difference to them. Anyhow, we can't get stuck in traffic like that. Go anywhere we please, and snoop on people and places without anyone realising, – nobody takes any notice of an air ambulance any more, not even this one."

"Charles, will you please come down to earth for just one moment. No, you idiot, metaphorically I mean. We can't go anywhere we like, we're stuck with Sorbo, remember? Where he goes, we go, – got it?"

"Yeah, yeah, OK. But I wish he'd go somewhere more exciting, or at least do something a bit different for a change. Let me think. Today's Thursday. Oh yes, Co-op in Borough Green. Bank in Sevenoaks. Not the doctor today, but wait a moment while I check back to 27th March. Bingo, five weeks today. It's haircut day! Wow, – this guy really lives it up. Anyway, should take the weight off his mind for a while."

"Doctor West, you're supposed to leave the corny jokes to me, – they're my speciality. Sometimes it feels like I probably even invented the really cringe-making stuff, and if you start coming out with it as well, between us we'll drive Andy completely bats."

"Well Andy flies. And bats fly. So maybe Andy's a ..."

"Charles, ... please?"

"Sorry, won't do it again. Promise. By the way, did you work out where he got his name? – Sorbo I mean of course, not Andy. No neither did I. Never heard of it before, even as a nickname. Google and Wikipedia were about as useful as a bucket of sand in a desert. All they came up with was 'Sorbo rubber – a very spongy form of rubber'. Grundy's a fairly common surname, but first name Sorbo, – absolutely no idea. However, that's his problem. Ours is to look after him, although what's going to happen to a boring old fogey like him, I can't begin to imagine. Andy, can you take it down a bit? Like to have another shufti at his house. What? Same as butchers or dekko, of course. Didn't they teach you anything at that posh school of yours Kate? Mmm, wouldn't mind living in that. Professional opinion?"

"Old, – probably really old. Georgian style windows don't mean a thing nowadays, but I don't think it's repro, – the brickwork's well weathered and the roof looks like it's genuine Kent peg tiles. Just look at the size of it though. And it's got a really well-designed annexe, maybe thirty or forty years old, but it fits in beautifully. And it's got two or three acres. Dream on Charles, – way out of either of our leagues. Anyway, we're supposed to be looking after him, not valuing his pad. Andy, can you take us back to the High Street please. We've seen enough to make us more than a bit green-eyed. No, I'm joking really. Quite like my flat in Croydon. Very posh part of Croydon I would have you know, big airy rooms, and handy for zillions of shops. And the trains to London, very fast and very frequent, not that I go there much any more. KS found it and organised my moving in, and they pay for everything, so I'm definitely not complaining."

Thursday – 20.05

"There he goes again. Dinner at the Rose and Crown, out of the door at quarter-past eight, turn right, over the High Street, left onto the pavement, twenty-minute walk home. At least then we can hand him over to home security and call it a day. And aren't we the lucky ones for a change. He's a good ten minutes early tonight, probably didn't stay for pudding or something. Andy, you'd better let Control know we'll be heading back in twenty. Thanks. Bit boring, Kate, isn't it? Just baby-sitting an old bloke every day, especially when nothing ever happens. Still, we get very well paid for it, so I suppose somebody knows something we don't, and maybe one day we'll find out just what it is. Night-night, see you both in the morning. Yes, ten-fifteen's fine. He never goes out before eleven, except to the doctor, and I gather he isn't going there tomorrow either."

Friday 2nd May – 10.00

"Hi, Kate. Lovely morning. Looking forward this wonderful new non-event day as much as I am? Right, and like time and tide, this job stops for no man, so we're going to have yet another rootin' tootin' action-packed Bank Holiday weekend, – I don't think. Could be worse though, I suppose. After shopping, he'll be home security's baby until he goes to the pub at six, so we've got the afternoon off. Fancy a visit to Hever Castle? Yes, I'll pay, and even treat you to lunch in the Moat Restaurant. Hang the expense, I'm earning enough and not a lot to spend it on. Great, you're on. Andy, could you drop us off at Biggin at 13:00 and pick us up again at 17:15? Superhero, thanks. OK Kate, let's see Sorbo through the morning's riveting stuff first."

Friday – 13.00

"Cheers, Andy. See you at five-fifteen for the next thrilling episode. Come on Kate, – Hever Castle beckons. It surely does. Didn't you see it waving its big flag at us a couple of minutes before we landed? Doesn't do that for just anybody."

CHAPTER 2

Friday 2nd May, 2014 – 16.00

Professor Hubert Drayton was one of the world's finest neurosurgeons. A modest man outside of working hours, he wouldn't express that opinion himself, but it was generally held by his peers in this elite, if somewhat arcane, profession. In the theatre, he was a different person. Authoritarian and dictatorial, he would not tolerate anything less than perfection, and he was well-known for swearing at the slightest provocation. He had devoted his long career to doing seemingly impossible things with brain and nerve cells that didn't want to perform as they should.

Now, he was looking forward to retirement after many years of hard work. He and Pru were going on a world cruise to celebrate their thirty-fifth wedding anniversary. At last they would make up for the gap years that didn't happen in either of their teens and twenties. Their children had long since flown the nest and had their own lives. Huw was a little disappointed that neither chose to follow him into the medical profession. Mark had once said 'one day you'll be able to poke about in someone's brain and find out exactly what it's thinking. That's scary-weird. Not for me in a million years, thank you very much.' So Mark was now a high-flying and respected banker. Huw wasn't so sure you could actually be both, but he never said that to Mark. No point in starting a family row that could go on forever. Nobody backing down and nobody winning, and it would upset Pru too, as she couldn't, and wouldn't, take sides between her husband and her son. No, Huw decided. Better to hope that Mark didn't do something stupid, or at least didn't get caught for it. Anyhow, it seemed that those guys had ways of looking after each other, even if things did go wrong. Funny, thought Huw, not the same if I mess up.

Jennifer was different. Two years younger than Mark. Academically bright, and hard-working as well. Not a stunning looker, but not unattractive either. Open, generous and highly popular with her contemporaries. The world was her oyster, so why on earth did she choose fashion designing? Some of her mega-bucks creations looked like she had run out of material when she'd only managed to cover about half of some aspiring young actress's body. Others had fabric designs which Huw thought would have looked better on a carpet than on the po-faced, anorexic-looking things who strutted today's catwalks in the name of fashion. Not a popular view with those who considered themselves politically correct, he readily acknowledged, but to them the truth often wasn't. However, Jen was successful in her job, and happy with the way things were turning out. Couldn't really ask for more.

Huw's thoughts turned to the weekend. For a change, the Bank Holiday weekend forecast was warm and sunny right up until Tuesday. Quick cup of tea, – then home before five. Oh, not again! Why does the phone always ring just as the kettle has boiled? "Drayton ... No Archie. In twenty minutes I'm away home. First weekend off in ages. What? ... Archie, I think you'd better come down. Kettle's hot, and I can just about spare another tea bag."

Huw liked working with Archie Prescott. A no-nonsense man like himself, Archie was the CEO of St. George's Hospital, Tooting, in Southwest London. Huw's domain was the Atkinson Morley Wing of the hospital, so Archie was technically Huw's boss, but their relationship had always been one of equals, and much appreciated by Huw.

"White – sorry, milk – one sugar. OK Archie, shoot."

"At two o'clock I got an e-mail from somebody calling themselves 'KS 1419'. No other ID but they did give a postal address of 77b, Whitehall Mews, London, SW1'. Reads 'Patient arriving your helipad 21:15 today. PRIORITY RED 1. Arrange and confirm soonest.' Never heard of KS 1419, so I Googled it and got a load of irrelevant rubbish. Rang my man at the Ministry and got him to check. The address exists alright, – it's an empty office. Couldn't trace KS 1419, so he asked up-line about it and 'Priority Red 1'. He got a very short answer. 'Action immediately as instructed without question. No further information required.' He strongly advised – no, virtually ordered – me to comply, so obviously I agreed. Did a bit more digging before I replied. As you know, our helipad is off limits between 20:00 and 08:00, so I contacted National Air Traffic Services (NATS) Control. Kent, Surrey and Sussex Air Ambulance given special clearance to use it until 23:00 today. Odd thing is, their HQ hadn't been informed when I rang them. Anyway, I e-mailed back to KS 1419 that we would act as requested, and asked for patient information. They replied immediately 'Repeat PRIORITY RED 1. Confirm arrangements. Details follow.'

So there we are, – and here it is." Archie passed Huw a three-page print-out.

"As you see, we must bypass A&E and admit direct to theatre 14, and we must have all staff there exactly as listed – you in the lead, for some reason."

Huw started reading. "Hmmm ... Pete Da Silva. Best dream merchant there is. I'd have him all the time if he wasn't so busy elsewhere. Simon Greenwood. Good old Simon, – top-notch orthopod, although he finds the easy stuff a bit boring. Prefers complex jigsaws and I'll swear he uses Superglue sometimes. Work on a Friday evening? Answer to me? You'll be lucky. And Warwick Hallibury, – Mr. Transplant himself, – but where's he going to find the bits? Matt Pottinger. Loud-mouthed, with an odd sense of what he calls humour. But I wouldn't want to be without him as he's such a damned good Registrar. Sister McCreedy. Highly organised, very precise, and red-hot on discipline. Great asset in any theatre, but don't slip up when she's around. She scares me, Archie. I've heard her tongue-lashing Consultants to their faces. Admittedly she was right, as usual. But in front of the entire theatre? Probably counts swabs instead of sheep when she's trying to get to sleep.

Think I've seen enough, Archie. Don't know some of the juniors, but the rest of them are all the tops, real A-listers. Couldn't have chosen better myself."

"Agreed, Huw.   And, until three this afternoon, every single one of them was rostered for the weekend off from their hospitals.   Difficult to believe, but I didn't get a squeak out of anybody, – except you."

"Not any longer, Archie.   Got me more than a little curious, so count me in.   Must be some patient."

CHAPTER 3

Friday 2nd May 2014 – 17.15

"Take us about ten minutes, Andy? Thought so. Might as well have a quick coffee before we go, – he never leaves home before six. Then, with a bit of luck, he'll be back by eight forty-five and we'll be off by nine. May not be everybody's idea of a Bank Holiday weekend, but at least we'll get some early nights."

20.00

"Shouldn't be long now. Main camera on Andy? Yes, superhero, I know, but procedure's procedure with KS as well, – not just the Royal Air Force. Captain's log stardate minus three zero eight six six six point two one, operation Babysit. Just pretending Kate, helps to fill in the time, and we've got about ten minutes before he moves. Oh, – some old TV programme. Come on Sorbo, don't be late tonight. Yes, here he comes. 20.13, – two minutes early. Out of the side door, turn right, cross over the High … What the? … Andy, quick, camera two on as well please, twenty-second sweep. Take her down to seven hundred feet and hold position."

"Alpha-Kilo-Sierra-Two-Six to Golf-Kilo-Sierra-Zero-Five report status please, over."

"Golf-Kilo-Sierra-Zero-Five clearing Maidstone two zero five five, over."

"Alpha-Two-Six, roger Golf-Zero-Five, thank you, disregard, out."

"Golf-Kilo-Sierra-Zero-Nine to Alpha-Kilo-Sierra-Two-Six, do you read me?, over."

"Alpha-Two-Six, affirmative Golf-Zero-Nine, go ahead, over."

"Golf-Zero-Nine clear in Wrotham. Have you in visual, can I help?, over."

"Alpha-Two-Six, affirmative Golf-Zero-Nine, thank you. RTA outside Rose and Crown pub, Wrotham High Street, soonest. single casualty, acknowledge, over."

"Golf-Zero-Nine, roger Alpha-Two-Six, High Street, single casualty, on the way, e.t.a. four minutes, over."

"Two-Six, roger Zero-Nine. On arrival driver to crowd dispersal, paramedics to casualty and load as soon as safe. West to end of High Street, at left bend turn right onto Kemsing Road, then west nine hundred metres. Field entrance on right adjacent to footpath fingerpost, and opposite first cottage on left. Rendezvous in field GR six-zero-one-zero-five-nine-three-five. Field cropped so get as close as you can. Both rotors active, retract aerial to max. two-point-three metres and avoid tail. Transfer patient soonest. Acknowledge and standby, over."

"Zero-Nine, roger Two-Six. Received and understood. Standing by, out."

"Alpha-Kilo-Sierra-Two-Six to Kilo-Sierra control. Do you read me?, over."

"Kilo-Sierra Control, affirmative Alpha-Two-Six, go ahead, over."

"Alpha-Two-Six, thank you Kilo-Sierra Control. Operation Babysit activated two-zero-one-four hours. Request instructions, over."

"Kilo-Sierra Control, roger Two-Six. Switch to channel four immediate. Inform pilot we will clear NATS. Confirm, over."

"Two-Six, roger Control. Confirm channel four live, pilot instructed, out."

"Andy, I hope you heard that, so consider yourself instructed. Can you put camera three on zoom? I'd like to get anybody in the High Street and the pub patio if possible. When they start loading Sorbo, we'd better move to the RV. Yes, in the field we sussed last week, but you probably heard me telling Zero-Nine. Soon as they transfer Sorbo, Kate and I will be just a little bit busy, so here's what came over channel four. Proceed to St. George's Hospital, Tooting, Southwest London. Helipad on roof, and lift straight down, not to A & E but theatre 14 adjacent. Anyhow that bit's Kate's and my problem, – you wait on the roof as long as it takes. Control said the hospital co-ordinates and flight plan are already loaded into your computer, – yes? Well I'm damned, these guys really are on the ball. Control will clear with NATS, but any problems quote Kilo-Sierra-One-Four-One-Nine, priority Red One. OK folks, time to go. All ready for our guest, Kate? Yeah I know, I know. Procedure, remember?"

"OK Andy, patient's nicely tucked in.   St. George's helipad, here we come."

"Alpha-Two-Six, good work Zero-Nine, thank you. Proceed direct to Biggin Hill hangar, strip off logo, then stand down.   You won't be needed for at least twenty-four hours, but monitor channel six, over."

"Zero-nine, roger Two-Six.   Channel six, wilco and goodnight, out."

21.07

"Here we are already, Kate.   Now let's get him off this rooftop and down to theatre pronto.   Wondering about wheels, but there they are.   Andy, we'll be back as soon as we can get away.   Then it's off to Biggin and go to ground."

21.15

"Good evening sir, – Charles West, – Kent, Surrey and Sussex Air Ambulance."

"Good evening, I'm Professor Drayton.   Who've you got for us?"

"Enough to ruin my weekend off, I bet."   "And mine." "Me too."

"Shut it Matt, – and the rest of you.   Let me hear these people."

"Thank you, sir. White Caucasian male. Er ... no ID, or known next of kin. No spring chicken, – guess late sixties. Pedestrian casualty of high-speed hit and run at 20:14, – say one hour ago. We picked him up from our road crew at 20:49. Left side severe external injuries. Odds-on he's got internals, but unable to assess extent. Likewise head, apart from the obvious contusion. When we got him we reckoned GCS, (Glasgow Coma Scale), at 9, but now less than 8. Systolic 92 and slipping. Couldn't get an accurate diastolic. Pulse 105. Temperature 39.6. IV insertion right arm, – 2.5 mg diamorphine at 20:56 – then saline until now."

"Thank you. We'll take him from here. Paperwork on the desk on your way out, please. Goodnight."

"Can't somebody please make the GCS 2.9, so we can all go home after all?"

"You can apologise for that later, Pottinger, – meanwhile just get on with it. And will someone turn off that bloody noise. Yes, I'm sure some people might call it music, but this is not a bloody concert hall, nor am I running an effing democracy, so turn it off. Now!

Sister, ... blood? Yes, I suppose I really should have known, but thank you all the same.

Dr. Da Silva, when you're ready."

"Anytime you like, professor. He wouldn't have felt a thing anyway, even if you'd started before me."

"For you, sir." Sister McCreedy handed him the phone. 'NUMBER WITHHELD'

"Drayton ... Yes, but ... Understood, sir. Yes we will. Thank you, sir. Goodnight, sir."

Professor Hubert Drayton didn't often call anyone 'sir'. Couldn't remember the last time he had. Something compelling about the voice, though. Vaguely familiar, but he couldn't put a finger on it. Anyway, what was said was far more important at the moment.

"Everyone listen for a minute. As you've probably gathered, tonight we and this theatre are not part of St. George's normal surgical operations. By request, we're all here for just this one patient. What we'd all been expecting, since early this afternoon, was a VIP. However, what we've actually got is a John Doe, casualty of an RTA only one hour ago. Except that this is not really a John Doe. Somebody knows exactly who he is, and his survival is crucially important to them. We've been told to pull out all the stops, no matter what. No letting go, no matter how hopeless it seems, or however long it takes. And, – and I've not heard it put quite this way before, so I quote – 'If necessary, tissue matches are available as required'. Right then, – questions later – now let's move it."

CHAPTER 4

Friday 2ⁿᵈ May 2014 – 21.35

"OK Kate, let's get back up to the chopper and out of here as soon as. I so nearly blew it then – Sorbo's name was on the tip of my tongue and I only just stopped myself with an – er … no ID, which I hope wasn't noticed."

"Was by me of course, but then I know. Anyway, why aren't we supposed to know who he is?"

"No idea Kate, – I don't make the rules, just follow the orders."

"And you didn't tell them we're both doctors."

"No. Service training, – never give information unless it's 'need to know' and this wasn't. I hope Andy hasn't dozed off as usual when he's shut the engines. We've got to get away before they look at the paperwork."

"Yeah, I was going to ask, – what did you put in the envelope?"

"Four blank sheets of paper. Hope they're not quick readers! Wake up, Andy, and out of here fast as you can, or even faster. Back to Biggin Hill and straight into the hangar – the ground ambulance should already be there – then lights off, lock up, and we all disappear pronto and lie low for a couple of days. Then they'll want you to take the chopper somewhere for re-painting. They'll let you know, but it won't be Biggin – too many eyes. Even after we covered up the KSS logo, it's been difficult to get it serviced there, – I think I mean here, as here we are. Thanks Andy, – see you.   Yes I'll call, – bye."

"Couple of days off, Kate. Know what I'd like to do?"

"Yes Charles. After two years working as close as we are, I know you perfectly … almost."

"Almost?"

"Yes, almost. You've never told me what this job is really about, how you got it, or why you picked me as your partner, – if you did."

"Yes, I did. And I'm glad I did. With my record, I never thought I'd choose the right woman for anything, but I was wrong – again. You're really special."

"Get off those knees and stop being such a creep. Where're we going now?"

"Your car's round the back, right? We'll leave it there for now and take mine – it's less noticeable. There's a great late-night takeaway in Westerham – excellent Indo-Chinese and veggies too – and we can go back to my place in New Addington. It's a bit of a tip, as Mo still hasn't taken the rest of her stuff yet, but it's comfortable enough and I've got some mineral water in the fridge. Yeah, OK, I do have some wine as well, but I'm no expert so it's probably plonk to a lady of your refined tastes. Ow – that hurt. Playful? Is that what you call it? What's it like when you're not being playful, I ask myself? You're right though, I owe you, and I'll tell you everything I know in the morning – if I've still got enough energy."

"Doctor West, you're being extremely crude and very presumptuous.   I happen to know that you have two bedrooms, so we'll use two bedrooms. No, not one after the other, you chancer. Separately. Me here, you there – capisci? Eccelente. That's all the Spanish I know, so come on then, let's go. What d'you mean it's not Spanish?"

Saturday 3rd May 2014 – 07.30

"Morning, Kate. Sleep well?"

"Yeah, thanks. Really nice meal – must go there again. Yes, I mean both of us. Last night I wasn't being prim, proper, or stand-offish, or whatever you like to call it – I really wanted to – but I won't do first nights, not even with a self-confessed useless woman-chooser like you. Ouch, – I suppose you'd call that playful too. Wonder what you're like when you're aroused. On second thoughts, forget I said that."

"Coffee in the kitchen. No room service I'm afraid, – must be the maid's weekend off. Plenty of towels in the bathroom. We can talk whenever you're ready. Apart from sorting out something to eat for later we've got all day, and it's probably going to take me most of it to tell you even the little I know. Anything to eat?"

"No, just coffee's fine for me thanks. Don't usually have much for breakfast anyway. Now you can start by telling me – how did Dr. Katharine Alice Gurley get involved with Dr. Charles ... have you got a middle name? ... thanks, Dr. Charles Simon West, in the first place? And we've got plenty of time, so don't leave anything out – not even the women. No, we haven't got that much time – just the important ones."

"OK. Fairly average sort of family. One older brother and a younger sister. Brought up in a three-bedroom semi on the outskirts of Swindon. When I was about ten my parents had the loft converted, so we could each have our own rooms. My father worked for a coach hire company just outside town and eventually became a supervisor. Mum worked on the checkouts at the local Co-op, and sometimes helped out at the cattery down the road. Didn't pay as much as the Co-op, but it was a bit of extra money and she really loves cats anyway. Sorry, – 1969, 22nd September. Isn't it rude to ask a gentleman's age, or is it the other way round? Yes, I know I'm getting on a bit, but there's still time for a bloke my age to have kids. I'm never going to get through this story if you keep interrupting. Where was I? Local primary school then I was lucky enough to get into Ridgeway Comprehensive. Not much good at games, but OK at schoolwork. Seven respectable O-levels, then Biology, Physics and Chemistry at A level. Only got two As and a C, but the Gods must have been on my side as, to everyone's amazement, Bristol Uni accepted my application to their Medical School. Always wanted to be a doctor but my parents couldn't really afford it, so as soon as I was at Bristol I applied to the Royal Army Medical Corps for a Medical Scholarship. Lucky again. Five years, and some Sandhurst, later I became a Captain MO. Thoroughly enjoyed myself to start with – completely different from my previous ideas of Army life – but then I started wanting a bit more action. My CO 'volunteered' me for special training. As I said, I wasn't much use at sport, but I've always been very fit and I've got a lot of stamina – mentally as well. Also done a quite a bit of orienteering and hill-walking in Scotland

and Snowdonia. Boy, did I need it. Firstly, I'd done no weapons training and that was an eye-opener, although great fun while I learnt a lot – particularly about safety, strange as that might sound. Then on to the course proper. Things like running and swimming were no great problem, but the rest almost defies description. Did things I didn't think a human body could – even with my medical training. And, near the end – well, let's just say I hope I never get grilled like that in real life. I think only eight or nine of us passed the course, and that's out of hundreds. Mind you, I was quietly chuffed about the loud-mouthed 'done-it-alls' who started with us. None of them got within a million miles of finishing.

After Hereford, I went here, there and everywhere. Mostly places you've read about in the papers, but quite a few you haven't. Bet you can't guess who was the Medic in our team, but I also learnt a bit about aerial support – quite useful recently. The postings were usually pretty gutsy, but by and large I enjoyed doing what we all knew was a valuable job, and I got on well with the guys I worked with. Then, towards the end of 2011, something very odd happened. I was brought back to England, accused of communicating with the enemy, court-martialled and cashiered. Just like that. No appeal allowed. Out of a job, lost my pension, nothing to do and nowhere to go. And all on a completely trumped-up charge. I was still married to Mo – or at least I thought I was – but I'll tell you about that later. And we still had this rented place here in New Addington.

After Christmas, I started giving some serious thought about what to do next. Checked the bank, to see if I could still afford to live, and got a bit of a surprise. There had been a transfer to my account of twenty thousand pounds and two further payments, on the 1st of December and 1st January, of exactly the same amount as my previous Army pay. The bank said they couldn't identify the sender of any of the transfers, so I was more than a little confused. The next day I got a text, which read 'Interview 77b Whitehall Mews London SW1 Tuesday 7th Feb 09:00 Confirm'. Very puzzled and more than a little suspicious, but I confirmed and went. Interview was by two men and a woman. No names. They said they were looking for doctors who were fit and active and used to working in difficult, and sometimes dangerous, situations. Recent work in overseas trouble spots was preferable. Honesty, integrity, loyalty and utter obedience to orders was absolutely essential, as was a genuine love of all mankind in general, regardless of race, religion or circumstance. Great so far, except for one small snag. But before I could mention it, they told me all about my discharge, and that they knew my version of events was true. They also said that they had made the bank transfers, and that unless I wanted out, as far as they were concerned I was already working for them. Whatever my decision, the money already in my account was mine to keep.

The job sounded simple enough. I would be part of one of a number of teams assigned to look after just one man, and to do whatever was necessary to keep him alive. No name given then, but now we know him as Sorbo Grundy, not that it means anything to me. The teams would work in shifts, and each team would comprise one male and one female doctor, a pilot and an Air Ambulance. There would be ground teams the same, except with a driver and a 4WD vehicle. Apart from necessary minor transgressions, at no time would our teams be asked, or permitted, to do anything contrary to national or international law. The teams would never normally meet, and there would be no communication between them and/or HQ, except by pre-programmed secure monitored radio transmission. What did I think? Even though I had a funny feeling that I'd been set up, I was quite intrigued and excited by the whole thing, so I said yes. They thanked me and said I'd made the right decision, then they showed me six photographs and asked me to select a partner. All of the women were quite attractive, but I had no hesitation in choosing you. Two years later I know I was absolutely right – makes a nice change for me."

"I've got news for you Doctor 'useless-at-choosing-women' West. You didn't pick me – I chose you!"

"What? ... Impossible ... I picked you out of six photographs."

"Yes, all pictures of me! I was asked to go to interview too, but on Monday 6th, the day before you. Two women and one man, but otherwise the same story as you. I jumped at the chance straightaway. They offered me six photographs, all of different men, but I only had to look at the first one. Actually, I really mean only the first pair of eyes. Then they told me you would have to pick one of six women, but I said I wasn't having that. They'd already told me enough about you that I wasn't taking any chances on you messing up yet again, so we arranged that I was photographed six times with different clothes, hairstyles, make-up, camera angles and lighting. Actually, true to form, you chose probably the worst picture ever taken of me, but I didn't care – and over the last two years you've proved time and again that I made the right decision – for both of us. Left to your own devices, a bozo like you would still be lost in the fog without a compass, and all your super training wouldn't get you out of it.

Is that everything Charles, – apart from the juicy bits of course? Seems to me you don't know much more than I do, but I'd better tell you my side of the story, so we're on the same wavelength. Yes, I know, but I'll tell you anyway. Now's the time to clear the air before phase 2 starts. They haven't told you yet? In that case they're bound to get in touch before the weekend's out – but for now I'm half a one up on you.

I was born …   no, I'm not going to tell you yet – you can guess later …   but I was quite young. Stop that right now or I won't tell you the story and I'll go home … I can get a cab. No, OK. I was born in Scotland and brought up in a lovely old house near Kilmarnock. Was a farmhouse once. Most of the land had been sold off but we still had about an acre for the garden and a small paddock. My parents are reasonably well off. Daddy works for a multi-national civil engineering company. Although he's about to retire soon, he still travels all over the world, but he's never happier anywhere than at home. He'd had a fairly tough upbringing in Glasgow, so as soon as he was earning enough he bought a house. The first one was quite small, but he did well and then bought the present place. Daddy calls it Gurley Hall, and we all humour him, but it's not half as grand as it sounds.

Mummy qualified as an accountant, and she's worked from her office at home ever since we were born. That's my twin sisters and me. They're two years older. Yes, you probably would, but you wouldn't get very far. They know me well, and they're both very fond of life. Anyway, the twins went to our local comprehensive which was excellent, but when it came to my turn, I was sent to a boarding school in Kent. Oh, – because mummy had a sister who lived near there and she thought that was a good idea, and because ever since I was eight or nine I had been dead set on being a doctor. Good as it is, they didn't think the local school would get me enough SQA Highers. I wasn't too keen at first, but I worked hard and got a load of A*s and As at GCSE, and then four A-levels. No, I did get two A*s, but the others were only As. Then I went to Cardiff University Medical School ... don't keep interrupting – daddy knew somebody there who said it was one of the best. Got my MBBS there, then spent two years at John Radcliffe in Oxford, followed by four at Glasgow Royal Infirmary. That was nice, as I could live at home then – it's only a forty-minute drive. In 2008, I decided to broaden my horizons, so I joined Medicins Sans Frontieres. I'd done French and Italian at GCSE, and that was just enough to get me posted to Africa. Quite difficult and sometimes dangerous work, but really rewarding when you can actually see what you have helped to do to make people's lives better. But then, in November 2011, some drugs went missing and I was accused. Absolute rubbish it was, but I was brought back to England and given the boot by UK Head Office.

My partner – yes, since you dare ask, it was a bloke – took their side, so it was 'goodbye Ray' a bit faster than the speed of light. So you see, you're not the only one who makes mistakes, – I just make fewer of them, as in one so far, and no more to come. Anyway, I paid a month's notice on the flat in Battersea, and took my stuff home to poor old mummy and daddy in Kilmarnock. Actually they were delighted to have me home again, but very upset for me, as they couldn't believe I was guilty. We had a lovely family Christmas and New Year, with my sisters and their husbands and children. They all live quite near mummy and daddy, and it was great us all being together again for the first time in ages.

End of January coming up, and I was still trying to work out what to do, when I got an e-mail from someone called KS1419. Like you, I didn't know who they were or how they got my address. E-mail read 'Interview 77b Whitehall Mews London SW1 Monday 6th February 09:00 Confirm.' Thought I'd take a chance it wasn't some kind of practical joke, so I e-mailed and confirmed. Went online to book my ticket, and I thought I'd better check my bank balance. You're interrupting again, but yes – twenty thousand pound credit, plus two transfers of exactly the amount of my previous MSF salary. I phoned a real person at the bank – they've still got a few you know – but they couldn't tell me who initiated the payments. More than a bit dazed, I went to London on 6th February. The rest you know. Oh yes – nearly forgot the other bit. Got a text yesterday afternoon. Hang on, I'll get it back. Reads 'Phase 1 completion today 22:00. Free time 4 days. Phase 2 report SW1 Wednesday 7th 08:00 Confirm.' Haven't done that yet. What d'you think? Oh, – and you haven't had anything at all?"

"Haven't had my mobile on for days – been using the secure RT set. Wait up. Yeah, same as yours, sent yesterday 14:00. Don't know about you, but I'm all for going on. If Sorbo, or whoever he actually is does pull through, I want to be around. This job's really got to me and, judging by the amount of time and money being spent, it's got to more than a few other people as well. Good, I hoped I knew you'd say that. I'll text back for both of us. Then we'd better start working out exactly what we do and don't know, and how we got to here. Seems to me that someone planned this well before we both got fired. And something Andy said makes me think he's in the same boat. He was an RAF Search and Rescue pilot, you know, and somebody did the dirty on him about the same time as both of us. All coincidence? Something tells me I don't really think so."

"Charles, – haven't you forgotten something? Yes, ... them."

"Not much to tell, really. No, honestly. I've always liked female company, but I've never handled relationships with them very well. If I didn't fancy what I saw, I just didn't bother with them – rather have another drink with the boys. When I did see what I liked, I used to get so immediately heavy-handed and intense that they'd run a mile, or more accurately, a marathon. Didn't help that most of my friends were much better looking than me, and good at sport and stuff, and all the girls I wanted were all over them instead. Mostly at parties and things, I was the wallflower who finished up in the kitchen. I was quite adept at serving drinks and food, and at least I got the chance to talk to some of the women for a minute or two. Same all the way through med school, so I concentrated on studying – probably a good thing actually, but it didn't seem so at the time. Sure, I had some one-night stands, and sometimes they lasted a bit longer, but they all ended one way or another, mostly in disaster. Trouble was I was always looking for the right one – you know, sort of soulmate, I suppose – but in the real world they don't seem to come along that often. Didn't occur to me then that if I met all three and a half billion women in the world, I'd still look for someone better.

Things seemed to improve a bit when I was commissioned. Never ceased to amaze me that a doctor in a uniform could be such a magnet. But then I got a reputation for always being seen with a different girl, and people always assumed – well, you know. None of them was right for me though. Every time we got nearly close, they either upped and went, or I found out they had a different agenda – not what was right for both of us, but what they thought was right for them. That didn't chime with my stupid utopian ideas. In a nutshell, it's that you both commit one hundred and ten percent to giving, not just to each other, but above that, to what is best for the partnership. Look – if you can do things faster than the speed of light, I can definitely do things better than one hundred percent.

Please may I continue? Thank you. I had another teeny-weeny little problem. My utopian partnership would never do something for its own benefit, if that knowingly disadvantaged other people. So I'd got to thirty-eight, and I was home on a long leave, when I met Mo – Maureen, that is. She seemed a bit, no a lot, more than alright. Thirty-three years old, well-presented, intelligent and sociable. PR consultant in London. Quite pretty to look at usually, but stunningly beautiful the time she came in from the pouring rain all soaking wet and stragglyhaired. Met her family and they must have been OK, as they even seemed to like me. We got on well, and after a little while she moved in here. I'd already rented this place as a base for when I was home on leave, and it was convenient for her. She could get the tramlink to East Croydon, and be at work in London much quicker than from her parents' place near Guildford. She'd moved back with them after a fairly torrid four years with Julian. I met him a few times. Nice chap on the surface, but he'd get really aggressive after a few scotches, and a few too many doubles is what he'd have most evenings. So I didn't blame her for ditching him.

As you'd imagine, I was back and forth on postings, but everything went well all the times we had together, and I thought this was probably what I should settle for. We got married five years ago. Thought about a family, but hadn't quite got round to it, what with thinking about careers, and buying a house and things. Then, in December 2011, everything blew up. Just like your Ray, Mo didn't believe me either. Sorry, but that was it for me. One of the few things I absolutely cannot stand is lack of trust, and I told her so, although she should already have known. She moved out in January two years ago, but to a bloke's place, not back to her parents. Don't know if anything had been going on before and my problems were just an excuse, but it doesn't matter now. I was fond of her once, and I still wish her well, but I wish even more, after two years, that she would take the rest of her stuff away. That's about it. Let's have a drink. No, it doesn't have to be mineral water, but not double scotches either. No, you, not me – I don't touch spirits. While you've been studying our not quite extensive wine list, I've been thinking. Yes, thinking. I know, terrible habit of mine, but somehow it's become addictive. Thirty-five – right?"

"No, naughty of me, I didn't mention the gap year – usually try to forget about it. Thirty-six. 5th March 1978. You're quite a good cook really, for a man I mean. Thought we'd probably have clay-baked hedgehog or stuffed rat or something like that. No, I knew it wasn't going to be smoked rattlesnake – I'd already looked in the freezer."

"Actually, we do eat proper food sometimes, Doctor Gurley, – and I've never had smoked rattlesnake, only pit viper and cobra. Seriously though, what do we know? Not a lot, is it? Sorbo is in St. George's, he's in a hell of a mess, and frankly I wouldn't give much for his chances. But KS1419, whoever they are, or it is, want us to carry on working for them. So they obviously think he's going to recover. From what we've seen so far, they're amazingly well organised and don't seem to leave much to chance. For instance, how did they know, at two on Friday afternoon, what was going to happen on Friday evening. So, let's assume Sorbo does pull through. What's our job going to be then? What's Phase 2? Roll on, Wednesday. London at 08:00? Never mind the body – they say starting early in the morning is good for the soul. Who're they? I don't know – just them."

CHAPTER 5

Friday 2nd May 2014 – 21.30

The light. It's so light, – like a beautiful sunlit day. But it can't be sunlight – not as strong and harsh as sunlight. And no shadows? And the light's more like a very pale amber, and glowing with a sort of warm luminescence. And it seems to be coming from everywhere and nowhere, and all at the same time. Must be dreaming.

"Welcome, Sorbo. Almost spot on time, I'm not surprised to say, but then we always do our best for special visitors, although we don't actually get very many. In fact, you are only the third real guest we've had in over four billion years, – all the others are here in transit, usually just for a millisecond or less."

"Where am I?"

"Where am I? That's a very human question Sorbo, and one that we are asked at least a million times every week, over fifty million times a year. But only by the souls from planet Earth. Never yet from a soul from any of the other planets anywhere in the Universe. So 'where am I?' is the normal question from souls who have just left Earth and for the moment I'll give you the normal answer. You are at what humans call the pearly gates or the entrance to heaven, or something like that. But there isn't any place such as heaven or hell in the way that most humans think of it, so you are actually at the screening and processing centre, from where we send all souls to their next appropriate destination. I'll tell you more about that later, but before I explain anything else, please tell me what you remember about the earlier part of this evening. I say earlier this evening, because on Earth it is still Friday evening in England – 9.31 p.m. to be precise."

"I had dinner at my local pub and I had just started to walk home, as usual shortly after eight. I'd crossed the High Street on to the opposite pavement, when a big black car came towards me out of nowhere. It was going so fast I didn't have time to get out of the way. I think I remember a bang, but nothing else at all until I woke up here."

"Nothing else at all? Excellent, that's just how it was planned. Yes, – it had to be planned. We needed you here for nearly a week, and that was our only option. When I say 'you', I mean your soul, or your spirit, or psyche. After the seven days, you may choose whether you wish to be reunited with your body on Earth, or let us decide where you should go next. I'm being a little unfair now, because we almost certainly know which choice you will make. Of course it is just possible that we may have miscalculated, but that would be highly unusual. In a while I'll go back a little bit, not to the beginning of the Universe because the Universe didn't have a beginning. So we'll start with the creation of your solar system which, you will be pleased to know, really did happen. And we need you to remember everything you learn here, exactly as I explain it in every detail, and with no alterations or omissions. Highly important, as you could hardly wake up in St. George's next Friday, with pen and paper in your hand, and say that you'd been taking notes for the whole week. Sorry, yes. After the collision, your seriously injured body was taken by road and air ambulances to St. George's Hospital, Tooting, in South West London, and it reached one of their operating theatres at 9.15 p.m. – seventeen minutes ago now. We extracted you, your soul that is, at 9.30 and naturally you came here, as all souls do initially. I'll have to explain that too, and you'll begin to understand why we need nearly a week for this. Only nearly a week, as if you choose to go back to Earth you'll wake up in St. George's next Friday at 3.30 p.m., exactly one hundred and sixty-two hours after you arrived here. And we have a very great deal of work to do in that very short time. So we'll start straight away and finish just about a minute before you return.

No, – we won't have any need to stop. Although human bodies must rest and sleep, souls and Gods do not. Actually cannot, as it is deliberately written out of our programmes. Yes. Everything in the Universe is programmed, although all souls have a certain degree of free will. When souls are in physical life forms, the amount of this free will is usually, but not always, approximately proportional to the complexity of the life form. Again, I'll tell you more later, – that's something I'll have to say a lot on this visit, – but for the moment I'll just talk about body and soul. That is, after I've explained what I'm going to say about you and the human race. During your visit here I'll be referring quite a bit to you. Some of the time I will be talking about you as a person, but mostly I'll be referring to all of humankind on planet

Earth.   No, don't worry, it will be quite obvious which I mean as we talk about it.

Anyway, I'll get back to body and soul.   All living creatures, even the most primitive ones, have souls.   They don't exist in what you would call a material sense, but in a highly complex electro-magnetic form, – a sort of invisible aura is not a bad description, if that helps.   In human terms, they can't be detected or measured, which is why many humans deny the very existence of their own souls.   For something to be real for them, they have to be able to see, hear, taste, smell or touch it.   In other words they need physical proof, and if they can't get this proof then they refuse to believe that it exists.   They will eventually realise that they do have a soul which is separate from their human body, but this may be a long time after their short existence on Earth.   Anyway, because the soul can't be measured by humans, the team at St. George's didn't notice when we took you on short-term loan and, of course, they won't notice when we return you either.   They're about the best medical team on Earth, by the way, as we couldn't take any chances.

To continue, on all planets which have life forms, the body and soul initially co-exist as one unit.   On physical death, the soul leaves the body and comes here for processing and onward transmission.   Usually, we have already determined its next destination, but we have some discretion and we can allow appeals for genuinely extenuating circumstances, although this doesn't happen very often.   We are governed by Universal Law, in no way to be confused with the laws which have been devised by the life forms on their respective planets, – Earth of course, in your case.   So, on physical death, the soul and body are separated. The soul comes here and the body, having performed its function, is disposed of as desired.

Incidentally, despite the almost countless different rules and rituals devised and observed by cultures, religions and races on Earth and sometimes in the name of God, God has absolutely no preference regarding when, where, or how the Earthly bodily remains are disposed of. After death, the human body has fulfilled its function and therefore becomes redundant. At that time, God's responsibility is only to re-direct the soul to its next appropriate destination. Humans should deal with the body as they desire, but they should not claim that their funeral traditions are a requirement or wish of God, or ever have been. It is very common for people to say that they act in a particular way about all sorts of things, because it is a part of their religious belief. And it is also very common for religions and their leaders to claim that this or that religious custom or tradition is a wish or order or commandment of God. Invariably they are wrong. Such a tradition is usually rooted in their culture and only adopted by their religion as one of the ways of distinguishing them from other systems of beliefs. Throughout the whole of your visit here I will also be telling you about some of the things which humans have done, and in many cases still do, in the mistaken belief that they are God's commands and therefore a part of their religion. As you will learn, God does not make commands. And that is something else which I will be repeating many times while you are here. God does not make commands. God gives guidance. And God's guidance is only in matters where humans actually need it. Of course that includes spiritual questions, such as the reasons for Earthly existence and the soul's progress throughout the Universe, but more importantly guidance as to what is right or wrong, what should or shouldn't be a crime in societies and nations, and what is or isn't a sin. Yes Sorbo, – as you will learn, there is a big difference.

Although it was understandable in early human history, it has always been wrong, and indeed a sin, for humans to claim God's authority in any matter on which God has not given guidance. We will talk quite a bit about all of this while you're here, but not in any particular order, as there is no such thing as a list of God's orders or commandments. No Sorbo, – not one, not ten and not more than a thousand. None at all. God's guidance as to how the soul should act, yes, – God's commands, none.

But I'll get back to funeral traditions and ceremonies. The only guidance which God has given regarding the disposal of an Earthly body once the soul has left, is that it should be done in a respectful and civilised way. However Sorbo, this doesn't apply to you at the moment, as although your body is very seriously injured, it will recover rapidly and if you so choose you will be reunited with it as soon as we have finished our discussions. And as I said, subject to your decision that will be next Friday afternoon at exactly 3.30 p.m. I'd better explain ... We needed to separate your soul from your body, temporarily on this occasion, and bring it here for a short explanation of some of God's guidance which, if you choose to help us, you will be able to take back to Earth. This temporary and reversible separation is a very complex, precise, and indeed highly unusual procedure, and in all of Earth's history there have been only two previous occasions. No, there's no point in trying to guess, because neither of them is recorded in any of your history books. However they are quite important, so if we have the time I will tell you about them before you make your decision, but for the moment I'm going to explain how we brought your soul here.

Essentially, the body must undergo a very severe trauma which would normally lead to death, not quite immediately, but within a few hours. However, if the patient is treated extremely rapidly, there is a short window in which the soul can be temporarily separated from the body without death becoming inevitable. This requires a highly skilled medical team to stabilise all vital signs very quickly indeed, as the window on Earth is only open for a maximum of about ninety minutes after the trauma. In your case, as a cushion to allow for human error, we aimed at getting you to St. George's in sixty minutes, where the medical team was already waiting. Your 'accident' occurred at 8.14 p.m., you were received by them at 9.15, and they acted immediately. And, as I said, we 'borrowed' your soul at 9.30.

On Earth everything is going as planned and the surgeons will be operating on your body throughout tonight and half of tomorrow. Amongst other procedures, you will need a total replacement for your badly damaged left hip. They will also give you a liver transplant. All organs conceivably required by you have previously been tissue-matched and are waiting at St. George's, but only a liver will be needed. No, – we could not allow those not used for you to be wasted, so they have already been allocated to various other London hospitals, where they have patients waiting on standby. By the way, we do apologise in advance for the fact that when you wake up your body will inevitably feel a little uncomfortable for a while. However, this will wear off much more quickly than the doctors could imagine and you will make a full recovery in no time at all.

Talking about time, I will explain that too in more detail later on, but first I would like you to look at this recording taken by the air ambulance. You've heard stories about people facing near-death situations, who felt that they could see everything from a sort of remote out-of-body perspective. Well, that sort of experience comes from multiple sensory perceptions giving signals which arrive at the brain virtually simultaneously, and cause confused sequencing and disorientation. What I'm going to show you happened over an hour ago, so you will understand that this is altogether different.

As you can see, the road from left to right in the middle of the picture is Wrotham High Street, and that's the Rose and Crown pub, at the junction with St. Mary's Road. Time is 8.13 p.m. That's you leaving the pub and crossing the High Street on to the fairly narrow pavement opposite. Now watch closely. From the left, the black car is now mounting the pavement and coming straight towards you at just over 60 miles per hour. You have no chance to get out of the way, and it hits you, throwing you into the air. You land back on the road. The car speeds off to the right. As you know, it's a dry but cool evening so the pub's patio heaters are on and it's quite busy out there, and six – no, seven – people come across the road to help you. One of them realises that you are very badly injured and quite rightly stops the others from trying to move you. You can see him trying to keep them back. 8.23, – and now look top right. You'll see the road ambulance just starting to move – blue lights flashing. No sirens, I'm afraid, – the helicopter engines drowned them out. The ambulance arrives in the High Street and three people get out. The driver moves the crowd back, and the two paramedics, – actually they're both highly-skilled doctors, – start to examine you. Sorry that's the end of the video, as the helicopter has to move to the rendezvous in a field off the Kemsing Road. The ambulance arrives there, and they transfer you to the helicopter which whisks you off to St. George's.

Why there? You do like detail, Sorbo, don't you? No, don't answer that, I know what you are thinking anyway. Why? – because we needed the best. You, – or rather your body, – would, and does, have a head injury, so we chose one of Earth's leading neurosurgeons, – Professor Hubert Drayton. His Atkinson Morley Wing is part of St. George's Hospital. St. George's has a newly-opened helipad and being in Southwest London, Tooting is a very short helicopter flight from Wrotham. We wouldn't disrupt any normal hospital activities, so we arranged a private hire of an operating theatre which would not otherwise be used tonight or tomorrow, so we chose St. George's theatre 14. And we arranged for a top anaesthetist, top orthopaedic surgeon for the fractures, and top transplant specialist. And, as I said, all of your organs had already been fully tissue-matched. Yes, we know that you've been quite surprised about just how many different clinical tests you've had recently, but now you can understand why.

Before I leave the 'accident', you may like to read this report in next Thursday's **'KENTISH CLARION'**.

'HIT AND RUN NO ACCIDENT', say eyewitnesses.

'At least five people who saw last Friday's hit and run accident in Wrotham High Street claim that the victim seemed to be deliberately targeted. The vehicle involved was a black Mercedes saloon, travelling about 60–70 mph, which mounted the pavement and hit the elderly pedestrian who was walking alone. No description of the driver was possible as the car had tinted windows, but three people gave Kent Police the same Registration Number. DVLA records show it as a 1954 grey Ferguson TE20 agricultural tractor, which is currently notified as 'off road'. Kent Police are continuing their investigations.'

And here's the **'WEST KENT GAZETTE'**, also from next Thursday.

'HIT AND RUN MYSTERY DEEPENS'

'Following a 'hit and run' incident in Wrotham last Friday, an ambulance was on the scene within a few minutes, although none of the witnesses interviewed had called the emergency services. The elderly casualty was taken to a nearby field and transferred to a waiting Air Ambulance. Kent Police have identified the victim, but are withholding his name until next of kin can be contacted. **This case is shrouded in mystery.** We contacted South East Coast Ambulance Service (SECam) to find out how they got both ambulances to the scene so quickly. They responded that no call had been received about any incident in Wrotham last Friday, and that at no time that evening had any of their units been deployed there. Wrotham resident 19-year old Andy Cox, a keen plane spotter, said that the Air Ambulance had a Kent, Surrey and Sussex (KSS) logo and it was a new type Bell 429, – the first time he had seen one. He added that the roadside vehicle was a Nissan Patrol 4WD in SECam livery.

Neither of these types is currently in KSS or SECam's fleets. St. George's Hospital, Tooting, in Southwest London, confirmed that a patient was admitted by Air Ambulance on Friday evening but declined to comment further. Our investigations continue.'

"Do you mean ...?"

"Yes, Sorbo. Everything that has happened to you tonight has been meticulously planned and executed. Not by God, as we can't physically affect life on Earth, but by people who we call kindred spirits. I will explain all about kindred spirits when I get round to it, but for simplicity's sake at the moment, just think of them as like-minded people who are concerned about life on Earth, and who pray to God for help and guidance. The only variable was that we weren't sure exactly when human behaviour would reach the point when intercession would actually become necessary. We decided it was now, so we advised kindred spirits, and they activated their plan immediately. And your short visit here is the result. By the way, you've obviously noticed recently that there seemed to be a lot of helicopters in your part of the world."

"Yes, I suppose I have. I assumed it was training flights from Biggin Hill."

"That's what we expected people to think. In fact, we have been watching over you very closely for a little more than two years now. All of your outdoor footwear has been fitted with nano-transponders, virtually undetectable by eye or touch, but reflective to our helicopters, which are liveried as air ambulances. We took the calculated risk that you wouldn't go out barefooted, and I'm pleased to say you didn't let us down. Don't look so surprised, – even God is allowed a little humour occasionally, – but I digress.

Both ground and air ambulances have been on hand at all times. They are crewed by the best pilots and drivers, and all of the paramedics are highly-trained doctors. And apart from one exception, all of the operatives are kindred spirits. Yes, – kindred spirits again. You realised many years ago that there must be billions of decent people all over the world who think about life in much the same way as you do, but you didn't think of them as kindred spirits, – just the silent majority who took whatever life served up to them. But they are kindred spirits, and their silent majority needs to find a voice before humanity continues too much further on its present course towards catastrophe. And deletion of your solar system, which would be the inevitable consequence.

I will tell you more about kindred spirits, but first I'll deal with the one exception I mentioned. He was the driver of the black Mercedes. It was crucial to the plan that you were very seriously hurt, specifically left-sided limb fractures, internal organ damage, and head injury, all added together to achieve the critical degree of trauma, as nothing less would allow temporary separation of your soul from your body. That initially gave the team on Earth a problem, as they couldn't find anyone in Europe sufficiently skilled to do the job without taking the risk of you being killed instantly. Then, as we do, we gave them an inspiration. Hollywood film studios in California, USA. They recruited Hollywood's best stunt driver and briefed him as to exactly what they needed him to do to make the 'movie' he was going to be a part of. He practised a lot with dummies, and on the night his performance was almost immaculate. Actually, he is a kindred spirit, but he has been so busy trying to be perfect at his job that he hasn't yet got round to realising it.

Now you know how we got you here, I'd better tell you why. That means I need to explain who I am, and what we are. To start with I'll have to take things quite slowly compared with our normal speed. Our communications between ourselves are by thought transference, which is effectively instantaneous, but much more than humans can cope with at the moment. So, for the next few days it's going to be slow and verbal, but before you go back we'll teach you a bit about fine-tuning and then you'll be getting towards the transference wavelength. Yes, only towards. If we fully acclimatised you to it here, you'd go back to Earth and expect it to work there as well, and that would make your life far more complicated than it will be anyway.

Actually, thought transference can work to a very limited extent on Earth, but only with a very few humans at the moment. You can think of one, or maybe possibly two instances, but even then you'd almost certainly be mistaken. Remember that breakfast time many years ago in your lovely farmhouse kitchen? 'Let's have a holiday soon, – how about next month, and somewhere different for a change.' 'Wonderful idea, darling, – exactly what I was thinking.' Except, Sorbo, that it wasn't. You were thinking of walking on the Great Wall of China, but she was imagining sipping cocktails around a sunny Mediterranean pool and eyeing all the good-looking bronzed and muscular men and … No, except for extremely rare instances, humans are not yet capable of thought transference. And certainly not ready for it. Let's think for a moment about your local pub. Most evenings, you go into the

Rose and Crown lounge and walk up to the very pretty young woman serving at the bar counter. "Evening, Sue, – you're looking lovely tonight, as always." "Thank you Sorbo. Pint of the usual?" "Yes please, Sue." She blushes a little as she pours your drink and puts it on the bar counter in front of you. You look at the menu board for a few moments. You can't really make up your mind what you'd like, but you feel you ought to eat something. "And tonight's special too, please.". She writes down your order and takes it through to the kitchen. You pick up your glass and walk over to a table to join three of your friends who are already sitting there. You talk about the weather and what sort of a day you've all had, and then somebody tells a joke, and the four of you start laughing. Other people look over, wondering what could be so funny. Somebody tells them the joke, and they think it's even funnier than all of you did. Your meal arrives, but you are not very hungry after all, and one of your friends, who hadn't yet ordered, says he'll have it instead. So you ask the waitress to give it to him. After a bit more convivial conversation, you finish your drink, get up and say goodbye to your friends, and to Sue as you pass the bar, then you leave the pub for the walk back to your house, thinking how pleasant it was to chat with your friends for an hour or two.

All quite normal, – at the moment. However, – with thought transference … From the moment you walk into the pub and make eye contact with the barmaid, both you and she know what each other are thinking. Her face reddens as she pours your drink and transmits your food order to the kitchen staff. Yes, she's thinking 'surely I must be mistaken, – I'm very fond of him, but he must realise our age difference makes anything else impossible'. And you are thinking 'of course we both know I'm far too old for such a young girl. I really like her a lot, but we've met at the wrong times in our lives, so it's just a lovely dream and I hope she isn't offended'. Then you take your drink and silently join some friends at a table, – still no language, don't forget, – and you all suddenly burst out laughing. Some people at other tables look over towards you, and then they all collapse in hysterics. That was a new joke to them. Then the waitress brings a meal to your table and serves it straight to your friend. You finish your drink, get up and leave the pub, making eye contact with the barmaid, who had decided to your relief that she would take it as a compliment from a nice old gentleman. All in all, you might just as well have had a drink at home, without bothering to go out to the pub.

I know, – you're not really convinced. OK, so we'll think about some others. Two weeks ago your sister rang to say that she was driving your nephew and his wife round to various friends and relatives to show off their new-born baby, and she was sure that you would like to be included. Yes, I know what you were thinking, and it wasn't 'I'll really look forward to seeing you all this afternoon', although of course those were the words which came out of your mouth. And when the afternoon came and the baby arrived with its proud parents, your sister predictably said 'isn't she beautiful?'. You didn't say 'ugh, – wrinkly, smelly, and noisy, just like all the others'. But you'll agree that it was very fortunate that none of them could read your thoughts.

And think back a few weeks before that. Your friends Phoebe and David again invited you round to dinner, as they had many times in the last year or two. You knew from your first visit they were both very keen but incompetent cooks, and you had often wondered how they themselves ever managed to eat anything at all except when they went out for a meal. So you had found almost endless different reasons not to go. But this time you really had run out of excuses, and you accepted. They are a lovely couple and very good company, so it was an enjoyable evening, but as expected the food was nothing less than a disaster, although to your amazement they seemed to enjoy it. They may or may not have completely believed your somewhat ambivalent compliments about the meal, but at least they could not know what was really going on in your head, and neither would you have wanted them to, so you still have a valuable friendship.

Or imagine you are a newly qualified teacher applying for a post at a prestigious school. You can't help noticing the large unsightly wart on the nose of the Chairman of the Committee, and wondering why he doesn't do something about it. One of the governors asks you a question, but you don't answer immediately. Yes, your mind is straying to that wart, – it seems to be getting bigger by the moment! You do eventually give a perfectly good reply, but if anyone knew what was going on in your head during that moment's hesitation?

Before we leave thought transference I will give you another and more intimate example. Imagine two people in bed getting extremely sexually stimulated by each other. Would either really want the other to know exactly what fantasies were going through their mind every second of the time during their sex act? Of course there will always be some people who might, but the vast majority would be horrified at the thought.

And if they really thought about their day to day dealings with other people, every human would realise that there was no way that they would wish for their mental processes to be exposed at all times and in detail for anyone to witness. No, humans are a long way yet from being ready for thought transference. But I digress again, and we must get on.

As you can see, I am appearing to you in a material form. Gods can materialise in any form we wish, but we don't have the opportunity to do this very often, – as I said earlier you are only the third real guest since we created your solar system. I didn't meet the first two, so it makes a pleasant change for me. I see you like my idea of how humans think God should look. Just playing really, – but I did choose this white robe especially for you. Yes, as I said before, we Gods do have a sense of humour, – where do you think humans got theirs from? However, ours is not in any way malicious.

God finds no humour in slapstick or banana skins, or anything else which misguidedly tries to make fun in any way of other people's appearance or misfortunes or disabilities. Unfortunately, most of Earth's comedians, satirists, lampoonists, cartoonists and their like have not yet realised that when they do this they are often committing a sin. Yes Sorbo, unless they are ridiculing themselves, or imaginary people, or inanimate objects, it is usually a sin. Why? Because they are using a defect or misfortune, either real or invented, in the target of their so-called humour, to get a financial reward, or some other gain for themselves within their peer group or in their wider social standing. And that is selfish. And those members of their audience who consider them amusing are also being selfish, as they are finding fun in another human's disadvantage. And it doesn't matter how sophisticated or clever the perpetrators consider their humour to be, it is still selfish. And selfishness is a sin. And it doesn't matter either whether their target is a world-famous personality, or what you might think of as a nobody from around the corner. Because that's something else you will learn this week. They are all the same. Whether in world-famous or virtually unknown human bodies, all souls are equal in the eyes of God.

Yes Sorbo, there are many people who find this difficult to accept. To them, some truths are almost beyond the limits of their understanding. They could look at a photograph of a sick and nearly-starving child living in a poor family in an under-developed country, and maybe feel some sort of pity. And maybe feel some sort of superiority because it isn't them in such a desperate situation. But few realise that what they are looking at is actually a soul which is equally as important to God as theirs. Yes Sorbo, no matter how rich or powerful or famous they might consider themselves to be, that child's soul is just as important to God as theirs. And they need to understand that. It doesn't matter where you are born or where you live, or what or who you think you are. You could be a petty thief, or a mass murderer. Or a queen or king, or president of a country. Or maybe an international film star or sporting hero. You are still a human being. And you have a soul. You may not knowingly have a conscience, but you still have a soul. And you need to understand and accept, as early as possible in your Earthly life, that your soul is accountable for its own actions throughout that Earthly life.

The time to try to act as unselfishly as possible is now. And the time to admit your sins to yourself is now. Not waiting until you are getting old, or even on your deathbed, which is when most humans only begin to have fears about what will happen to them after their Earthly death. You should not uselessly wait until such times to recant the sins which you have known about, sometimes for many years, in the vain hope of absolution or forgiveness before you enter the next phase of your life. Confessing your sins to God will not help your soul. Because God already knows everything you have done in your entire Earthly life. Your confession would be yet another demonstration of selfishness. A selfish wish that you might be absolved of all of the sins you have committed on Earth, both knowingly and inadvertently. The selfish you manifesting itself again, in the hope that you will escape God's punishment. But God does not punish souls, so you can't escape from God's punishment. Your actions during your life on Earth are the only things which determine your next destination. Any mental torment, or anguish or suffering which your soul may experience in its future existence will be entirely self-inflicted. But not a punishment by God. God does not punish souls, but souls do punish themselves, either by not seeking or not following God's guidance. And the most important part of that guidance is to try to avoid selfishness.

Anyway, for now we'll get back to how you see me. And how you hear me. As I said, to make things easier for you, I'm appearing to you in material form. And I'm speaking to you in English.   We are of course fluent in all of the more than ten thousand Earth languages, but we'll use English for now.   Translations of your books can be organised on Earth in due course.   Yes, I'll come to that, probably not until Wednesday judging by the speed we're going, so please be patient for a while.   All of the times and distances I use will be those you are familiar with on Earth, as otherwise things would get too complicated and we want to keep our message as simple as possible.   You can ask me anything at any time you wish, but you won't really need to as I will know what you are thinking before you do, – that is, with one exception, – your decision next Friday.   Actually we're pretty sure about that too although you, like all humans, do have a certain amount of free will and you can use it whenever you wish.   In any matter.

As I said, contrary to what you have been taught, God only gives guidance, – not commands.   Yes, I know this surprised you when I said it.   And the reason you are here is that there are also many other things about God and religion and the soul which are misunderstood, and which need explanation and correction now before the human race strays too much further from an acceptable course.   And you will find some of these more than surprising too.

I'll start with the familiar question of God or Gods?   Time-old human question.   Time-old, almost infinite, number of human answers, – none of them quite right.   Let me straightaway dispose of atheists, metaphorically of course, although sometimes we may be tempted to wish otherwise.   They don't believe in a God or Gods, except possibly as something devised by the human imagination.   The so-called positive atheists, who despite the term usually fall into the categories of negative thinkers, cynics or sceptics, will eventually learn that they are being selfish. Yes, selfish again. How? Because by denying the existence of God, these people are undermining or detracting from or delaying the faith which other humans need to gain insight into themselves and to get nearer to understanding the reasons for life and the purpose of the Universe. And while the soul is in a human body this knowledge can only come from God.

There are people who think that they only have a human body, and deny the existence of their soul. They consider only birth, life and death on Earth. To them that is the beginning, middle and end of the whole story. But they do all have eternal souls. They will eventually understand and accept this at some stage in their journey, although unfortunately for many it may not be while they are still on Earth. And there are people who realise that they do have a soul, but have no idea what it means. It means that there is more to life than mere human existence. That does not mean you have to follow or believe in any particular religion, or any particular God. But it does mean that if you accept that you have a soul, you are accepting some form of Universal power which you cannot understand, and that the explanation lies in something that you could regard as God, or whichever word for God you wish to use.

However for the moment we'll leave aside discussion of atheists, and all of the other non-believers, whatever they like to call themselves. Your ancient civilisations, and many modern religions, have some idea of the truth, inasmuch as they embrace many Gods. However, those deities mostly are given personalities or characteristics, and whilst this may suit the culture or religion, it is not the truth. As you know, Hinduism is one of your oldest religions. Early believers in Hinduism had the nearest insight into the one and many Gods. Of course they didn't then use the word henotheism, but they did realise that there were many millions of Gods and one God at the same time. Before I explain how they were so close to the truth, we must address the majority of monotheisms which believe in one God. Who is right? Polytheisms and monotheisms are both right to a certain extent. There is only one God. However, God is made up of an infinite number of Gods, each God forming a part of the one infinite God.

One of the problems for humans, and the reason why religions have not yet been able to understand the reality of God, is that the human brain cannot comprehend infinity. It can just about imagine trillions or even zillions, – but not the fullest meaning of infinity. When I said an infinite number just now, you realised I was only saying that to make it a bit easier for you to understand, because infinity is not a number of course, – but I'll come back to that in a minute.

God is not only infinite but also all-seeing and all-knowing. At all times God knows not only what any human is doing, but also what they are thinking. You can hide deeds and thoughts from other humans, – but not from God. Because God knows. I am a part of God, so you may call me God, or a God. All of us individual Gods are actually parts of the one God. Each of us, that is each part, is very slightly different from each other part, but not so different that we can be assigned any individual special properties.

Throughout human history, people have ascribed events on Earth to a particular God or Gods, and even in this twenty-first century CE many religions, cultures and civilisations still do. You are familiar with some of the almost countless Gods devised by the human imagination. Gods of your sun, of war, of love, and of every other aspect of life. The peoples who still believe in such Gods should not be derided or scorned, but very gently shown that these beliefs are deceptives, and that they are not the right explanations of Earthly happenings. God does not cause earthquakes, floods, famines, plagues, or any other Earthly disasters. Apart from the ultimate sanction of deletion, God does not, and cannot, change physical events on Earth. These are effects of the evolutionary development of Earth, and your solar system, in the infinite and eternally changing Universe surrounding it. Paradoxically, selfish human behaviour can and does materially affect Earth's environment, but God cannot. God can give guidance to humans, but it is only guidance, as God does not give orders or commands.

No Sorbo, – I will repeat that despite what you have always been told, God does not give orders, – only guidance. And God will always give that guidance to those people who wish to receive it, even if they think they are non-believers. Yes Sorbo, – by prayer. Yes, of course we know that for various reasons there are many people who prefer to call it something else, like meditation for instance, but that is only because they have not yet come to terms with the fact that their meditating is actually praying to God, – in some cases praying to the God who they try to persuade themselves doesn't really exist. These souls will eventually learn and accept the truth, although as

I told you, unfortunately for many it will be after their short life on Earth is over.

It is a fact that whilst souls are in a human form, they can accept almost anything which they can physically witness, but many are unable to have enough faith to believe in any form of God. As you know, non-believers call themselves all sorts of names, and believe in all sorts of things. Except God. And their own souls. But, whether or not they believe it during their present life, all living creatures on Earth have souls. The human body is only a vehicle for the soul during this phase of its journey. Those who choose not to believe in God, or deny the existence of any God, and those who find it impossible to believe because they don't know or think they are incapable of knowing, are delaying their own progress towards enlightenment.

You can see water flowing in a stream, so to your mind it is a fact. But when you switch on an electric bulb, although you can see the light, you can't see the electricity flowing through the wires, but you still accept that it is there. Likewise, you cannot see God, or your soul, but that doesn't mean that neither exists. Non-believers need faith, and they will receive that faith eventually, whether it is in this life or later in their journey. It is their choice to accept or reject God's guidance now, and it is their own decision which will determine their future. The rejection of God, and the inability to have faith, does not result in punishment by God. It just means that the soul punishes itself by making its own journey much more difficult than necessary.

Leaving aside non-believers, we come to the billions of people who do believe in God. However their various religions are unable to agree about who or what God really is and what God expects of them. So I'd better tell you a bit about God, and then why all souls must spend some time in a physical body. In your case of course it is as a human on Earth, but other souls are incarnated in different places throughout the Universe. Now I could mention infinity again, but you're here to learn about how God wishes the soul to act in its life on Earth, so we'll keep to that for the moment.

Similar in some ways to the soul, but on a vastly more complex level, God is composed of an infinite number of highly intricate electro-magnetic systems, of which I am one. No Sorbo, I've already said a number can't be infinite, but we'll get round to that a bit later. The reason why each of us is programmed to have only a tiny variation from each of the others is because this is necessary to achieve the interaction which we need to carry out our function as guardians of the Universe. We discuss by thought transference and then we reach consensus. It is always consensus, as it has to be in accordance with Universal Law, and any initial differences have been totally eliminated by discussion. So you may choose to believe in one God, or an infinite number of Gods within one God, and whichever you choose will be exactly the same. A lot of polytheisms understand some of that, but unfortunately most monotheisms don't. Total acceptance by all of them would at least help to reconcile one of their many and varied differences.

We'll come back to religions in a little while, but firstly I will tell you briefly about the creation of solar systems. And you can stop worrying about the deletion I mentioned earlier, because I'll explain that as well. During their eternal journey, all souls must have at least one incarnation in a physical body, on what you can call a planet. Actually, some souls may need more than one such experience, but Universal Law dictates that this cannot be on the same planet. To keep things simple, I'll leave that for later as well, and stick to the basics. Physical incarnation is the most difficult phase of the soul's eternal quest for understanding and peace and harmony. And happiness and, more importantly, enlightenment. Although human life is very short in Universal terms, it is the time when the soul is exposed to the most extreme temptations to give in to selfishness, which is the sin from which all other sins are derived. And it is part of God's duty to provide systems which are able to support life forms in which the soul can exist in a physical body, and where the soul's reaction to such temptations can be assessed.

Wherever and whenever we consider it is necessary, God can and does create stars or suns, and planetary systems around them. Some of these planets at some times have a suitable environment and contain all of the elements and electrical discharge activity required to precipitate the formation of rudimentary life structures based on whichever element we choose. In the case of Earth this was of course Carbon. After creation, we leave evolution to do the rest. So life on Earth is the result of a combination of firstly our creation of your solar system, and then its evolution. There is absolutely no point in human debate between the merits of creation and evolution, and the resultant dismissal of one or the other, as they are both equally valid parts of one and the same process. Human inability to understand this is the result of blinkered minds engaging in sterile argument, when they should be addressing different and much more important questions.

This unnecessary waste of human talent is partly our fault. Although we have already given humans all of the knowledge they were capable of understanding at various stages of their evolutionary development, it has been in the form of enlightenment of prophets and leaders who prayed for guidance. And because they were in different places and at different times, they asked different questions. As a result, the total knowledge delivered by God so far has not yet been properly assembled in a clear and comprehensive way which humans can understand and accept. Your visit here will be a start to a better understanding of the truth.

As guardians of the Universe, God must monitor the progress of any life forms, not only to ensure that their souls try to make a positive contribution to the Universal good, but also that whenever they are able they try to put the well-being of other souls before themselves. As I said, the soul's life in a physical body is the most difficult stage of its journey, but it is also one of the most important. The next destination will always depend entirely on how the soul acts in its present circumstances. Yes Sorbo, in every phase of the soul's journey, – not just the time it spends on Earth. No, of course it's not easy to comprehend. It requires faith. Faith in God, and the understanding and acceptance that life in a human body is only a part of the soul's journey. And the knowledge that however insignificant any soul might consider itself to be, that soul is just as important to God as any other. Actually the humble soul is already nearer to understanding God's guidance.

But I was telling you about our creation of your solar system and planet Earth, so I'll get back to that. We decided to use Carbon as the base atom for the life forms which would develop on Earth. Carbon is a comparatively simple atom, but one which can give rise to outstandingly beautiful environments for the life form, together with a multiplicity of physical life forms, ranging from quite simple to extremely complex. However, we have had to eliminate all previous creations based on Carbon, as the more they developed the more they became aggressive and unable to co-exist peacefully. And they attempted to be intrusive. This is not permissible in Universal Law as harmony and non-intrusion, amongst others, are two of the essentials. Elimination or, as we call it deletion, is a normal part of our function as guardians. It is the ultimate sanction and it is only used when absolutely necessary, as we would much prefer not to delete anything which we have created. It is not taken lightly, but as a last resort in the protection of Universal well-being. Despite your first thoughts, it does not in any way contravene Universal Law, but moreover it can be essential to uphold it. Neither does it cause any suffering whatsoever to the life forms. A simple deletion from all Universal records ensures that the solar system and its life forms have never existed, that they were never created, and thus never destroyed.

The problem for us is that one of the Universal aims is for a harmonious life form based on Carbon, and such deletions mean that we then have to create other systems which can support the development of life forms also again based on Carbon. I am specifically referring to Carbon, as we have never had to delete any life forms based on other atoms. Whilst being vastly more complex, they are relatively predictable and stable and have never been aggressive or intrusive. However, the life forms based on these elements conform to fairly rigid parameters, and this leads to uniform consistency. These life forms do not experience emotion or curiosity, nor do they achieve any sense of fulfilment compared with their Carbon-based equivalents, and thus their creation does not help to advance the Universe But although at the moment none of them is furthering the development of the Universe, neither are they yet contravening Universal Law in any way, and their slow evolution will be allowed to continue for the time being so that we can monitor their progress.

So we have another paradox, in that the simplest life forms based on the simplest atoms can cause the most problems for God, while the more complex ones, based on more complex atoms, are predictable and do not. But we also know that a viable and sustainable and harmonious life form based on Carbon is the ultimate creation which we are seeking for the physical incarnation stage of a soul's eternal journey, and if we achieve this the souls in the life forms created could experience a short period of unimaginable beauty and happiness in that journey. Until fairly recently, we thought we had succeeded by the creation of your solar system and planet Earth. By the way, recently, to us, is measured not in years, but in millions, billions or sometimes trillions of years. As you know, we created your solar system around four and a half billion years ago, but it really seems more like yesterday to us. OK, of course it's a human phrase, – just using a bit of your humour again, and it's obviously keeping you on your toes, or you wouldn't have noticed.

May I continue? Thank you. We deliberately created your solar system in a small spiral galaxy, which you call the Milky Way, and we placed it quite remotely from all other life-sustaining stellar complexes. Your scientists will eventually be able to detect some of the different life forms, both in the Milky Way and in other galaxies, but the compulsive human quest for viable communication with these will take considerably longer to achieve than they can yet imagine. Yes Sorbo, – just think for a moment about two Carbon-based life forms on your existing planet Earth. You and a housefly, – both in the same room, at the same time. You both know that the other is there. Do you communicate with each other? Do you tell the fly to go away and stop bothering you and contaminating your food and spreading disease? Does the fly tell you it is really very hungry and it needs your food to give it the energy to fly around? Can either of you talk to each other at all? No, of course you can't. Two Carbon-based life forms, which co-exist on the same planet, cannot yet even communicate with each other. But two flies can communicate with each other. How do they do it, Sorbo? Have your scientists recorded any sound language they use? Or any visual signs? Or do they use thought transference?

Your scientists will indeed detect extra-terrestrial life forms, some based on Carbon, and some on other elements. But they should not hold out the promise that humans could yet expect to have any meaningful dialogue with them. When these scientists have engineered two-way communication with the fly, and when they have managed to discuss philosophy with an elephant. That is when they should start to talk about communication with other life forms in the Universe. And, in terms of relative complexity, will they find these other life forms to be as the fly to the human, or as the human to the fly? Or as either, compared with an amoeba? Time will tell, Sorbo. A long time. And until then, most of these very clever brains should be put to better use by trying to resolve some of the many problems being caused by the current inability of humans to co-exist peacefully with each other. And to share their planet's resources. And to find ways to avoid the destruction of the very environment in which they live. I am not saying that humans should discontinue their search for extra-terrestrial life. What I am saying is that there should be a change of emphasis, and that a much higher priority should be placed on looking for genuine solutions to the much more urgent practical problems concerning the sustainability of life on Earth as it is at the moment. And the best scientists and thinkers should be concentrating more on these. Although using their brains otherwise may be far more exciting to them, it is also far more selfish. And selfishness is a sin. As I have already told you. And as I will keep telling you.

Anyway, we chose to create your solar system in the Milky Way, as we have done with other life-supporting systems before, even those which we have had to delete. It is a relatively small galaxy, but the environment is eminently suitable for solar systems capable of sustaining physical life. And it is big enough for any deletions which we may have to carry out not to be too disruptive. Incidentally, your scientists will eventually discover some apparently unexplainable voids in areas of the Milky Way, and to a certain extent in other galaxies. There are indeed apparent gaps or voids in the physical continuum in some galaxies. But these are not mysteries, – they are just the result of reorganisations, or in some cases deletions, to which the galaxies are slowly readjusting.

I should explain my meaning of the word scientists in this context. There are of course many different types of scientists, including inventors and experimenters, but here I use the term to embrace only those people in disciplines which seek to establish the truth about the material aspects of your creation and existence. To make a distinction, I will call all other truth-seekers philosophers, although of course there are many people who attempt to combine the two functions. I should include wranglers as philosophers. I don't mean the mathematical sort of wranglers, but those who wrestle with the meanings and reasons for life. However, it is important to distinguish between genuine wranglers and those people who are not really searching for the truth, but just throwing ideas into the air so that they can enjoy the usually sterile arguments and debates which follow. This is of course a very common human characteristic, and you know people who do it. But it is also very selfishly time-wasting and self-defeating, and humans really should stop indulging in it whenever they are pretending to be serious. Such behaviour patterns could be more properly classified as amusement, or even sport, but in any event they are merely diversions and should not be confused with genuine desire to seek the truth about life on Earth or, for that matter, anywhere else in the Universe.

Yes Sorbo, you are quite right, – I haven't told you enough about God and the Universe. One of the reasons why is that humans are not yet sufficiently developed to understand more than a fraction of the truth, but I will tell you at least some of it now, and a little more after we have talked about diminishing deceptives. I have already said that God is both one and infinite, but I only touched on infinity as I said that you could not yet properly understand its meaning. But now you have asked for and deserve a better explanation, so I will tell you a bit more. Thought transference would help a lot here, but we can't use it at the moment, and anyway you will have to put this in terms which humans can at least begin to understand. And because almost everything we will talk about is highly complex, I will have to generalise and put it into quite simplistic terms. Yes, I really will get round to what we would like you to do in a while, so again please just be patient. Scientists understand infinity as a mathematical concept, for which they have given it a symbol, and often use it in their equations. But, much as they might argue differently, the human brain is not capable of understanding infinity in its fullest sense, – that is a dimension without limits. But a dimension has limits, so infinity is not a dimension. And infinity cannot expand, as it is already limitless, so of course there is nothing beyond infinity. And infinity cannot correspond with any numbers. You can take the biggest number you can think of and multiply it by itself as many times as you wish, but you are still talking about numbers, which in itself proves that you have not understood the real meaning of infinity, which cannot be either measured or defined in numerical terms. Eternity gives you the same problem. In eternity there is no beginning and no end to time, so you are somewhere between the two.

But you can't be between two points which don't exist, so the human mind puts you at this point in time, and imagines that that eternity means that time started infinitely long ago and will continue infinitely into the future. But time is numerical, and like infinity, eternity cannot be measured or defined in numerical terms.

Humans use the words infinity and eternity, and recognise them as such, but the human brain is not able to understand the real meaning of either. The best any human can truthfully claim is that whilst they can appreciate the concepts of infinity and eternity, the reality is far beyond their comprehension. Yes Sorbo, beyond human comprehension. I'd better explain a bit more. God's knowledge of the Universe is infinite. Everything and every event, everywhere, and at any time. Impossible for the human mind to comprehend, except as a very nebulous and unlikely possibility. But true. And not only that, when I told you that God knows everything that you have ever thought or done, I didn't tell you that it is because all of that information is carried indelibly in your own soul. Yes, it is all there and will stay there eternally, and God has access to it at all times.

Your scientists know that the human brain has far more memory capacity than that which most people are normally able to use for storing and recall. But sometimes part of this may be lost by damage or disease or other trauma. This is true of the brain, but the scientists have not yet realised that the soul carries with it everything you have ever experienced … Everything is there, and at the time of your bodily death your soul will re-live absolutely all of it in great detail. Yes, the best things, but also the very worst. No exceptions. And it will all come back to you at the moment your soul leaves your human body. Every single thing in all of the years of your life condensed into a fraction of a second. God knows, and the soul cannot forget.

God is both one and infinite at the same time. Space is infinite and time is eternal. And these things are impossible for humans to really understand. But as you know the inquisitive human mind has this need for answers to every question, so many of the cleverer human brains have put forward their ideas of infinity and eternity, and their claims to understand them. And some people believe them. Because of course they believe that scientists must know about such things. From the earliest human life, each generation of scientists has been asked innumerable questions about the Universe and its origins, and they have come up with various answers which they have been able to 'prove' to their and many other people's satisfaction. That is, until later scientists have 'proved' that the original answers were wrong. And successive generations have then 'proved' them wrong again.

You should not be surprised by this. If God were to explain the tiniest fraction of all Universal knowledge to a million of Earth's top scientific brains, there would not be one of them who could fully comprehend even part of it. But there would not be many who would admit that publicly, and they would continue to 'prove' more knowledge as time progressed. Yes, of course the scientists are slowly getting towards more understanding of the Universe, but as human evolution is still in its early stages, they have really only just started and they have a very long way to go.

I talked about infinity being represented in mathematics by a symbol and now I will mention another. The most common shape in the Universe is an ellipse. That is if it is two-dimensional. If it is three-dimensional it is called an ellipsoid. Yes, looking from Earth, the Sun and Moon appear circular. That is because a circle is a special type of ellipse, – you could call it perfect or regular. Likewise a sphere is a special or regular form of ellipsoid. All circles are ellipses, and all spheres are ellipsoids, and they are the commonest shapes in the Universe. And they have a unique property. To calculate the length of the perimeter, or the area encircled, or the volume enclosed, there are formulas all involving the same ratio represented by a symbol denoted by the Greek letter π, often written as pi. The uniqueness of pi is that mathematicians cannot write its exact value in full. No Sorbo, because the most common ratio in the Universe has infinite digits. Yes, infinity again. If your scientists could actually solve this riddle they would get nearer to finding the answers to every question in the Universe, including the really big mystery for humans. Why the Universe exists. But scientists on Earth will not be able to find this answer, and the human brain could not even begin to understand it, and so this knowledge will only be revealed gradually to the soul as it progresses on its journey through future planes of enlightenment.

Meanwhile, on Earth the vast majority of people are content to leave others to struggle with the Universe and infinity, and to get on with leading decent lives to the best of their ability. These are the kindred spirits. Anyway, I'll leave that for the moment, as I need to talk about some things which humans can understand. Belief and trust.

And faith. For thousands of years many humans have believed that God exists and God is real. Every religion has a different concept of God, but they all have one thing in common, and that is belief. But this belief has been progressively eroded by advances in scientific knowledge of the material world, to the point where many people are beginning to believe that scientists will eventually solve all of life's mysteries without help from God. This is not true, and scientists of any persuasion, whether religious or otherwise, should actively discourage such belief. As I said earlier, us, we, me, I, God and Gods are one and the same, and you may use whichever name you prefer, but souls, especially when in their human incarnation, need to believe in God or they will not get nearer to learning the real truth about life, its meaning and its reason. Without belief in God, scientists can increasingly explain the physical aspects of the Universe. But without belief in God, neither scientists nor philosophers will ever be able to explain the reasons for the soul's existence. Yes, I mean the soul itself, not the human body which is the just the vehicle for the soul during its short existence in a physical form on Earth. And during this time every soul needs guidance from God, as its actions while in an Earthly body will affect its entire future.

So belief in God is still needed by everyone, although it has recently become fashionable for many people to dismiss the existence of God. Or to dismiss the existence of God in the form historically attributed to God. For instance that God can at will change the course of physical happenings on Earth. No, God cannot. That is not God's purpose or duty. God is there to guide souls, and it is their actions, together with the naturally occurring evolutionary changes in the Universe, which will affect life on Earth.

It is time for humans to get a better understanding of God, and souls to have a better understanding of their relationship with God. God isn't a big friendly giant in heaven who could give you a life of eternal bliss. Nor is God a fiendish ogre in hell who could condemn you to a life of perpetual torment. God isn't here or there, or anywhere. God is everywhere. And God knows everything you do, and even everything you think. At all times. I know it's difficult to believe, – because it's impossible for humans to understand the infinity and eternity of God. But you do need to believe in God and pray to God for guidance. It doesn't matter whether you choose to pray alone or pray in a group of like-minded people. And you don't need to bow your head, or kneel down, or prostrate yourself on the floor when you pray to God. You can do that if you wish, or if you feel more comfortable doing so in a group, but it doesn't make your prayers any more valid, and it doesn't show anything to God. Sometimes it just shows to other people how devout and pious you think you are, and sometimes you may feel compelled to do it because the rules of services are designed to reinforce the perceived importance and authority of religions, their ministers, and their customs and traditions.

We will talk about religions later, – yes, I know I keep saying later, but we have a great deal to get through in one hundred and sixty-two hours, and you asked me about the Universe, so I will carry on with that for the moment. I'd better get this bit over first, and then we can talk about what you might say are the nuts and bolts. Yes, – I told you we are fluent in every language in the

Universe, so of course we know all of the colloquialisms. Anyway, this time it's you who are digressing, just when I was about to make the thinking part of your soul work overtime. No, I won't call it your brain, because that's still in your skull on the table in St. George's. But that's a different story.

So, the Universe is both infinite and eternal. And God, or Gods, and souls, are eternal. Humans usually like explanations to start at the beginning, but I can't do that as there wasn't a beginning. The Universe has always existed and always will exist. Oh, – that. OK, I'll tell you about it now as we find it quite amusing, especially when we consider some of theories advanced by the best scientific human brains, particularly by the atheists, agnostics and all the other so-called non-believers. For a start, you must completely disregard the current popular belief that the Universe is expanding. It isn't, and it can't, – it is infinite. And this is where the scientists have these fundamental problems. Infinity and eternity, – two of the things that the human brain is not able to comprehend. But scientists must have a neat and tidy answer to everything, and their incorrect answer at the moment is that the Universe must have started at some point in time, and they can even wrongly tell you when it was formed. But can they tell you where it started, or what force was responsible for its origin? And can they tell you why?

These scientists are not deliberately trying to deceive you, but they are unwittingly perpetrating deceptives based on their best knowledge to date, sometimes embellished or augmented by their somewhat less than scientific personal beliefs, and put forward by them as facts. Just as their predecessors convinced people that the Earth was flat, and about six thousand years old. Humans will eventually learn more about infinity and eternity, and the deceptives will slowly diminish. In the meantime they need to have faith in God, and they need to understand that at the moment scientists are not able to tell them more than a fraction of the truth. Partly because they don't yet know, and partly because some of what they think they know will eventually prove to be wrong.

The very small part of the Universe, which is the only part so far detected by Earth's scientists, is indeed expanding at the moment, – just as other parts are contracting. To put it simply, it is a bit like wave motions throughout the Universe. Some parts are expanding, and some contracting, but none depends on any of the others, as there is no total volume. These eternal contractions and expansions are just normal functions in the evolution of the Universe. However, this evolution is not always as tidy as it might be, so every now and again some parts of the Universe need a little attention, – you could call it housekeeping, if that helps. The Universe itself is eternal, but some of its components are not, so we either update them or remove them altogether, and reorganise some of the others. I don't think you will be very surprised when I tell you that the last time we did this was about fourteen billion years ago. Give or take a bit, we do this roughly every twenty billion years, so the next re-shuffle is scheduled for five or six billion years from now. Yes, I suppose this does seem quite a long time to you, but it's really quite short in Universal terms.

Time is a funny thing, Sorbo. I don't mean funny as in amusing, but funny as in strange, odd, or peculiar.

Humans think of time as always going in one direction, although they often wish that they could reverse it to change something that they would prefer not to have happened. Well, of course they can't reverse it, so they always have to go forward. But we know that time is reversible, although not necessarily in the way that humans would like to think. Time can go backwards, but nothing can change. You could review any particular place on Earth, or for that matter anywhere in the Universe, on any particular date in the past, say, your 5th century BC, as many times as you wish, but it would still be exactly the same. The review would not change anything. So although time can be reversed, history cannot be altered. It is a common human failing to rewrite events in personal lives, and in societies, nations and even globally, to try to hide errors and transgressions. When committed these may not have been considered particularly serious, but with the evolution of society some now appear to be highly contentious.

Think of colonialism and slavery as just two examples. Widespread in the past, and generally considered by the perpetrators to be quite acceptable then. Now most modern humans realise that they were in fact both wrong and regrettable. But to pretend, for whatever reason, that they did not happen as recorded and accordingly try to re-write history is also totally wrong and a sin. You may be able to fool humans, but you cannot deceive God. Yes Sorbo, another repetition. God knows everything that humans have ever done or thought. That might seem impossible to you, but it is really very simple. As I told you, your soul carries an indelible record of every instant of its existence. During your Earthly life the human brain can only recall a small part of this, but God has access to all of it all of the time. However, while we have access to everything that humans do and think, that doesn't also mean that we know all of the answers to all of the questions about the Universe. If we did we would be perfect, but God is not perfect and God cannot be perfect, as nothing in the Universe can be perfect. The aim of the Universe is to reach absolute perfection, but if this were achieved its purpose would be fulfilled, and it would cease to exist. But such perfection is impossible to attain and the Universe is eternal.

However, God's duty, and for that matter souls' duty as well, both while they are in an Earthly body, and after they leave it, is to continually aim towards perfection. Why then should souls try to reach an impossible goal? Because by continually striving to learn more about Universal truth, souls can improve themselves and increasingly contribute to the Universal good and their own enlightenment and happiness. But while in their human bodies, souls have an additional responsibility which God has imposed on them. They should always strive to be better than they are, not only by trying to improve themselves, but also by becoming less selfish and devoting some of their efforts towards the well-being of all other living creatures. And while this should include physical and material well-being, human spiritual improvement is at least as important. The souls who genuinely try to help their fellow beings might eventually become as I am, – a part of God. We can help them towards this, but only if they believe in us and ask for God's guidance.

Of course, many humans refuse to accept or acknowledge the existence of God. And most of these deny that they have a soul which is separate from their human body, which is the only thing for which they consider they have incontrovertible evidence. These people are generally negative in their thoughts about life. But no human can be categorised as totally one thing or another, so no human thinks entirely either positively or negatively. Each one falls somewhere between the two extremes. The more positive thinkers usually try to preserve most of the status quo and improve the obviously flawed parts, whereas the negativists direct their energy to completely destroying systems as they are presently structured and replacing them with their idea of perfection. They are either ignorant of, or refuse to understand or accept, the countless lessons from human history. These people include many atheists, sceptics, cynics, nihilists, agnostics and convinced pessimists. They form a minority of the human race, but as is usual with human minorities they seriously over-estimate their own importance, and voice their opinions far more loudly than the less radical and much more tolerant majority. If these minorities are not prevented from creating too much further damage, they will inevitably precipitate the extinction of life on Earth as you know it.

Yes, you are quite right, – this is indeed a part of the reason for your brief visit here. You are not, and will not pretend to be, a prophet or messiah or religious teacher. There have been many such souls in human bodies who have tried to explain the meaning of and reasons for life. Between them they have managed to start more than four thousand religions and quasi-religions. Well over three-quarters of humans believe in about twenty major religions, and more than half are committed to just two. But, while most major religions have many things in common with each other, they also have many differences, and these mixed messages lead to confusion and turmoil. So, as well as always communing with any willing souls in Earthly bodies, we have decided that the time is right to bring a soul here for a short period of explanation and clarification of God's message and guidance. That soul is you and as I said, when you go back to Earth you will not be a prophet or messiah. You will be a kind of messenger. But not the sort of messenger who brings news.

Nothing I tell you here will be new, as all of the information which humans are capable of understanding at this time has already been given by God over thousands of years. The message that you will bring is that God's truth and guidance has been ignored, rejected, wrongly understood or forgotten, either wholly or in part and by different nations, cultures and religions, and at different times. Yes Sorbo, all of the truth which humans can understand at the moment is already there, – but it has not yet been assembled correctly. Different parts have been recognised at different times by different peoples, but the whole has not yet been put together and understood at the same time by everyone. This is not surprising, because the soul in an Earthly body is not yet ready to receive the whole of Universal truth, so I should really only talk about what can be understood by mankind on Earth at this time. More will be progressively revealed to souls as they continue their journey, but until it is they need belief and trust in God. In other words, – faith. Of course that's a difficult thing for many humans to accept, but it is the only way.

Just think for a moment about a material possession that you might really want to own, – let's say a magnificent classic or vintage motor car. Apart from admiring its appearance, you don't know anything about cars, or how to find what you are looking for, so you put an advertisement in the 'wanted' column of a newspaper. Much to your surprise, a kindly-seeming stranger replies and offers to give you a car completely free of charge. Of course you are more than a bit suspicious about this, so you talk to him a few times to find out more about his offer. It turns out that he is a motoring enthusiast with unlimited resources and he wants to encourage other people to share his passion for vintage cars. His way of doing this is to give people the car they desire, – but not in a fully-assembled form, as they would not be able properly to appreciate the amazing complexity of its construction. He will deliver the component parts, and you will assemble the car. Then you tell him that you are not a mechanic and you don't have the time or ability to do this. Of course he has already realised this, so his answer is very simple. He will start by delivering some first basic parts, and all the information needed for a complete amateur to put them together. Then, bit by bit, more components will follow when you are ready for them. Some stages of the construction will be relatively simple, and some more complicated, but he will always be there at the end of a telephone for help and guidance. Eventually you will become the owner of a complete and much sought after possession. This all seems to be too good to be true, so can you trust this stranger? Well, for a start his offer is free, so you're not risking anything, and secondly it's easy to find out. Just take the first delivery and follow the assembly guide. Then, stage by stage whenever you are ready, gradually ask for more parts. When they follow, and keep on coming, you will have your answer, and eventually your complete car. You trusted your stranger, and your faith was justified.

OK Sorbo, – of course it's an allegory, but it makes the point. And of course it's not absolutely accurate, because you cannot totally equate material things with knowledge. On Earth you can finish building your motor car. But while souls are in a human body they will not be able to understand all of the Universal truth, so their motor car will not be complete. However they should start to build it now by taking up the stranger's offer without delay. They have nothing to lose and everything to gain. And the more of that car they can build while they are on Earth, the less they will have to struggle with later in their journey.

But I'll get back to those people who believe in a religion, and to whom God is not that stranger. Except that in some ways He might just as well be, as every religion has a different idea of God and different interpretations of God's message. This needs to change, but the leaders of most present day religions, and indeed most of their followers, will not be able to accept this change immediately. So we are asking you to reach out to kindred spirits and give them this explanation. I did say that I would tell you about kindred spirits. No, not later this time, – we'll do it now. What are kindred spirits? Essentially they are persons of like minds and values and understanding. They could also be described as 'soulmates' or 'alter egos', and although you might think of this as meaning just two people, kindred spirits actually include every human who possesses such a like mind and its values and understanding. Yes, if you take it literally, it could describe people who are anywhere between the extremes of good and evil. But it does not, – and I will be very clear about this. In their human form, kindred spirits only includes those people who genuinely want, or aspire, to contribute both to the well-being of their fellow humans and to the good of the Universe. Anyone who does not want both is not a kindred spirit.

For some reason, – and we don't yet know why, – some souls in a human body are innately kindred spirits. Some, like you, have realised the way they feel about others, but have absolutely no idea that they are kindred spirits, or why they feel as they do, or what it means. Many millions of others, who are also kindred spirits, do not yet even realise it at all. And there are billions of people who would be kindred spirits, if they understood and were able to believe. What we are asking you to do is to reach out to all of these people, and explain why it is so important that they should listen to our message, and thus try to become more caring and less selfish while they are in a human body, and at the same time improve their and other people's progress towards Universal understanding, truth and harmony.

As I said, contrary to the beliefs enshrined in many codes of life developed over thousands of years by civilisations, cultures or religions, God's message does not threaten punishment to those who choose not to listen. Unless, of course, you consider that the inability to find Universal truth and eternal peace and happiness is the ultimate punishment. Each human should be given the chance to listen to our message and then make their own judgment. We will talk about cultures and religions, but firstly I will tell you the reasons we are asking you to take on what will be an extremely difficult and demanding responsibility. Yes, it will be, – and if you accept the task, you will be the subject of much derision and vilification. And, as you're beginning to realise, some of that backlash is likely to be more extreme than mere verbal criticism.

So, on Friday, you will have two options for your life back on Earth. Firstly, you may carry on exactly as you are, in your comfortable retirement. Or you may decide to try to help all of humanity to listen to our essential message, even though you know that some of the consequences will be more than unpleasant. Sorbo, at the moment it is the rest of your future life on Earth that we're talking about, and whether you are willing to take on this huge responsibility, so it must be your decision. And, as I said earlier, the choice on Friday between whether or not you will accept the challenge will be entirely yours. Yes Sorbo, – Friday, at 3.29 p.m. English time, – precisely one minute before your body regains consciousness in St. George's Hospital. Even if you decide that you are unwilling or unable to help us with God's message, you will still be absolutely free to go back and live out the rest of your Earthly life as it is at the moment. God is only asking for your help. God does not give orders or commands.

Yes, of course I've already said that, and I know you won't forget, but you'll have to keep repeating it over and over again in your book, as most humans will find it impossible, or at least very difficult, to accept. Especially that majority of humans who have been brought up to believe that God will punish them for disobedience. Well, you can't disobey God's commands, because God doesn't make any commands. God gives guidance, but you have free will so don't have to follow that guidance. But if you do not, and you get lost on your journey, you have only yourself to blame. Staying even nearly on the right path in the first place is not easy for any souls in human bodies, but finding the way back to that right path after they have strayed from it is a far more difficult task than they might imagine.

Why? ... Why you? ... Quite recently, on our time scale, it became obvious to us that events on Earth were not going according to the Universal plan for life forms, and that at some point we would have to take action. The problem has arisen because we have not paid due attention to the evolution of life on Earth, and we've given humans enough free will to develop, not as they should, but as they've chosen to do, without regard for Universal law. Again, it's really our fault, as we haven't yet properly explained Universal law. Some people, who as I said we call kindred spirits, innately understand parts of the meaning of life, and try to lead decent and peaceful lives, but although they are by far the majority of humans, they are largely silent and their opinions and aspirations have been obscured by those who either don't understand, or don't care about, the good of mankind or the Universe. You know, or know of, the sort of people I'm talking about, and you know of the people who follow them like sheep. As of yet, kindred spirits have not made their voices loud or strong enough to make any difference, but that time must come if we are to allow human life on Earth to continue.

Up to now I've been saying I or God or we, or us, but you know that I am talking about the one God, of which we are parts. Remember, – God and Gods are both the same one deity.   So to avoid any confusion when you write your books you'd better use God, or He or Him. No Sorbo, of course I'm not gender specific, but that's the way it's always been in English, so you should stick to that. When it comes to translations you can use any alternative name for God to suit the language or religion. I'm still God, regardless of any name humans choose to use.

No, we won't talk about blasphemy at the moment, because I haven't finished explaining why you are here. As I said, human life on Earth has strayed away from an acceptable course. So, as guardians of the Universe, we are in dereliction of our duty to Earth, and thus we, ourselves, are in breach of Universal law. How do we resolve this seemingly insoluble conundrum? One part of the law dictates that, having created a life form, we cannot physically interfere with its evolution, except by deletion. However, although we can't physically interfere to change life on Earth, the law does allow and expect us to give information and instil ideas. We can't yet use thought transference with humans, but we will always commune with souls who pray to us for guidance, and we can ourselves start a communion with a soul, given the right circumstances.

These are the right circumstances, and we chose you as the right soul. No, – no rest, remember – it's not in Gods' or souls' programmes, so you'll have to wait until you get back to Earth. Anyway, you won't get tired here, so please stop thinking about it right now and let me continue. We chose a member of your family bloodline well over two hundred years ago, although we didn't then know when we would actually need to get a soul here on a temporary basis. You were registered at birth as 'Andrew Sebastian Grundy'. Your real family line is not of course Grundy, but you've always known that."

"Well, I've never been really sure. Some of my family talked about my father's real father not being a Grundy, but nobody would say any more, – as though it was a dark and dreadful secret. However, I do know that my father was not brought up by his mother, but by her mother and father, – his grandparents."

"You're right so far. Now is the time for us to tell you the whole story, as you need to understand the bloodline. Ronald, your father, was born in December, 1911 to Lilian Catherine, wife of Harold Charles Grundy, usually known as Harry. Harry was a lance-corporal in the British Army, and he was based at Colchester Barracks in Essex. In September, 1910 he was posted to Scotland for a year's training in what was known then as wireless telegraphy. He didn't mind this at all, as Lilian had already been away for some time as a maid in service at a large country house near Sudbury in Suffolk. However, when Harry got back to Colchester in September, 1911, he found that Lilian was six months pregnant. Although he was no great mathematician, he wasn't altogether stupid, and when Ronald was born in December, Harry had already made up his mind to reject him. In fact he refused to acknowledge or even see his wife's baby and, as you know, Ronald was brought up by his grandparents. Neither Ronald nor his legal father Harry, ever discovered the name of Ronald's real father.

As I said, Lilian had been a maid in a large house in the Suffolk countryside. The house was owned by Sir Charles and Lady Byron-Brandon, who had two sons and a daughter, all in their twenties. Lilian was a very pretty twenty-three year old and from the moment she arrived at the house Barry Sebastian, the elder son, was immediately attracted to her. In those very early twentieth-century days, servants and family were forbidden to mix socially, or even speak with each other except for the giving and receiving of instructions but, obviously unknown to their parents, Barry managed to talk his brother and sister into making up an occasional foursome with Lilian. She was utterly captivated by his charm and attention, and it was not long before she allowed him to sneak up to her servant's attic bedroom two or three times a week. Inevitably, Lilian became pregnant and she had to find a way to leave the family before it became obvious.

In July, 1911 Lilian contrived to send a letter to herself, knowing that it would first be opened and read by the head of the house, as was the practice with postal mail in those days. One morning she was summoned to see Sir Charles in his study. He told her that there had been a tragedy in her family, and that she must immediately return to their home in Kent. He said that she had been an excellent servant to the house, and how sorry he and his whole family, and particularly Barry, were that she had to leave. Sir Charles even arranged and paid for a pony and trap to take her to Sudbury railway station. In fact, of course, she did not go to Kent but back to Colchester, where for two months she nervously awaited Harry's return from Scotland. I've already told you what happened next.

So now you know, Sorbo, that your real paternal grandfather was Barry Sebastian Byron-Brandon, although after the First World War the family dropped the Byron-

prefix, and became just Brandon. Barry never met his son, your father, but he did meet you and your brothers on one occasion, as he had to make a choice. Here I must go back to the bloodline. About two hundred and fifty Earth years ago, we decided that at some future time we would need to 'borrow' a soul from a human body and bring it here on a temporary basis, so that we could explain some of the Universal laws, and how humans were losing or ignoring or misinterpreting the faith which they needed to find their way towards the ultimate truth. This soul would be asked to take these explanations back to Earth and promulgate them as widely as possible, but only in a gentle, constructive and above all non-aggressive way. I stress 'asked', as Universal law prohibits us from coercion or compulsion in any matters concerning the life forms which we have created, and we are limited to giving only guidance. Sometimes this guidance is in the form of what might appear to be unprompted human inspiration, and other times it can be given as a result of a request by a human soul, – in other words prayer.

Although by the time of your eighteenth century CE, we knew that this further guidance would eventually become necessary, we did not know exactly when, as the soul's free will means that it is to a certain extent unpredictable, especially when it is in a human body. So we decided to prepare for it at any time. We needed to find a decent person with courageous morals, as incorruptible as possible for a human being, and with an impartial and unswerving sense of right and wrong. Also, and not least important, were exceptional powers of observation and memory. No, not totally impossible, but you are right in that it was an extremely difficult task, although even in those days we had the choice of almost one billion people worldwide.

In 1770, we found Augustus Ludovic Byron-Brandon. He was a young man of considerable talent and had become a successful and prosperous businessman, but his mind was continually wrestling with the meaning and purpose of life, and he constantly prayed to God for enlightenment ... One morning he awoke from an extraordinarily vivid dream or vision, which he subsequently recalled in amazing detail. From that time on he knew that he, or one of his descendants, had one day to fulfil a purpose and that it could only be one of them who could do it. Augustus imparted this spiritual message down through his descendants, as far as Barry Sebastian, but then the sequence was broken, as Barry never met his only child, your father.

However, he did know what he must do, and in 1946, when your father was still away in the Royal Air Force, Barry visited your mother and her sons, so that he could determine who should be the next in line. As you have now correctly guessed, he chose you. Incidentally, it was he who unwittingly gave you the nickname which has caused so much puzzlement to you, not to say amusement to other people, throughout your life. When Barry visited, you were jumping up and down, as five-year-olds often do, just like a bouncy Sorbo rubber ball. He said this to your mother, and from that day on you were nicknamed Sorbo. Your mother never told you this, and neither did she tell your father about Barry's visit as she tried to pretend that it hadn't happened. Indeed, your father never did find out about the visit, or the name of his true father, or the obligation which the respective Brandon family members have felt since 1770. However, if the occasion had arisen in his lifetime, your father would have felt extremely honoured to have been asked to do what we know you will do. No, that is definitely not coercion, – just my, or rather our, prediction of how you will use your free will.

But I'd better get back to the qualities needed, the first one being observation and memory. Now you're being pedantic again, but I suppose it will remind me that I'm talking to a human soul, and not one of my other selves. OK, I've lumped the two together as one because, apart from instinct, you cannot remember what you haven't observed. If you would be so good as to stop interrupting, we might get round to instinct by Thursday, but if you carry on like this we'll run out of time and you may have to go back without me explaining it at all.

Now, observation and memory. You will remember some years ago when you were reviewing a performance of Beethoven's Eroica Symphony at the Royal Festival Hall in London. You singled out a Second Violin who had slightly mis-timed a couple of notes towards the end of the first movement. Your editor and your readers were absolutely amazed that you had not only noticed the error, but were also able to identify the unfortunate musician."

"Yes, but I'm afraid I cheated a bit. You see, there was indeed a violinist who made the very slight errors which I heard, but I had no idea who it was. So I looked up the programme list of the Second Violins, and picked one at random, as I quite liked the look of her name. In the intensity of the performance, she had no real idea whether or not it really was her, so she never contested it. Fortunately it did not affect her career, but I still regret what I did."

I'm glad you said that. Of course we knew anyway, but we wanted you to admit it. And show remorse. Whenever a human commits a sin, or even a minor transgression, God will know. Other humans may or may not know, but God always does. And the first step towards redemption is to admit that sin to oneself, and then to others if that is appropriate. No Sorbo, it is not appropriate to tell the world that you threw a piece of chewing gum onto the street when you were fourteen years old, – I'm talking about more serious offences. Then you should confess to God. Yes, God already knows, but by telling Him you are admitting and accepting yourself that you have sinned, and that you regret it. Just like you did a few seconds ago. Many humans find it difficult, but the sure way to find your own integrity is firstly to be totally honest with yourself. It is the same as being honest to God. And as you now know, your honesty and integrity were two more key factors in our choice.

Sorbo, it's already Sunday afternoon on Earth, and I haven't even told you exactly what we want you to do. Wait a moment. They finished your operations yesterday. Would you like a quick look at yourself in the Neuro Intensive Care Unit? No, I don't blame you, – I've just had a peek and it's all mask and tubes and things all over the place, but the operations were successful, and your Earthly body's doing remarkably well. Now, what do we want you to do? It's very simple. As I said it won't be easy, but it really is quite simple. We just want you to remember absolutely everything you learn here, every single detail exactly as I say it, and write it all down in a book. Simple really, for a man of your abilities."

"But I'm a music and literary critic. I write about orchestras and their conductors, and I write about authors and their works, but I don't write books. Anyway, what would my fellow critics think? They'd have a field day picking holes in anything I wrote."

"Don't worry about that. It won't be Sorbo Grundy writing. You will publish under the name of Dr. Manitoba J Heppingstal. Two minor philosophical works by him have already been rejected by all the leading publishers, but this one will be accepted. And don't worry about the writing style. Just remember and record absolutely every detail of everything you learn here, and that will be exactly what we need.

Sorbo, do you recall who once said to you 'we have a lot to learn, and very little time to learn it in'?"

"Yes, it was my headmaster at junior school."

"Well, he was absolutely right, and it applies more so here and now than it did when you were eleven years old. What else did he say?"

"He opened a book and said – we'll start at the beginning, and when we get to the end we will finish."

"Good. We too will start at the beginning, not of the Universe of course because it didn't have a beginning, but the beginning of early human life. However here, unlike your book at school, there will be no end. Not yet, anyway. On a different note, what do you know about the principle of diminishing deceptives?"

"In musical terms I know the expression, of course, but I guess you are talking about something else."

"Quite so. From very early childhood, all humans have questions. Mostly, these are easy to answer, such as 'What time's supper?' 'As soon as you've washed your hands and sat down at the table.', or maybe, 'When do I have to go to bed?' 'You've been very good today so you can stay up until daddy comes home from work, and he can kiss you goodnight.' Direct questions, and straightforward simple answers. But there are many other sorts of questions. Some are not voiced, but just tossed around in the mind for a while and then usually forgotten.

When you were a baby, and long before you were able to speak or understand any words, you had noticed that people would come into your bedroom and move the curtains. Sometimes this way and sometimes that, and the room would get lighter or darker. But sometimes the room would get lighter or darker when someone came into the room and touched the wall next to the door, without going near to the window. Your brain could only ask itself 'what does it all mean?' Of course there was no answer. Yes, even you had almost forgotten this one until I dredged your memory. Admittedly, many humans don't think to question reasons for all sorts of things that happen in life, but you are one of the more inquisitive types, – always looking for answers to everything. I would call you curious, but in the nicest possible sense.

We haven't got round to semantics yet, but we will before you go, because the real meaning of words and how they are used is where a lot of human misunderstanding arises, deliberately or otherwise. But before we temporarily leave semantics, I will explain why we use the word 'deceptive' instead of 'deception', and why we use it as a noun and not as an adjective, because you won't yet find this use in any of your dictionaries. A deception is known by the perpetrator not to be true. A deceptive is something which appears, or is believed at the time, to be true but later transpires not to be so.

So now we come to the questions which, for various reasons, are not answered properly at the time of asking. Either the respondent does not know the answer, or does not wish to give the correct answer, or cannot explain the answer as the questioner does not have sufficient knowledge or experience to understand. We know that your very earliest conscious memory goes back to when you were just nineteen months old. Your mother was in bed in the back room of your house and just about to give birth to your baby brother. You wanted to see your mother, but you had whooping cough, and your grandmother stood in front of the door and said that you couldn't go in and see her. You were desperate to see your mother, and you knew that she really wanted to see you. 'Why can't I see her?' 'Because you can't'. Your grandmother would not give you a deception, but neither could she give the real answer as it was beyond your comprehension, and only some years later did you learn the truth.

And what about the moon? One day it's only a small funny shape, and the next day it's a bit bigger. A few days later, and it's different again. Sometimes it's a big round circle, but sometimes it's only half the size. Why does it keep changing? What a mystery. Then your elder brother ruined it all by telling you that the moon was always big and round, but you could only see the bit that was lit up by the sun at the time. But of course you knew the sun didn't ever come out at night. So was he telling you the truth, or just teasing again?

Thunder and lightning, – although it's a mystery, even to us Gods, why many humans put it in that back to front order. Your father told you that lightning was caused by electrical discharges in the atmosphere, and these heated the air and made it rush about, and this caused the thunder. At your age, he might just as well have told you that God lit a candle in the sky just before he went to bed and started snoring. You didn't understand the answer he gave you, but you wouldn't have understood who or what God was either, so you couldn't really learn anything then.

Your baby brother came from mummy's tummy. How did he get there? Surely she couldn't have eaten him? Or was it that God again giving them such a lovely present? Doesn't seem much like a present to me, you thought. Who on earth would want an ugly wrinkled piglet like that? And the smell. And it never ever stops crying. But it's all baby this, and baby that. They seem to have forgotten about me and my brothers. If that's a present, I hope they never get another one.

Of course as you grew older, you gradually learnt the truth about these things, and bit by bit the deceptives gave way to understanding. Sometimes they disappeared completely in one go, but other times you only learnt the whole truth bit by bit, over a period of time. Which is why we call them 'diminishing deceptives'.

You are now a little bit older and standing on a railway station platform. They built the track so straight you could almost see it for miles. But they must have got something wrong, because the track is quite wide apart here and it gets narrower and narrower, until the rails join together at that point you can see in the distance and where the train must fall off the track. That much is absolutely obvious. 'No, dad, if I can see it quite clearly, surely you must be able to as well.'

Now imagine for a moment that you are a very young child, living in a Ticuna village beside the Amazon River in Brazil. 'Papa, I've just seen the biggest bird ever. It was enormous, and it made a terrible loud screeching noise. And its feathers were all shiny but it didn't flap its wings. How does it stay in the sky? What kind of bird is it papa?' 'I don't know, Moaca, but I'll ask the captain.' Beni himself hardly knew what a jetliner was, let alone how to explain it to a three-year-old. OK Sorbo, but you're being pedantic again. No, an aeroplane wouldn't normally have been that close to the ground in that location. I was just giving you another example of the many things that children do not understand, and that cannot properly be explained to them until get older.

And so it goes on throughout human life. Almost daily, something happens to explain a little puzzle or mystery, and you think 'so that's why this or that happened', or 'now I understand'. But the principle of diminishing deceptives doesn't just apply to each human, but to whole groups in society, and indeed to the entire human race. There are countless examples in Earth's history, but I will only give you just a few, purely to illustrate the point. How old is the Universe? Around the time of, and before the Christian Era (BCE), depending on who and where you were, it was generally 'known' that the Universe was between 4,000 and 6,000 years old. Not much more, and not much less. Not much difference really from what your scientists now say they 'know' to be approximately fourteen billion and four-and-a-half billion years for the

Universe and your solar system respectively. The original deceptive was not deliberate, as it was the best guess of the scientists and philosophers of the time However, it was indeed a deceptive as it was a widely accepted belief which turned out not to be true. Just before I leave that, I'd better remind you that the so-called age of the Universe is still a deceptive, although they've at least got your solar system about right.

The Earth is flat. The sun is the centre of the Universe. The sun revolves around the Earth. These so-called 'truths' were all at one time unwitting deceptives, which gradually became challenged and bit by bit they diminished to the point that they completely disappeared and humans now know the realities.

Nothing can exceed the speed of light. Almost 'absolute truth' for over a hundred years, although it was disputed by a few people. Now your scientists have discovered that some particles may possibly be breaking this 'law'. Will other particles join them in future? And, whilst I have mentioned thought transference, I haven't yet explained that it is instantaneous. Albert Einstein was undoubtedly what you would call a genius. But he was also a human, and therefore not infallible. Before I leave Einstein, I'm going to give you the only quotation from a human that I will use this week. "Two things are infinite: the Universe and human stupidity, and I'm not sure about the Universe." As I said, a genius, and he was fairly close to the truth. The Universe is indeed infinite, but most humans are not totally stupid. He just used the wrong expression – human blindness would have been more accurate at that time. But in this context, blindness is of course not the physical inability to see material things, but the inability to understand all of the Universal truth. And while infinite was to all intents and purposes correct at the inception of human life and reasoning ability, some of your original deceptives are gradually being diminished.

Scientific progress in the last few centuries has been very effective at finding many physical truths about the Universe. However, humans want all questions to be answered immediately, and your philosophers and wranglers have been spectacularly unable to keep up with your scientists. This should not be surprising as, although humans can largely understand material facts, they are as yet unable to comprehend many things which cannot be proved to their satisfaction. As examples I've already briefly mentioned infinity, eternity, thought transference and of course God.

Throughout the whole of this week I'm going to tell you some of the things which humans need to understand about the reasons for their short life on Earth, and also what God expects from them. As I said earlier, I know what you are thinking at any time, but you cannot yet receive my thought transferences, so I'll have to express them in words. And one of the problems I have in communicating with you in words is that we are programmed altithonically so there are infinite thoughts circulating at the same time, and I have to select only those which you can comprehend. No Sorbo, – well, not yet. Many of Earth's computer experts are rightly convinced that altithonics must be possible for humans, and they are actively working towards it, as it will lead to whole new concepts of instantaneous thought and communication. But, because it requires a new mindset, and different and unfamiliar paths of instruction, it will not surprise you that many disagree and totally dismiss the possibility. Humans may indeed eventually find and use altithonics, but at the moment the only thing they can all agree on is that, even if it could work, it is still only a distant dream. And when they do discover how to use it, they will of course give it another name anyway.

Although I will tell you everything that you need to know while you are here, it may not always seem to be in what you think is a logical order. In fact there really is no absolute logical order to anything, either on Earth or in the Universe. You hadn't really thought about that before, so as a very simple example I'll give you five topics and ask you to arrange them, – climate, sex, leadership, food, space. Or another five, – hair, carrot, aeroplane, dog, geography. Yes, you're right, – there is no logical order. Everything we will discuss interacts with, and in many cases depends upon something else, but not always in any particular sequence or priority. And while I'm talking about communication, I should mention that in one short week, you will be learning the answers to more questions than most humans think about in their whole Earthly existence.

I'd better explain that too. Although many humans have a compulsion to wonder about the reasons for their existence, the average person only gives it a moment's thought from time to time. Contemplation of life itself doesn't get the priority we would like, but of course we do understand why that is. Far too often most of their energy and effort is consumed by the struggle just to survive. And sixty precious seconds a week would be more than the average human even realises that they are questioning the reasons. I have to say average, because as with all humans there are exceptions, so I am talking about the average of seven billion people. And the time you will spend here learning about God's guidance will be the equivalent of more than one hundred and eighty years of thoughts about life in the average human mind.

We will talk about religion in a while, but firstly I'd better explain why, during the whole of this week, I'm going to say quite a lot of things which to you would appear obvious and probably unnecessary. When you write the book, you must remember that many of your readers may not have had the benefit of much, if any, education as you know it. Indeed, some will be partly or wholly illiterate, so your book will have to be read to them. And of the people who can read it for themselves, there will also be many who will need someone else to explain some of things you have written. And the book should be published in printed form. Yes Sorbo, many people have access to computers and electronic publishing, but there are also many who don't. The book will not be just for the privileged and educated minority. It is for the entire human race. This also means that you will have to begin a lot of things with simple explanations of what is often already generally accepted knowledge. Inevitably, you will be accused of being over-simplistic, or not telling people anything they didn't already know and understand. You must ignore them and start every subject with very basic principles, and gradually enlarge on them by adding the further learning which you will take back from here. When the doubters have read all that you write, they will come to realise that it was indeed necessary for you to begin in this way. And of course I haven't forgotten the people who will learn to believe, but who will afterwards, very smugly, say 'well of course that's what I've known all along'. You know the sort of person, but you may be surprised at just how many there are.

And another thing before I forget, – although as you know I'm just saying this for you, – Gods can't forget. When I repeat something I've already said, and as you will do when you write, it's because it's deliberate. Most humans are not able to understand something new to them the first time they hear or read about or see it. Nor even the second, third, or sometimes the umpteenth time. So repetition is absolutely vital. As you have realised, I have repeated quite a lot of things I had already told you, and I will continue to do this freely whenever I consider it necessary. And therefore so will you, as eventually you'll be writing everything I tell you.

Before we discuss some of the differences between God's will and the way humans and their religions have interpreted it so far, we must talk about sin. And wrong. And crime. And the differences between them. Yes Sorbo, it should seem very simple, but unfortunately, as is the case in many things on Earth, it has become more than a bit blurred. So we'll start with the basics. And because crime is purely a human invention, and indeed it varies between different systems of justice, we'll start with sin. Yes, I know some crimes are sins, and most sins are crimes wherever they are committed, but it is very important that we separate the two. God's will isn't necessarily incorporated into human law, and human law does not always reflect God's will. I say God's will, but as you know now, this is what humans should try to observe, and not something that we dictate.

So we'll talk about God's guidance to the soul while it is in a human body. As I said, we have deliberately created solar systems and planets so that each soul can have a brief existence in a material body during its eternal journey towards Universal truth and understanding. I don't wish to confuse you, so for the moment I'm not going to discuss other planets, but only your solar system and planet Earth. We can talk about the others later, as I'm well aware that humans have this fascination to know everything about everything, even though this curiosity often leads to them straying from our guidance, and ignoring what they should be doing in their Earthly life. Right now, we will talk about Earth and humans. And souls and God. The soul is in a material human body for a reason. OK, I know yours isn't at this precise moment, – but it will be again on Friday, if that's what you choose, so don't be so pedantic. Yes, – picky, if you prefer that word.

Anyway, I'll continue. Like every other part of the soul's eternal journey, life in a human body is a learning process. At birth, you know very little, except what is in your inherited genes, which you sometimes call instinct. As you grow older you accumulate knowledge, and you use this in your development. And you have a certain amount of free will, and you sometimes use this, if circumstances allow. But although the eternal soul is not innately selfish, while in a human body it is often tempted, and many souls give in to this temptation in one way or another. This is not necessarily a sin, or even wrong. That depends entirely on the temptation and your choice.

We will discuss a whole range of topics where humans have mostly got things right or wrong, but first I'll give you two apparently simple everyday examples. We'll think about the excessive consumption of food or drink, which is a common human habit. Many cultures and religions call this gluttony or greed or a similar word, and consider it to be a major sin. Historically, and even today in areas where food is in limited supply, it is indeed a sin. But is it still a sin in regions where food supplies are more than sufficient to meet the need for reasonable sustenance for the whole population for their everyday activities? You know somebody who enjoys eating. And, because they enjoy eating, they eat more than their body needs and they become overweight. Is this a sin, or is it wrong, or is it both? Yes Sorbo, apparently simple, isn't it? But we have allowed humans to develop in a way in which they may enjoy pleasure, as long as it does not cause disadvantage to others.

Over-eating, leading to overweight, is not ideal for the person concerned, but is not necessarily a sin. However, it would be a sin if it caused such a shortage of food that meant that other people would not be able to get their reasonable share of the available resources. Or if the deliberate over-indulgence caused obesity or illness which put such unnecessary strain on the services providing medical care and attention that it jeopardised the treatment available to those other people who were ill through no fault of their own making. That sin would be because you were putting your desires before the needs or desires of other people, – in other words, you were being selfish. Yes Sorbo, you are quite right. Everything concerning humans will always have exceptions. In this case, one of those exceptions is that there are people who cannot stop themselves from being compulsive eaters or drinkers. They are addicted to their habits. These people need to and should seek help and treatment for their addiction. In these circumstances their failure to do so would demonstrate selfish disregard of others.

Now I'll try to make the second example a bit easier. Last week, you drove through your town at a speed of 32 miles per hour. Yes Sorbo, 2 mph above the speed limit. In human terms, this was both wrong, and an offence. But it was not necessarily a sin. However, if you had been driving recklessly and had an accident in which you had killed or injured someone, or damaged property, you would not only have been wrong and committed a crime, but you would also have committed a sin. Your reckless driving would have shown a lack of consideration of the safety of other people, and again your sin would be that of selfishness.

By the way, remorse after committing a sin does not alter the fact of the sin. I'm telling you this now, as many humans have the erroneous belief that remorse after the event might lead us into deleting the sin from the assessment of their Earthly lives. Genuine contrition is highly desirable, but cannot completely atone for sins committed while the soul is in a body. Each soul will spend a brief time in a material body, – in your case as a human on Earth. I could be having a discussion such as this with any soul from any other planet, but as I said earlier it is human life on Earth which is causing us concern at the moment, so I will only talk about humans and Earth. In time, humans will learn about other planetary life forms, but they are not yet quite ready for that. The material incarnation phase of a soul's journey is different from any other. It is where we assess not just thoughts, as is the case at all other times, but how the soul in a physical body reacts to temptation away from the search for eternal truth. Actually, where we assess whether it succumbs to being selfish, which is the greatest sin of all. Selfishness has to be eradicated before a soul can proceed to higher planes, and it is this progression which is the fundamental purpose of Universal existence. Yes Sorbo, I know you are struggling with that, so I'd better explain a bit more. And again to make it as simple as possible, I'll still only talk about humans.

We have created the solar system and Earth, to put the soul into a human body. This is the most difficult part of the soul's entire eternal journey, as here and at some times, it is always tempted beyond what it can completely resist. We have done this deliberately, – as we do in everything, – because it is our duty, as guardians of the Universe, to guide the soul towards Universal understanding. We observe the soul's entire human life, and of course we give guidance when asked. And when the human life is over, we send the soul to whichever plane is appropriate. That depends totally on how it has acted in its human body. On Earth, there are always temptations to stray from what is right, and many of these seem irresistible, at least at the time they arise. As I said, the soul is not innately selfish, but in a human body it usually becomes so, to one degree or another. There are exceptions, but these are very rare, so I will leave them aside.

We have allowed life on Earth to evolve in such a way that the physical life forms themselves, – but not the souls within them, – have historically had to be selfish just to survive, and for human evolution to continue. So we have another paradox. Innately unselfish souls within instinctively selfish human bodies. No Sorbo, – it's not at all insoluble, – but yes, it will take time. Humans must learn to recognise, and fully understand, that what seems to be their one body is actually made up of two different parts. Their physical body may seem to be the important part. But it isn't. It's just a short-term vehicle for the crucial part of them, – their mind or psyche, or actually their soul. Although it may not be obvious, many humans already realise this. They just don't do anything about telling other people. As with so many things on Earth, they say to themselves 'I'm only one of billions of people, so whatever I do or say won't make any difference'. But they are wrong. Even if they don't feel able to shout about what they believe, they can lead by example. And they can talk about their beliefs with family and friends. And bit by bit they will come to realise that they have kindred spirits, – often in the people they least expected. Yes Sorbo, there are many billions of kindred spirits, but not that many who realise that they are, or that there are indeed billions of other people of like mind.

We would like this to change. But the change must be gradual, and it must be done in a very gentle way. If you choose to help in this change, your visit here will be the beginning of a wide acceptance of kindred spirits, so I must tell you more about them. They are not, and will not be, an organisation such as those you are familiar with on Earth. Essentially, they are all of the humans who instinctively know the difference between right and wrong. They may have a religion, or they may be religious without belonging to a particular religion. Yes Sorbo, just because you believe in God doesn't mean you have to belong to a religion. In their inner thoughts, all kindred spirits know that there is some form of God, and that there is a reason for their existence on Earth. Those who currently do belong to, and largely believe in, an organised religion, also know that there are some aspects of that religion which cause them a certain amount of mental discomfort.

Think for a moment about a devout member of a major religion. They know that their religion gives all the answers to all their questions about life, both on Earth and in the hereafter. All the other religions must be wrong, as theirs is right. But how can so many billions of people believe in other religions which obviously give the wrong answers? If they really think about this deeply enough, it does indeed cause a little discomfort. The answer is the truth, and as so often is the case, the truth is actually very simple. So simple, that very few people can see it. And because they can't see it, and because scientists are increasingly seeming to give all of the answers to life and the Universe, many humans are turning away from religion. That is, of course, excepting religious zealots. There is no good place in the Universe which is truly suitable for such misguided souls, so they are confining themselves, after their human death, to long periods of corrective contemplation in limbo, or whichever of the thousands of words you choose to call it. As I said, it is not a punishment imposed by us. It is self-inflicted by the actions of the particular soul. All religions have produced zealots at some point in their history, and unfortunately some still are. Paradoxically, their actions have exactly the opposite effect to their aims, inasmuch as that they very often turn the majority of decent people away from religion. This is not what humans should be doing, as belief in God is essential to the proper way to enlightenment.

Scientists are also misleading humans. Whilst they are indeed giving some answers to the physical questions about the Universe, they cannot give the answer to the most important one. Only belief can do that, and if you believe in God, you are religious. Yes Sorbo, in a way you are right. We must talk about religions. But we should not talk just about their different beliefs, or even the different beliefs within one religion. As I said earlier, major religions try to give answers to the reasons for the soul in its human existence, and guidance as to how humans should conduct themselves. Should be simple. But the soul is not simple, – it is highly complex. And in a human body it becomes more so, as it has to adjust to the needs of that human body. And humans need leaders who, at this stage of evolution, are of course also humans and therefore have all the fallibility of humans.

We'll talk first about the codes of conduct developed by religions. And now you must remember that God has never given any orders or commands. No Sorbo, – none whatsoever, – only guidance to those who seek the truth. All of the rules of any of the religions have been dictated by a succession of humans, some following our guidance and some, because of the necessities of human survival at the time, with or without our guidance. So it follows that different religions have in the past laid down different rules of behaviour. With some exceptions, most of these rules were quite acceptable to us when they were formulated. However, life on Earth has developed substantially since then, and most religions have failed to alter or amend their rules to take this into account.

Now is the time for change, but this can only be done by humans. God will give guidance whenever asked, but God will not dictate.

So Sorbo, just for a start, every religion should examine its bibles and alter the texts accordingly. All reference to rules dictated by God should be amended to show clearly that they are God's will, but not God's command. No, that will not change the fact that humans should try to follow God's guidance. If it helps you to understand what I mean, try to think of God as a very friendly and caring schoolteacher. Not the sort who punishes children who don't behave properly, but who really encourages children to learn as much as they can take in. If they refuse to listen and learn, their only punishment is that they won't get to understand the truth. And, while we are talking about God's will, some religions and cultures have written into their sacred books beliefs which they consider to have been dictated by God, but which actually are misunderstandings of the guidance given to humans by God over many thousands of years.

As I said, from the time that they are able to use conscious thought, all humans, no matter how difficult their circumstances, sometimes wonder about the reasons why they exist. Indeed, pre-humans also had the same curiosity, but we won't go back as far as that. Many thousands of years ago, there were of course no real means of communication, except largely within the communities in which people lived. Like individuals, whole communities also wondered about life and its reasons and meanings. And because they were human, they had to have answers. But they didn't have any answers. So, gradually, answers had to be formulated. And, over a long period of time, theories were developed about who or what created the Universe and life.

Most of these theories involved a God or Gods as the ultimate supreme power. A power to be worshipped and obeyed. Along with these beginnings of religions, usually came some forms of rituals and codes of behaviour. So humans had their embryonic answers as to how life started and how they should live it.

But communities were scattered all over the Earth, so their religions developed differently and therefore, while they had some beliefs in common, they also had many which were not. As I also said earlier, there are now over four thousand religions on Earth, and this includes more than twenty major ones. I'm not going to talk about the minor religions, and I'm not going to include atheism, agnosticism, secularism or similar things as religions, even though some of their adherents do. Most of the major religions are the combination of the thoughts and beliefs of communities and cultures, developed over thousands of years. But, as you know, some were established as a result of the lives of prophets or messiahs. I'm only going to discuss those religions which believe in a God or Gods, or as you might say, monotheisms and polytheisms. Now you know that they are both the same, so that difference is irrelevant. And I'm going to exclude any theisms which do not accept that God is benign. As guardians of the Universe we must be benign. So we're left with the religions which believe that God created the Universe, and that God is good. But none of these religions is completely right. Yes, we are good, as we must be, as guardians of the Universe. And yes, we created your solar system, in which human life then evolved. But there's also the big 'No'. God did not create the Universe. As I've already told you, God and the Universe are eternal.

Some Earth religions have understood that for thousands of years, but the clever modern scientific brains, the academics, the scholars, and the religious teachers, cannot come to terms with it. In a way, we are amused by the sort of argument that if the Universe is indeed eternal then we, that is God, are redundant, or at least irrelevant. The purpose of the Universe is to continually strive towards the perfection which we know will not quite be reached. God's function and responsibility is to be the guardian of the Universe, and to assist that purpose. To put it very simply, – God is the eternal guardian of the eternal Universe, and both are inextricably essential to each other. Without God, there would be no Universe, and without the Universe, there would be no God. That does not mean that God created the Universe, – it just means that both are eternal. No, I did not say it was going to be easy, or even possible for you to understand that – at the moment eternity and infinity are beyond the reach of human comprehension. One day, if we allow your Solar system to continue, the human mind will be nearly be able to understand what they really mean, but that day is far into the future.

In the meantime, the only way towards Universal truth is belief, or faith. Sorbo, – if you flashback to Friday, – you will remember that we have given humans a certain amount of free will, so they may initially refuse to have faith. But, like Gods, all souls are also eternal, so they will eventually have to accept the Universal truth, even if they are not yet ready or willing to accept it now. I'd better tell you what happens to the soul when it leaves its Earthly body, – permanently that is, – not temporarily, like you this time.

We'll start with the historical belief which in various forms was generally accepted by a majority of religions. You are born, live and die on Earth. After death your soul goes to Heaven or Hell or somewhere in between, depending on how you have lived your life. Quite simple and straightforward, and a good basis on which to form early codes of behaviour. But not one which is accurate, or sufficient for today's humans. Actually, quite a few of Earth's ancient civilisations, cultures and even religions, understood many things about the soul, but unfortunately this knowledge has been progressively disputed and dismissed by scientists and philosophers throughout the modern centuries and most, but not all, of it is now regarded as primitive folklore. Of course some of it really isn't true, – for instance, despite some continuing belief, we do not send souls back to Earth as a reincarnation in any life form. During their eternal journey, some souls do indeed need to progress through one or more further existences in physical bodies, but these are always in different places.

However, some of these earlier thoughts or beliefs are actually true. We do indeed process all souls, and we then send them to wherever Universal law dictates that they should be. And their destination does depend entirely on how they have performed in the past. And the time they spend there depends on their willingness to learn and accept Universal truth, and thus conform with Universal law. But we don't give these destinations any Earthly names like heaven or hell.

As you know, the human brain is extraordinarily complex. But because it is a physical structure it has limitations. One of these is the inability to fully comprehend something which it has not itself experienced. For instance, consider a strawberry. You know what it looks like, but can you describe it verbally in such accurate detail that someone who has never seen one will have a perfect picture of it in their mind? And how can they know what a strawberry tastes like until they have eaten one? Yes, of course you can tell them everything that it doesn't taste like, but that won't get them any nearer to the actuality. And although everybody might agree that a particular taste is that of a strawberry, as each person's palate is slightly different, so their personal experience is slightly different and unique to them.

Childbirth is another example. Until the expectant female has actually given birth it is impossible for them to understand exactly what they will experience. They can read and talk about it as much as they like with mothers and experts in pre-natal matters, but that cannot not fully prepare them for the reality of the actual event. Even then, each childbirth is different, not just for different mothers, but also for the same mother on second and subsequent occasions. So while females can empathise, they still cannot totally comprehend the uniqueness of the experience of any other mother's childbirth. And of course men are completely unable to do either. Men can understand that a cracked rib or maybe acute appendicitis is painful. But each person has a different pain threshold, so while each occurrence will give pain in a similar location in the body, the severity to the sufferer will be to a different degree which is impossible to describe accurately to other people.

So it is with death. Until they actually experience death, humans cannot really understand what will happen to their soul after it leaves its physical body. But to give you an idea, try to imagine the Universe as an enormous building. There are many rooms on many floors or levels of this building. The lower rooms are the most unpleasant and most undesirable and could be likened to the dungeons in a castle. Extremely cold, damp, dark and miserable. So oppressive that if you were here you would feel that ceasing to exist at all would be far preferable. But that is not an option. The room you are in was chosen by you, as a direct result of your actions on Earth. And you will remain there until you can prove that you deserve to be moved to a higher level. Each level above is progressively better and more comfortable and lighter. If you can rise further the windows become larger and you will be able to see more and more of the view, until if you could reach the roof you could survey the entire Universe. But you cannot actually reach either the roof or indeed the basement of this building. However far you go up, there is always another floor above you, and no matter how far you descend, there is another level below. And on each floor there are always more rooms in front of and behind you and to each side. Yes Sorbo, the universe is infinite in every direction.

When it leaves Earth the soul will initially be sent to the appropriate level or plane of the Universe. This will depend entirely on how the soul has acted in the past. The more selfish the disregard of the best interests of other souls and the good of the Universe has been, the lower and less desirable the initial plane will be. Every soul will have acted selfishly to some extent during its life in a physical body, so its initial plane will depend on the extent of that selfishness. The more serious the sins, the lower the level of the plane. For example a sin such as deliberate murder would commit the soul to the dungeons or hell in human terms. Lesser sins result in allocation to higher planes. So the soul's initial destination will depend on how it has acted during its time in a physical body. And this is dictated not by God, but entirely by the way the soul itself has used the freewill it was given.

As I said, there are no human terms to properly describe the soul's destination. But old words like heaven, paradise and nirvana, or hell, purgatory and limbo are much closer to the truth than modern thinking will admit and for the time being we are happy with their continuing use. With the exception of one aspect of hell. Hell cannot automatically be a permanent state. Souls are eternal, and therefore they could acknowledge their sins at any time, although there are some who have always strongly resisted this, and have so far shown absolutely no signs of repentance. But God is patient, and time and souls are eternal. And all souls can seek to improve themselves by asking God for guidance and then acting upon it. Genuine remorse and repentance for past sins will in time give the soul the opportunity to start to make amends for the selfish negativity of its physical life and adopt a positive benign attitude to other souls and the Universe itself and thus advance to higher levels. All souls could eventually reach the higher planes of contemplation before Godliness. In your sixteenth century CE, Thomas More coined the word utopia, and this word could be used for those planes of contemplation, as long as utopia is properly defined as being a region as near as possible to perfection, and not understood to suggest perfection itself. As I said, perfection is not possible in the eternal Universe. It is to be strived for, and not quite gained, but the souls which genuinely seek true enlightenment will find peace and harmony. And their eventual reward will be eternal happiness.

But I'll get back to those religions which believe in God, and that God is good. Some quasi-religions have very acceptable codes of behaviour, but they don't include God or the reasons for human existence, so I will exclude them. Some others are so misguided that, in human terms, you could justifiably call them the work of the devil, – but that's a different story which doesn't have any place here. I'm only going to talk about religions which have beliefs and principles and laws, rules or codes of behaviour, – usually set down in the form of books of scriptures. These books have many names, but I will call them all bibles. No Sorbo, I am not referring just to the Jewish or Christian Bibles or the Quran, but to the definitive written scriptures or sacred texts of all religions, and I will use the word bibles to mean all of these authoritative books.

We've talked about the origins of religions. As you know, many of them have beliefs in common with each other, and a lot of these beliefs are largely true. But problems arise where there are differences between religions, and these problems are made worse by all religions' refusal to accept that they are wrong in any respect. Mostly, they will not even consider altering their bibles to take account of subsequent human scientific knowledge which proves that some parts are historically wrong. Although you now know that God did not create the Universe, it will take many years before all humans will be able to come to terms with this. Until then, we accept that many religions will continue to believe that He did. However, He did create your solar system which of course includes your planet Earth. As I said earlier, God is not male or female, but I'm using the word He, as that's the way most humans do. I, or we, would be more accurate, but we can stick with He for the time being. And, of course, the world as you know it was not created six to eight thousand years ago, nor did the creation take six days. In your twenty-first century CE you won't have much of a problem in explaining those, but others will be more difficult.

We'll take just a couple of stories from the Jewish and Christian Bibles first, then we'll talk about all bibles. The Jewish people have a covenant with God. Right from the beginnings of recorded Earth history humans have prayed to their God for guidance. And God has given that guidance. Many people consider that Adam and Noah were two of the earliest Jewish prophets. They prayed to God for understanding of life and God's message. In return and as a part of God's gift of knowledge to them, God also made a covenant with them. That covenant was that they belonged to God's chosen race on Earth. Adam and Noah both felt highly honoured and privileged that God had chosen humans above all other life forms on Earth to be the recipients of His wisdom and His guidance and blessings, and they gave this knowledge to their peoples. This was passed down through many generations and to later prophets and God re-affirmed this covenant with each one of them who prayed to Him. These prophets knew that God's covenant was with the entire human race, but as time passed this part of the knowledge was given less emphasis. While most of today's Jewish teachers and leaders also fully understand and accept the entirety of God's covenant, there are still many in their communities who do not. As a result, even in your twenty-first century CE, somewhere around half of the Jewish people are not aware of the true history and meaning of God's covenant, and many still believe that their race alone among humans is the chosen race of God.

Now is the time to correct this misunderstanding. The enlightened Jewish religious leaders need the courage to explain to their people how it came about, and they need to do it without hesitation or equivocation. And as it will indeed require a great deal of courage on their part to explain this clearly and unambiguously, there will be many who will be tempted to shrink from carrying out this difficult task. And there will be many more who will argue that it is not possible that their historical religious texts are wrong. But all religious texts were written by humans, and are still analysed and interpreted by humans, and humans are frequently wrong, sometimes due to accidental errors, sometimes to misunderstandings, but sometimes deliberately to reinforce their argument. No Sorbo, that is neither racist nor anti-semitic. Anti-semitism is one of many forms of racism, and it is a sin. It is hostility to or persecution of the Jewish people in any way. And persecution in any form of any race, religion or culture, or of any individual who is different from the majority by reason of physical or mental disadvantage, is a sin. But it is not persecution to explain to a Jew, or for instance to an Inuit or Balinese, that to God they are the same as every other member of the human race. They and their customs, beliefs and way of life may indeed be different from other peoples, but their souls are all equal in the eyes of God. Likewise it is not persecution to explain to a Hindu that the cow is no more sacred to God than any other animal. All animals are sacred to God and God loves all animals equally.

It is indeed a sin to consider any person or race to be inferior to any other, but it is not a sin either to believe or to tell them that they are equal. So I will repeat that the Jewish people have a covenant with God. Yes, they do. And every other nation or race on Earth has exactly the same covenant. In God's eyes, all humans are equal, and always will be equal. God has chosen the human race to be the life-form on Earth to which, if their souls are willing, God will impart guidance towards eternal truth and understanding. The entire human race is the chosen race. And God did not make this choice by random selection.

At this point in Earth's evolutionary development, the human is the only animal sufficiently advanced to receive and understand God's spiritual guidance Many other creatures will eventually evolve as far as this, but it will take much more time. So God has chosen to impart to souls, when they are in in human form, His guidance as to how they should behave in their own best interests, which although many souls do not yet realise it, is actually also in the best interests of all other souls and the Universe. But only if they ask to receive it. And as I said before, and I will say again and again, they do not have to ask for this guidance, nor do they have to follow it. But failure to do so will mean a selfish disregard of the good of the Universe, and will inevitably result in the soul's unnecessary self-inflicted suffering.

So all humans are equal in God's eyes. And all humans are not only equal but, since God created your solar system and planet Earth, they are also therefore in that respect all children of God. God who created your Earth, and also created the means for the evolution of all of the life forms on it. There is not, and never has been just one child of God. All humans are children of God. Regardless of their sometimes seemingly desperate and inexplicable circumstances, every human is a child of God, and is just as special to God as every other. God who created your solar system so that souls may have one short incarnation in a physical Earthly body, as a part of their eternal quest for Universal truth. But only one on Earth. As I said Universal Law does not permit the soul any re-visitation or reincarnation on the same planet, and of course that includes Earth. Any soul needing a further period of exposure to selfish temptation in a physical body will be incarnated on a different planet in a different solar system.

So we must talk about bibles and their stories, and I'll also come back to these two stories again, as they're relevant to human understanding of life on Earth, as it was thousands of years ago, and still is today. With some exceptions, bibles are not contemporary diary records. They were mostly written well after the happenings which they describe. Therefore, as both individual and collective human memories are very prone to error, there are inevitably many inaccurate accounts of events and claims.

For instance, right from its recorded beginning, in many cases well over five thousand years ago, most folk-lore and every religion has stories about miracles. But then, almost every human being can recall having experienced something which seemed miraculous at the time. These are events which are apparently inexplicable, but they are not miracles. Going back at least as far as religious chronicles, there are also many other records of miraculous events. Partly to demonstrate that these were miracles of God, they often happened in temples or other places of worship. Although it was not known, or even imagined, at the time, most of these were actually performed by magicians, conjurors, illusionists or the like. So there are many biblical, and non-biblical, stories about miracles, but these are all either inaccurately chronicled, or they are deceptions or deceptives. Some of these recorded events, such as the miraculous opening and closing of the temple doors at God's will, have already been explained. When this 'miracle' was first witnessed, it was for its time an exceptionally advanced and sophisticated application of hydraulics and mechanics constructed by very clever engineers who were employed by priests to demonstrate both their own authority and the power of God. And to its audience at the time it did exactly that. Thousands of years later, the workings of this 'miracle' are now fully understood. So it has been exposed as a deception and an illusion. But not a miracle. Some other so-called miracles have also now been explained, but many have not. But they do all have explanations. They are not miracles. Miracles do not happen, – they only appear to happen. And in time, humans will come to understand the explanations of all of them.

Yes, Sorbo – you're thinking that we wish to discredit religion. But we don't. We would like all humans to believe in God, – even those who, at the moment, choose not to believe in anything. Sometimes we wonder whether we have given humans too much free will, but only time will give us the answer to that. I'm digressing again, so I must get back to basics. We want humans to believe in God, and we would like humans to believe in some form of religion. Yes, you're right, – it's almost the same thing, but not quite. And we don't expect all religions suddenly to merge into just one religion, – humans are not yet able to come to terms with change at that sort of speed. But neither do we wish to see the continuation of over four thousand different interpretations of what should be essentially one fundamental belief. Our guidance is for humans to believe in God, that God is good, and that if a soul genuinely seeks the truth about life, God will offer enlightenment. No soul can reach full enlightenment in its short life on Earth, but every soul should strive towards it. No matter how difficult the struggle may be on Earth, even just for day-to-day survival, each soul should try to find some moments for prayer for the strength to continue, and for guidance towards their and other souls' improvement. The power of prayer should never be underestimated. Proper prayer, for the right reasons, will always be answered.

While the soul is in its human body, and therefore not yet able to use thought transference, the only way to commune with God is by prayer. And prayer will only work if you believe in God. But there are a lot of misconceptions about prayer, and this leads to many people praying for the wrong things. Proper prayer is the soul asking God for guidance, either for itself or for other souls or sometimes for both, and if asked for the right reasons, God will give this guidance. As I said much earlier, we, that is God, cannot physically interfere with life on Earth, so it is in vain and useless to ask us to do so. For example, farmers would be misunderstanding the nature of God if they prayed to us for rain. So would holidaymakers who prayed for good weather. And don't pray that someone will have a safe journey. You may sincerely desire these things, but they are all hopes or wishes. They are not prayers which God can answer. In your places of worship, or in your homes or anywhere else, you may, and often do, individually or collectively, pray for someone who is ill to make a speedy recovery. Again, this is a wish, but not a prayer However, if you add or include a prayer for that person's soul to find peace or harmony or understanding, you are praying for the right guidance, and God will give that guidance if their soul is willing to receive it.

I must come back again to God's guidance and tell you a bit more about it. It is only guidance. Despite the beliefs of many religions and as recorded in their scriptures, God does not give rules, laws, commandments or any other sort of orders. It is God's duty and responsibility to help souls towards the understanding of Universal truth, because that is where they will find peace and harmony. But as I also said earlier, souls have free will, and God does not use coercion or compulsion in any way. Souls must wish to seek the truth, or otherwise they will not find it. When souls leave their human bodies, they firstly come here for assessment and redirection. We send them to the appropriate place for them to reflect and contemplate, and if they genuinely wish to improve, then we gradually move them to higher planes, or levels of understanding. If they refuse or reject the truth, there is no punishment visited upon them by God. The peace and harmony and enlightenment which they could find is merely being delayed by their choice, and they are prolonging their own mental turmoil. Eternity being what it is, they will eventually wish to seek the truth, but until they do, they will stay in what we said humans might consider the undesirable state of limbo, hell, purgatory, tartarus, or whatever you wish to call it, for far longer than they should. And it is indeed an undesirable state for the soul, – a state of torment and hopelessness, from which the soul feels it will never be released. But of course, never is just a human word, with a human understanding. And on Earth, this human understanding gives it both a past meaning of not yet and often a future meaning of impossibility. But in eternity, while never still has the same past meaning, it has no future meaning.

Anyway, I'll get back to prayer. When I talked about prayer, I also mentioned inspiration. If you believe in God and pray to God for guidance, you will receive it, but you may not understand how you receive it. You may suddenly realise something, and think that you've had an amazing inspiration. That is the nature and power of prayer. So true prayer is the request for spiritual help and guidance. A request to God for intercession in physical events on Earth is not prayer. You could call it false prayer, as it means that you do not understand or accept the nature of true and proper prayer. There are of course humans who do understand this, but for each of those there are thousands of people who don't, and they need to be given this explanation. And here I should also talk about those people who witness the terrible suffering caused by natural disasters such as earthquakes and floods, and the follies of war and the consequences of other avoidable human actions, and thus dismiss the existence of God. Because to them, if God existed He would not allow such events. But that is to misunderstand the reality of God. Except by deletion, God cannot physically interfere with the evolution of your solar system, or the actions of humans. God can and always will give spiritual guidance to those who ask, and the future of life on Earth will depend on whether or not the majority of humans can collectively agree to try to follow God's guidance.

Now we'll think again about religion and bibles, and the patriarchs who inspired most of them. Yes, Sorbo, it was largely patriarchs. Thousands of years ago, we hadn't instilled the idea of equality of the sexes, – nobody would have understood or accepted it then. Even now more than half of the world population can't really get their heads around the fact that while there are some things that men can do better than women, there are also many areas where women are superior to men. Yes, we will talk about women and aggression and war before you go, but for the moment just imagine this scenario: About four thousand years ago Abraham, or Abram or Ibrahim, – we'll call him Abraham, – prayed to God for guidance for his people. We said to him 'well, Abraham, – it is good that you are praying to God for the guidance which we will give you, but you're a man, and there are some things which are beyond your comprehension. Ask Sarah also to commune with us, and we'll impart to her those parts of the knowledge which only a woman can really understand.' No, Sorbo, – more than a bit difficult even today, – absolutely impossible then. Particularly for Abraham, because he'd been talking incessantly about God for many years, – and Sarah didn't even believe that God existed. As far as she was concerned all of the hours Abraham spent praying to that god of his could be far better put to doing something really useful. But now it's you who are digressing this time, so let me return to bibles.

Bibles were mostly written with the very best of intentions. Apart from many stories, they often include basic explanations of life, how it started, and how it should be lived. Leaders of almost every religion regard their bibles as being immutable, and setting out God's testaments and commandments. But God does not give rules or commandments. God gives guidance. And bibles were written by humans, so of course they contain human errors, and most of these errors have not yet been corrected. Over the years, millions of scholars, academics, religious teachers, and other very wise people, have minutely examined every word in every bible, and every translation and revision of every bible, – looking for errors, inaccuracies and contradictions, – historical or otherwise. But they have been looking for the wrong things, so they have either arrived at the wrong answers, or no answers at all. Fortunately, Gods don't weep, – otherwise the Universe would be permanently flooded. Sorry, – just borrowing a bit of your humour again. Actually, we quite like it, as it doesn't make the discussion any less serious, but it does add a bit of interest. Anyway, as I said, they have been looking at things the wrong way.

Many early bibles were inspired by patriarchs. Patriarchs who were leaders, most of whom genuinely sought to do what they considered were the right things for their tribes, races, or nations. And some of them prayed to God for guidance. And we gave them guidance about what is right or wrong, and how to improve themselves and their peoples by striving towards Universal truth. But, as I said, we cannot physically interfere with or change evolutionary development on any planet, except by our last resort of deletion. And we do not give rules, laws, commandments or orders. Those are human concepts and inventions, and humans needed them many thousands of years ago, as indeed they still do today, and will do so for many years yet. Not eternally, but for a very long time. Although it is not accepted by many people, human evolution is still in its early stages, and rules, laws, and the people who formulate them, are still required at the moment. Yes Sorbo, – I did say human evolution is still at a very early stage. And that many people are not able to come to terms with that. But that's nothing new either.

Every generation discovers more about the Universe, and often wonders how their forebears could have lived in such ignorance as they obviously did. But so far humans have only discovered a tiny fraction of available knowledge, and most of that is only about the physical aspects of the Universe. This should not surprise you, as humans as you know them have existed for just thousands of years, and even your solar system is over four billion years old. Each generation has discovered scientific facts, or more accurately what they considered to be facts. And each present generation will believe that they now know almost everything they need to know about the Universe and their existence. And each future generation will learn more, which will modify and in some cases contradict the previous accepted knowledge. And so it will continue, adding all the time to the sum of knowledge of the physical Universe. Yes, I did say physical Universe, because that is the only part which the scientists can understand or explain. What will take a lot more time is for all humans to realise and accept that there is a reason for their existence on Earth. And a reason for other life forms throughout the Universe. And the soul's short existence in a physical living body is only a small part of that soul's journey.

It is an unfortunate fact that religions have been unable to keep up with scientific discovery, and therefore have allowed themselves to appear increasingly less relevant to the material facts of twenty-first century life as it is on Earth. Because scientists can find more and more about the mechanics of life, but scientists cannot explain the reasons, and religions have so far not provided the spiritual assurance which humans need to fill the void between physical knowledge and Universal truth. Indeed, humans are not yet sufficiently developed to fully comprehend the gift of life which is both body and soul, and that is why they need faith and trust. Faith and trust in God. God who will freely give guidance to any soul who wishes to receive it. And humans need religions. But they need religions which will give God's proper spiritual guidance. Not religions which insist on outdated or compulsory rituals, teachings or services. Religions should be there to help their followers to seek the truth about life and God, but not for the self-advancement of the religion or its ministers. And those ministers should be humble servants of their congregations, not dictatorial masters. To remain relevant to humans, or indeed to regain that relevance, religions must evolve as life on Earth evolves. And God needs religions to embrace this change. What I am telling you is what we would like the rest of humanity to read and try to understand. Of course many people will not believe anything that you write. And of course that is their choice.

Let's go back again to about the third millennium BCE, and patriarchs, – or leaders. Historically, humans have always needed leaders, and many people have been either eager, or willing, – or sometimes both, – to assume such a role. The early patriarchs are good examples. They were generally well-intentioned in their efforts to lead their people, but they needed to demonstrate some form of authority, and many of them chose to use a God, or Gods, to provide this. Indeed, many of them did pray to us for guidance, and of course we gave such guidance, according to Universal law. But, whilst the leaders mostly understood and respected this guidance, in those early times they had to modify it to suit the actual conditions in which their peoples then lived. So, using the word of God as their authority, they laid down codes of practice and behaviour to be adhered to by their followers. They were well aware that these rules would have to be altered over time, to adapt to changing conditions, but of course they could not say that. In those days, they could not say 'these are the words of God for today, but tomorrow they will be modified'. Yes Sorbo, you are absolutely right, – even though you must try, you will indeed find that you can't even say that today to sophisticated and well-educated twenty-first century CE humans.

But those leaders of the past had to lead, and so they did provide codes of behaviour which were, and mostly still are, valid and decent principles which largely follow God's guidance, and which humans should try to respect. But there are some rules, founded in religions or otherwise, which do need both explanation and then modification. I am not going to talk about those of any specific religion or belief, and I won't put them in any particular order, – I'm going to leave that to you. Except, that is, for the two examples I briefly mentioned. Abraham prayed to God for guidance, and we gave it to him. And we also explained, – and he fully understood, – that whilst this guidance was what we wished individual beings to strive towards during their lives, and the whole human race during its evolution, it was not something which could happen immediately. Abraham needed to, and indeed he did, explain our guidance to his people in the only way that they could have accepted at that time. We do not give rules, laws, or commandments, but Abraham needed them, and he set some out and gave them as God's word. We were content for him to use our authority then, and for him not even to suggest that the passing of time would necessitate some changes to God's perceived laws. He simply could not say it then. And he was right not to say it. And the same goes for Moses, and all of the other prophets, sages and messiahs of any and all religions and beliefs.

But over the ages, humans should have realised that what Abraham did say needed further explanation, or clarification or modification. So-called wise people, of whatever calling or profession, and for whatever motives, have vigorously resisted this, and largely contented themselves with analysing actual words as they were written, and of course translated, many thousands of times. Wonderful scholarly brains have wasted trillions of hours analysing millions of words, – and all to little or no avail. They're simply looking at what they have got, – and failing to come to terms with true meaning of God, and God's role in furthering the development of the purpose of the Universe.

Before I leave the subject of prophets, and get round to human rules, I promised to talk specifically about one more, – Jesus. The Christ or Messiah, to his followers. More recent than most of the others, and to Christians far more special. But special is a human emotive word, and God does not have emotions in that sense. I will call him Jesus Christ, although he was not a messiah but a prophet in the true meaning. Many prophets before him had conveyed some of God's message to their peoples. But right from the time when humans started to have any rational thoughts, no human before Jesus Christ had fully understood and explained all of God's guidance in the loving and caring and selfless way which he did. He was well aware that he would be punished by humans for giving God's message to the world, but he had the courage and determination to continue. And in human terms he made the ultimate sacrifice. And so did many of his apostles, disciples and followers. For telling the truth about God's guidance to humans. Too many powerful people in both the religious and secular communities of that time were afraid of losing their authority over the people who they regarded as their subjects. And of course, to themselves, those leaders were far more important than God or God's message. They had to be, because that is what they believed and said. And many of their subjects followed them like sheep. Yes Sorbo, you are quite right. In that respect not a lot has changed in two thousand years.

And now I should tell you a little more about Jesus. Most of the accounts of his life and teachings were written by different humans and at different times, so there are of course some contradictions, although these do not alter or invalidate his essential message in any way. Many Christian leaders and thinkers have already realised that there are some events written in the Christian New Testaments which are probably inaccurately or incompletely recorded and thus not wholly true accounts. It is these which need further examination and consideration. God does not place specific souls in particular human beings. Souls are sent to wherever is appropriate for the next part of their eternal journey. In the case of Jesus, it was to be on Earth for a short time about two thousand years ago. Almost from birth he knew that God's message, much of which had already been correctly given by numerous prophets before him, was being ignored as being too inconvenient or difficult to follow, or just totally rejected as being wrong or irrelevant. Jesus constantly prayed to God for guidance and spent the whole of his life explaining exactly what that guidance meant. As you know, it was largely for this that he was vilified and killed.

Many humans, both then and still now, are unable to face the truth and react by punishing the messenger. So it was in the case of Jesus, even though he was showing souls the path of righteousness and the way to their own salvation. I said that God does not specifically place souls in particular physical bodies, so you might think it was timely that Jesus's soul came to Earth when and where it did. You could call it a fortunate coincidence. Or you could believe that God chose Jesus. Or that Jesus chose God. And as humans will eventually come to realise, it all means the same, so you would be right in whatever you decided.

Sorbo, you ask whether Jesus actually claimed to be the son of God? As you know, the overwhelming majority of accounts of his life record that he did, or at least that he did not deny it. It may seem to you that it was unwise at that time and with his audience. But he was a son of God, as all humans are children of God. The difference between Jesus and other humans is that he was giving God's message in a clear and accurate and comprehensive way which no prophet before him had been able to do. His teachings were God's teachings and God's exact guidance to humans, so he was entitled to call himself the son of God. And despite knowing the inevitable consequences, he needed God's authority as a reinforcement of His message. And God gave Jesus that authority. Sorbo, you also ask about blasphemy. An ugly human word for an ugly human concept. If you mean that claiming any form of deity for oneself is blasphemy, then you are right in that it offends humans. But it does not offend God. Jesus was right to claim insight into God's mind and God's purpose for humanity. He was explaining God's message. That is not blasphemy.

Another misconception of blasphemy is swearing at God. But it is a normal human reaction in many circumstances, and whilst it is a sin in human eyes, it is not to God. God knows the frailties of humans and God is understanding and patient, but not offended, –

that is a human emotion. Deriding or dismissing the validity of other religions or their gods is also considered as blasphemy by many people. It is certainly wrong, and a sin in the eyes of God, to deride or scorn other people's beliefs. That is a demonstration of intolerance and lack of consideration, which is selfish, and selfishness is a sin. Instead they should be gently shown that there is a better way to the understanding of human life and its purpose. But regardless of what other people might think, you cannot sinfully blaspheme their god, as their god is your God. There is only one God, and God does not recognise any form of language against Himself as being a sin. It is at worst a human weakness, but not a sin. Many humans make much of their ideas of the sin of blasphemy against God. But they are wrong. In God's eyes it does not exist.

There are two more aspects of the life of Jesus which I should explain. I told you earlier that there is no such thing as a miracle, but that what appears to be a miracle is really a deception or illusion. But the early Christians actually witnessed Jesus performing what appeared to be miracles and some of them were recorded many times. So was Jesus a trickster or illusionist like so many people before him who had claimed to perform miracles? No Sorbo. Those events did happen much as they are chronicled, and to humans at that time they were indeed miracles. In reality they were extraordinary demonstrations of Jesus's utter faith in God and the powers given to him by God, and needed by Jesus to convince his followers that his message and teachings were the truth and brought to Earth by him on God's behalf. It is not possible in this life for Christians to understand how Jesus performed these apparent miracles for God. Only for them to have faith that their souls will learn in the fullness of time.

And in the fullness of time will Jesus return to Earth as Christians believe he promised? I said that no soul could have more than one existence in a physical body on Earth, and Jesus knew this. Although not properly realised by his disciples at the time, and therefore by some people misunderstood and inaccurately recorded, Jesus did not say that he would be re-incarnated on Earth in the same body and with the same name. The truth which he did give was that at the appropriate time a soul with an identical message would again come to Earth to continue his work. Christians would identify and recognise this soul as that of Jesus and thus to them his second coming would be realised.

From what I have told you so far, you now know that, although it was rejected at that time, Jesus was accurately giving God's message and guidance to the world. So why aren't all humans Christians? And why doesn't God's guidance mean that all humans should try to live their lives according to Christian values? For a start there is not a single aspect of God's message conveyed through Jesus which does not form a part or parts of many of the other thousands of world religions, and a large number of these religions have a lot of teachings in common with those of Jesus. So Christians cannot claim uniqueness for any of their beliefs or moral principles. What Christians could claim is the uniqueness of the entirety of Jesus's message as he delivered it.

But in your twenty-first century CE there are now thousands of different churches professing the Christian faith, almost all of which have very similar views of what Jesus preached, but with different interpretations developed over the years. So there is not any longer a single Christian church or single set of true Christian values. And the same applies to all of the other major religions. What often started out as one set of beliefs or morals based on the teachings of prophets or other founders, is now divided into many different codes. A believer can give a general indication of their faith by saying that they are, for example a Christian or Hindu, Muslim or Buddhist, but they cannot describe their particular beliefs further than that without explaining which of the divisions or subdivisions of that religion they adhere to. So now you have thousands of religions and hundreds or thousands of subdivisions of many of those religions. And billions of people who follow one religion or another, – well, sort of. Yes Sorbo, – sort of. They totally believe in their religion, – except for the bits of it which they don't believe in, because those are the bits which other branches of their religion believe in. But those bits don't matter because they believe in all of the other bits. And there are many billions of such people. Actually God doesn't mind this too much, as mostly it is better that humans believe in some form of religion rather than nothing at all. I'll tell you more about this when we get back to non-believers again.

No, Sorbo, I have not forgotten Mohammed, Mahomet or, as I shall call him, Muhammad, – the great messenger and prophet who founded Islam, – nor will I omit to mention that there will be other prophets in the future. These are, and will be, acceptable to us, as long as they do not seek to destroy the genuine faith in God which people of other religions hold dear to themselves. The important thing is the true belief in God, and any religion which is sincere in this will, in time, learn to accept and tolerate the alternative interpretations placed on this belief by other people of different faiths. And, of course, it will need to modify its own interpretations to take this into account, as failure to do so will only prove that such religion is not a true religion of God. Yes, intolerance of other peoples' understanding of God and God's guidance is a sin, and we'll talk more about this when we discuss aggression and violence. I have put that quite clearly, and so will you when you write your book.

Just to remind you Sorbo, as you already know, you won't be a messiah or prophet, Yes, that's a very good question. We could make up a new word, but that would only cause confusion, and probably endless unresolved debate about what it was actually supposed to mean. And there's already far too much wasted human argument about the real meanings of words. No Sorbo, – I told you that Gods can't forget, – so yes, we will talk about semantics. Yes, later. But for the moment, we've got to give you some sort of description, – something that people can call you. Never mind what you can call me, – that comes later too, – in the meantime we're talking about you. We can't say translator or interpreter, even though you will be explaining how God would like humans to receive His message, – which in itself will be a new interpretation of some of God's wishes. Moderator and mediator would both be quite good descriptions, but again they would be misinterpreted. So, as I said much earlier, we could call you a messenger, because that's exactly what you will be. But even that would be misunderstood, as the true prophets are generally held to be messengers from God, and as I said you will not be a prophet. And you won't be telling anybody anything new. No Sorbo, everything I will tell you this week has already been given to humans by God on countless occasions. So nothing you write will be new, but the way it is put together will be.

You will be guiding the human race towards the right way to assemble and interpret God's message in a way that can be clearly and properly understood. Think of yourself as being like a steward at a football match, or an usher at a wedding. You are an absolutely insignificant part of the event itself, but you are crucial to guiding people in the right direction. And that is exactly what God is asking you to do. To guide the human race in the right direction to properly construct, and listen to, and understand the entirety of God's message in a way that the majority of people have not yet been able to. And which, with Earth's increasing scientific and technological advances, they are finding even more difficult than before. But they should try to understand that God's spiritual help and guidance is far more important than the scientists' discoveries of the material facts of life.

And now we'd better get round to other things, as we have a lot to do and little time to do it in.

Yes, I did say that you could choose the order that we talked about things, – so yes, – let's talk about God's name, or my name, or our name. It won't surprise you at all when I say that, over the past ten thousand years or so, – starting from well before most major Earth religions – I have been called by many thousands of names. What may surprise you however, is that as long as you genuinely believe and trust in God, we do not in any way mind which name you prefer to use. I have already told you that in God's eyes there is no such thing as blasphemy against God. No, Sorbo. You can swear by or at God, but it won't be blasphemy in God's eyes. It is a normal human reaction to stress or anger or frustration, and it is quite understandable to God. And it does not in any way offend God. But it does offend humans, who wrongly think that it is derogatory to their God and their religion, and who coined the unnecessary word blasphemy to describe it, and who consider it a sin. But it is not a sin.

It is undoubtedly unwise and very foolish and indeed a sin to denigrate other people's religions, but you cannot denigrate other people's God, because there is no other God. All of the thousands of human religions have the same God, even though they don't all really understand that yet, and some totally refuse to believe it. To put it all another way, – the belief in God is important, but the name and how it is used is irrelevant. When I'm speaking to you I do use the name God, as it's a word understood by far more than half of Earth's population. It will eventually be the only word used by humans, but that will take a long time. Yes, even those people who deny our existence will use the word God, if only so that they can demonstrate to their own satisfaction that God is an imaginary creation of the human mind. And we don't mind how you spell God, or whatever name you choose. Capital letters or not, and written and spoken in full, or with letters deliberately omitted, – it matters only to humans, but not to God. By the way Sorbo, leaving letters out of the spelling, or using another word instead, to show a mark of respect to God, is not only unnecessary but also silly and outdated in Earth's twenty-first century

CE. And it doesn't show any respect to God, – it just shows that you don't understand the nature and purpose of God No, since you ask, these sort of things don't happen on other planets. Their life forms don't use or need spoken or written communication, so it doesn't arise.

Anyhow that's another matter altogether, so I'll get back to Earth. The important things are belief and trust. And love and respect, – but not worship. No, not worship, – I knew you'd be surprised by that, too. It's another example of the real meanings of words, which we're going to talk about later, but I'd better explain this one now. Worship would be quite acceptable if it meant true spiritual love, but then only love of God. And to some people it did, and still does. But worship now means so many different things to so many people that its meaning has become confused and contaminated, and thus debased. So humans can now worship anything they like, whether it is material goods or money, or people like film stars or sporting heroes. Of course, this form of worship is idolatrous, so it has no place in the love of God. While we are talking about this, I'd better tell you that idolatry in itself is not necessarily a sin, although it usually demonstrates ignorance, which often can be.

And now I will repeat what I have already said more than once. You cannot obey God. No Sorbo, you cannot obey God. God does not give orders or commands, so there is nothing to obey. God gives guidance if or when humans ask for it, and then it is up to them whether they accept it or not. I know this is all difficult for you to understand, so I'll go back again to a part of Earth's history. As I said, when the early religions were being formed, it was necessary, at those stages of human evolution, for the patriarchs, prophets, messiahs or sages, to impose what they said were God's laws or commandments, and to dictate that these must be obeyed, or otherwise the transgressor would suffer God's retribution. Rules, laws and punishments were set out like this in many religions, and with our blessing and agreement, as it was the only way possible in those times. But times, and human understanding, have changed. Unfortunately, the need for religions to gradually modify to accommodate such change, has been so strongly resisted that they are largely condemning themselves to being irrelevant to modern human life. I say unfortunate, because humans really do need religion, – the right sort of religion, that is, – to guide them towards truth and understanding. Many religions consider their bibles to be sacrosanct and absolutely immutable. But they are wrong. God's love is immutable. Religions and their bibles are not. And if modern religious leaders pray to God for the right reasons, we will give them the guidance they need, and help to instil in them the courage to act on that guidance.

Sorbo, I told you that the universe is evolving, but of course you already knew that. And that almost all of Earth's living creatures are slowly evolving is also quite obvious. But what about evolution of other things? What you call the 'Industrial Revolution' was actually no more than industrial evolution. And in the last hundred or so years you have had very rapid evolution in all sorts of technology, particularly in electronics and communications. Yes, you could call these things discoveries or inventions, but they are really only inevitable effects of human evolution. And human attitudes and behaviours are changing, although not yet quite quickly enough to keep up with recent technological advances. There is however one area of human life which has not properly accepted evolution. Yes Sorbo, – religion. The most important influence on the soul's journey while it is in an Earthly body, but the one which stubbornly refuses to accept that evolution is just as inevitable and essential to religion as it is to any other aspect of life. When I say religion, I mean not only religious texts and bibles, but more importantly the sages, leaders and teachers who interpret them and impart their message.

The prophets and leaders who inspired religions and their bibles knew very well that religion must evolve as human life evolved, but most of the guardians of those religions who have followed them have so far failed to understand. They still consider that their bibles and the teachings in them are immutable. But they are not. Like many of the living species on Earth, religion must evolve or die out. And modern religious leaders need to accept and act on this, or religion will eventually become an irrelevant part of Earth's history. Properly chronicled, but only as a part of that history, and therefore outdated and obsolete. And that would be wrong, because, imperfect as they are, religions are a way to guide people to belief in God and the understanding of the reasons for human existence.

Of course God does not expect religions to suddenly re-invent themselves and change all of their teachings and beliefs. But some things do need explanation and correction. And the most important of these is the nature and existence of God. The existence of God, or their God or Gods, is already accepted by believers of most religions. But the nature of God is totally misunderstood by almost all of them. God is not a ruler or dictator who issues laws or commands and then punishes people who disobey them. Yes Sorbo, I did say that many things will need repetition, and this is just another of them. God is a teacher and guide and God's responsibility is to lead souls towards Universal understanding, peace, harmony and eventual happiness. But guidance is not the same as commandments. Commandments were devised by the prophets and leaders of their respective races, cultures and religions, and they were highly important in those times. They were taught as commandments of God. But they weren't. They were human rules. And so were the lists of mortal or deadly sins which you will find in many bibles. Mostly they had and still have the approval of God, but only as guides and not laws.

As you know, many of the old religious commandments are incorporated into modern religious practices, and national and international laws, and this is largely acceptable to God. But one area where God's guidance and human laws differ is the punishment for transgression. God does not punish, but humans do. Human laws and human punishments for breaking them are necessary at the moment. And since different religions, cultures and nations are at different stages of their development, their laws and punishments also differ. Of course this cannot change immediately, but it does need to change. One example of this is the death penalty, which humans have used right from their early existence. Many nations still consider that exacting the death penalty is essential to deter people from breaking the more important of their laws.

Whilst the maintenance of law and order is necessary for the harmonious co-existence of peoples within their communities, apart from a few specific exceptions, the killing of any living creature is contrary to Universal law, regardless of who carries it out. And yes, that includes governments There are exceptions when the human race faces impending or immediate threats by such as viruses, bacteria and pests which threaten food crops or human life. Another exception is when human life is endangered by other people. It is quite acceptable to use physical force, if necessary including the killing of the perpetrator, to halt or prevent crimes being carried out at that time or in the immediate future. But the later use of physical punishment of humans for past crimes is not the same and it is wrong and should be eventually consigned to history. Yes, that includes all forms of physical and mental torture and capital punishment. Of course nations and their leaders will not be able to change their laws immediately, but they do need to understand that change will eventually be necessary and very slowly start to modify their systems of crime and punishment accordingly. Yes, this will take a lot of time. Time to understand and accept that it is wrong, and then time to change their laws. God only asks that leaders will pray for guidance and receive it, then act upon it when they are able to do so.

While I have so far been talking about governments and their laws, I haven't forgotten the codes of practice adopted by cultures and religions. Some of these consider themselves to be outside the jurisdiction of national laws, and some quote God as their authority. Earth's history is littered with countless examples of cultural and religious strife. Some have been called religious wars, either between different religions or between different systems of beliefs within what started as one religion. They are wrong. There is no such thing as a religious war. It is a contradiction of terms. All wars between humans are regrettable, but in the past some have been necessary to counteract many forms of injustice in respect of actual or threatened physical, material and territorial invasions. But there is no justification whatsoever for any form of aggression as a means of trying to impose any religious beliefs on those people who either follow another religion or no specific religion, or even on those who do not believe that God exists at all.

The so-called religious wars of the past, and those of the present, were and still are perpetrated by bigots, zealots and extremists who completely misunderstood the true message of the religion they claimed to be furthering. And in their human terms, far from reaching the 'paradise' they were expecting, they were actually consigning themselves to their form of 'hell'. And their sins were compounded by the leaders of those religions who not only failed to condemn their actions, but also failed to tell them that they were acting totally against God's guidance. Those sins of omission committed by religious leaders were equally as bad as the actions of their self-professed disciples. Yes Sorbo, you commit a sin of omission by deliberately not acting when you know, or ought to know, that you should act. And it is often as bad as, and sometimes worse than, a sin of commission. So far I've been talking about the past, but exactly the same applies to the present and the future. God would like humans to follow the religion of their choice. At the moment there are differences between religions in the interpretations of the observance and nature and meaning of God and the Universe. These differences will eventually be resolved by peaceful discussion and explanation. But this will inevitably take a great deal of reasoned argument and gentle persuasion over a long period of time.

Any system of beliefs which accepts a form of God could call itself a religion. But if that religion tries to impose its beliefs on anybody else by any form of aggression whatsoever, then it is not a genuine religion acceptable to God. No Sorbo, in the eyes of God it is not a true religion if, in your twenty-first century CE, it cannot or does not now utterly eschew and totally condemn violence and aggression as a means of spreading its beliefs. Most major religions were founded in times when it was considered that violence was an inevitable part of life on Earth. However, even then strife in the name of religion, regardless of who carried it out, was misguided, wrong and a sin. Human evolution has now reached the point where this should already have ceased. And it is the responsibility of the leaders of all religions to examine their bibles, their beliefs and practices, and their consciences, to see what changes need to be made to allow their religions to evolve as the human race is evolving. It will take great courage to accept the need for this. And even greater courage to carry it out. But it is the only way for religion to have any lasting and meaningful part in human development.

Although any soul can commune with God at any time, many people find it better and more reassuring to do so through their chosen religion, often at services held in their religious buildings. But leaders and ministers of religion are not there to make or enforce or even countenance the furthering of unreasonable or outdated human rules, laws or behaviour. Nor are they there to try to impose their religious laws and codes upon other peoples of the nations in which they live or hold sway. Their responsibility is to help people to commune with God so that they may gain insight into their own souls and the reasons for their existence on Earth. God is always there to give guidance. And religious leaders have a duty to seek this guidance and pass it on to those of their followers who themselves find it difficult to commune directly with God and to those who need further explanation of God's message. And I will repeat that a part of this message is that any system of beliefs which still accepts, tolerates or condones any form of aggression as a method of furthering those beliefs is not a religion acceptable to God. All past and present religious strife is both wrong and misguided and any religious leaders who lack the courage to make this absolutely clear to even the most extreme elements in their followers, and any other people who claim to be their followers, are committing a sin. And until they fully acknowledge and atone for that sin, in God's eyes they are not fit to hold their office.

And this brings us back to the reason why you are here, and why you are here now. Over three-quarters of the Earth's population have historically believed in over twenty so-called major religions. These religions believe in a God or Gods. But each religion has a slightly different understanding of the real meaning of God, and different rules as to how humans should love, respect, and yes, even worship, God. The result of this is total confusion about what is or isn't true, and humans' tendency to give gradually less importance to any religion. Scientists have accelerated this process, by implying that they will eventually be able to explain everything about the Universe, without the need for God, and humans are increasingly accepting this pernicious belief. So, belief in God, and belief in the necessity to accept God, is slowly appearing to become less relevant to human life. But the scientists are wrong. They can explain material facts, but they will never be able to explain scientifically the spiritual truth, – the meaning and reason for life on Earth, or indeed anywhere else in the Universe.

Only belief in God can lead the soul towards true enlightenment. Yes Sorbo, – the soul again. It may come as a shock, or even an unpleasant truth to some people, but every living being has a soul. And that includes every non-believer, even though some might think that all they consist of is a human body. Well, it isn't. The body is just the vehicle for the soul while it is on Earth. Of course you can't see or describe or analyse the soul, and that is why some people refuse to acknowledge its existence. But it is the soul, and not the body, which gives humans a certain amount of free will. Those people who are unable to recognise this, and those who choose not to pray for guidance, are delaying their own journey towards understanding. And if they try to spread their lack of belief, they are actually hindering other people on their journey. And yes, as I said earlier, that is selfish and therefore a sin.

We've talked about worship and obedience, so I'll get back to love, – and prayer. Anyone who genuinely believes in God will know that God is a benign teacher.

And they will love God, as God loves them. And they will trust and respect God. And they will pray to God for enlightenment and understanding. Their prayers can take many forms, and God does not mind which form of prayer people choose. But there is a very important exception to this, and that is that prayer should never be compulsory. We would like everybody to pray to God however they choose to do so, and as often as they wish to. God will always listen, and if the prayers are for the right reasons, God will always give the guidance which is sought. But we do not demand that people should pray to God in any particular way, or at any particular times, – that is entirely up to the individual. For reasons which I've already talked about, some religions do have strict rules about prayer, – but these are based on historical misunderstandings of God's guidance. Their rules were laid down by human beings, but not by God, and in time these religions will need to change. It is not compulsory to accept God's guidance, nor should it be to observe religious rules. It is the duty of true religions to help people to commune with God, – not to enforce unwarranted or unreasonable human discipline.

Yes Sorbo, you are quite right. I really must tell you more about prayers to God which are made properly, and in the way we can answer them. I've already said that they must be for the right reasons, and that if they're not, they aren't proper prayers. Prayers can be made by an individual, at any time and in any place. Or they can be by a group of people, and if it's a group, the prayers could be led by a religious minister, or a lay member of the group, or by more than one person, either taking turns, or together, by sharing parts of a prayer. Again, this could be at any time, and you could pray in a field, a cave, a mountain top, or any other chosen place, always as long as it does not interfere with the peace of anyone who does not wish to be involved.

And now we get round to the more widely accepted, and more widely practised, forms of group prayer. Yes, alright Sorbo, – we can say worship, if you like, – as long as you remember why we don't need the word. Some of the buildings which humans have constructed for their religious observations are the most beautiful examples of design and workmanship, although when marvelling at their splendour, you should also always contemplate that a great many of them were built by slave labour or conscripted workers who had to endure much pain, suffering and even death, during their construction. And you must appreciate the irony that this slave labour was often used to build places ostensibly designed specifically for the worship of God. And you must also understand that the motive behind the building of many of these was not actually the worship of God, but the desire of rulers to demonstrate their power and importance. But you also have many other religious buildings, maybe not quite so exquisite visually, but perfectly suitable for meetings for communion with God and each other, and for prayer, – and yes, worship. You see Sorbo, – the importance is the spiritual use to which the building is put, not the building itself or its architecture, or even the direction which it faces. Many religious buildings were aligned to a particular direction, often to the rising and the setting of the sun, as the sun was then God to many people. But the sun is no longer God, – and anyway God is all around, in every direction, and always has been. Your prayers would be equally valid if you were in an underground train or on a roller-coaster, when you would have no idea which way you were facing. Of course, there is nothing wrong with praying towards a particular direction, – as long as you understand that it is in no way a requirement of God, but just an early human misconception that God had somehow decreed it.

And another human misunderstanding of God's wishes is in the rules made by many religions about when, and how often, and on what days or occasions a believer must take part in prayers and other observances to God. These are human rules, made in the name of their particular religion. But they are not God's rules. God does not make such demands or obligations. And any religions which claim otherwise are trying to put their words into God's mouth to suit their own interests. That is the true meaning of taking the word of God in vain. And of course it is a sin.

Neither has God has ever placed a duty or obligation on any follower of any religion to make a journey or pilgrimage to any place of worship. Whether these pilgrimages are easy or difficult for religious believers, and when and how often they should be made, is irrelevant. They only show observance of rules mistakenly made by humans in the name of their religion. And they only show this to other humans. They are not necessary, or even desirable, to show respect to, or belief in, God. God does not need or wish for this demonstration of faith from any human believer. At all times, God knows what is in their hearts and souls. Of course you are right in thinking that there are many people who themselves choose to make journeys to ancient or modern sites of historical or religious importance, whether involving people or buildings. These can be very uplifting and inspirational for the pilgrims, but they should always be made entirely of their own free will, and not as a result of any compulsion or any order made by humans in the name of their religion.

Now I'll get back to the forms of services, most of which are conducted by religious leaders. There is no harm in praising God, although God really doesn't need it. And there is nothing wrong in thanking God, – although again, we are just doing our duty as guardians of the Universe. So praise and thanks are quite acceptable, but not in any way essential. The important things are belief in God, love of God, and prayer. We have given your soul a brief life in an Earthly body, on a planet which can give you truly beautiful physical surroundings. At this moment in time, many humans are in circumstances where they cannot enjoy the wondrous gift of Earthly life, and even day to day existence is the greatest imaginable struggle. But there are also many others who are in far better circumstances. It doesn't matter how extremely difficult or very easy it is, but all souls should try to pray to God for guidance and understanding to improve themselves, and try to help others who are less fortunate. And God will listen. The way you act in this life will determine the next destination for your soul. This is a simple message, and religious leaders of all faiths should keep it simple. Complicated services and rituals are not just unnecessary, but also undesirable, and for many people they make God's purpose more difficult to understand, and thereby often seemingly less relevant. Whilst they serve to perpetuate the emphasis of the power and importance of the religious leaders, they do nothing to bring God's message closer and more relevant to their congregations. Indeed they often have the opposite effect.

No, not yet Sorbo. We'll get round to men wearing frocks in a little while. But first we'll have a quick look at your planet. It's Wednesday morning in London, England.

CHAPTER 6

Wednesday 7th May 2014 – 07.55

"Good morning, Doctors Gurley and West. Excellent timing, but of course you wouldn't have passed even the first selection if you weren't always punctual. You've probably realised by now that we were screening you well before your unfortunate events of 2011, and that we might possibly have played a small part in them. Please don't look so surprised at the greeting, Dr. West. I addressed you both in alphabetical order – not because we're at all concerned about being politically correct, but because we don't believe in male supremacy either. We didn't introduce ourselves last time we met, so I will do so now. I'm Alan Bululough, although it's such a mouthful we pronounce it Bulow. On my left is my wife, Roxanne. To my right is Christine Arberry, and next to her is Dr. Michael Raine. You may remember your meetings here with me and Roxanne in February 2012 One of you also met Christine, and the other saw Michael. This is our London base. To the outside world it looks like an empty building, but you will have noticed that it is actually a fully-equipped hi-tech office. Now to KS1419. It's shorthand for 'Kindred Spirits 2014/2019'. The dates are obvious.

A very simplistic definition of kindred spirits is 'those people of like mind, who have in their hearts the best interests of the whole population of Earth, regardless of species or of race, religion or circumstance'. You will both recall the brief reference made at your interviews in 2012, but you wouldn't have realised the significance. Everybody in the world, even those in the most dire circumstances imaginable, sometimes wonders why they are alive, but nobody has even the remotest inkling of an answer. What makes kindred spirits different, is that they realise that there must indeed be a reason and, whatever it is, they have to believe that it is benign. To them, it cannot be acceptable to imagine that a malicious God, or Gods, created life for their own sadistic pleasure. So, – whilst they have no real ideas why, – kindred spirits believe that they should try to make a positive contribution to the lives of their fellow beings. They do not do this out of fear, or any other expectation of anything which may or may not happen after their life on earth, but largely because they think it is right and, to a lesser extent, to show some appreciation for the gift of life itself. Of course, this is a utopian description which most people can only aspire to, but you understand what I mean. Kindred spirits is not an organisation which you join, – either you are or you are not. Some people have to be told, but deep-down some already know. So you're in no doubt, you both are – otherwise you wouldn't be here.

I think now is the time that we start using first names. I've already told you them, except that these two are shortened to Roxy and Mike. We'll tell you everything we know about Sorbo Grundy, but we also know it's only a fragment of the whole story. We have only been given enough information to carry out our role as guardians, with the expectation of learning more as the reality unfolds, – a sort of combination of 'need to know' and 'diminishing deceptives', – if you're familiar with the latter concept. KS1419 is only a codeword for this operation, and will not be known to the outside world. I'll deal with the structure and funding later, but first to Sorbo. A nickname of course, but we don't know the derivation. We have been told only that he was registered at birth as Andrew Sebastian Grundy, which leads us to believe that he might also have another name. He is seventy-two years old and retired, from what we don't know, although it would seem that he has wide experience in many fields, – no, Kate – we do know he was not a farmer. He lives at Owl Barn in Wrotham, Kent, but you already know that. Dr. Gurley, we are well aware of your schoolgirl humour, and I've just won a bet, but it's really not that much of a hoot.

I'll continue. We know that Sorbo is a kindred spirit, that he himself recognised it over fifty years ago, and that since then he has been waiting to learn what he has to do. We also know that his life has been in danger for at least the last two years. Hence your jobs, and those of the ground crews and home security teams. He has been under surveillance twenty-four hours a day since you all started in March 2012. Last Friday you learnt why. Nasty accident and, as you know, he was in a critical state, but we'd already been told when and what to expect. We'd been asked to get him to St. George's within one hour of the accident. You actually took sixty-one minutes because Andy Lowe had a problem with the NATS controller who hadn't read his briefing properly. Otherwise you'd have been four minutes earlier. Andy didn't bother you with that, – he thought you just might have other things to worry about. Ex-Squadron Leader Lowe is, of course, a kindred spirit and another very great asset, and I'm glad to say that he'll be working with you for the next five years as well. Yes, – I'll come to that in a minute. Sorbo was in theatre for around fifteen hours. Dr. Raine – sorry, Mike – will give you the gory technical stuff."

"Thanks, Alan. I'll keep it short. Extensive left hip damage necessitated a total arthroplasty. Severely ruptured liver beyond repair. We don't know how, but a tissue-matched organ was already at St. George's and the transplant was successful. You're both doctors? Good. Acute large left-sided subdural haematoma – surgically removed. Fifteen hours quite short really, in the circumstances. I'm pleased to say everything went well and Sorbo is making a remarkably good recovery, although he'll still be in a coma for a while yet. This next bit is not technical now, and I don't understand it, but we've been told that he'll regain consciousness at exactly 3.30p.m. this Friday. How so precise? Well, I'm tempted to say 'God knows', but I'm not a swearing man. Anyway, we shall see."

"Thank you, Mike. Kate, Charles or Charles, Kate. We'd like you to visit Sorbo around 4.30 on Friday afternoon to get properly acquainted with him. Avoid the medical staff if possible, but anyway use different names if you do get asked. Sorbo will know who you actually are. We don't know how, but he will know you. Meanwhile, use today and tomorrow to get ready to move all of your things into Owl Barn annexe this coming Monday. It's quite large and well-furnished, and there's plenty of room for anything you want to take. It's got two bedrooms, but that's up to you. We'll get some keys cut and let you have them over the weekend. General housekeeping, cooking, cleaning, shopping, driving, gardening, but above all, protection. He's apparently going to need it. We'll set up a housekeeping account with an automatic top-up, and you can draw on it as needed. Anything gets too much for you to handle, home security will be on call 24/7. Just use your RT handset, and it'll be answered immediately, as you've already found out.

Job will initially last for another five years, then we'll see how things are going. Can you both put up with each other for that long? Good, we were sure you would but please, both of you, try not to look so smug about it. Sorry, forgot to tell you. Milk is delivered daily. Small convenience store and newsagent in the village. Most other shops and a couple of banks in Borough Green. GP practice in Sevenoaks – about five miles away. Very professional, capable and understanding partners, all of them – and the staff. Sorbo's happily seen most of them from time to time but, given the choice, there's always one he prefers. Don't know why, really. Like the others, she's very good and very caring, but her mind is different – maybe it's that. She's up to her eyes with work and family, but she seems to find time for Sorbo. Seen him through some problems in recent years. No, mostly the usual age things, – nothing out of the ordinary, although she has found a few things early and nipped them in the bud before they got nasty. And yes, she's a kindred spirit. Didn't have to be told – knew it herself, probably long before most of the rest of us. Yes Kate, she does have a name. Dr. Karen Katto. Kate, I think we'd all already guessed that. Charles, are you really sure you can cope with this for five more years? Of course, I'd forgotten about the mental aspect of your stamina.

Before you go, I'd better tell you about this office. As you've seen, everything above the ground floor appears to be an empty building, with the usual 'To Let' sign. But it's only the shallow front rooms that are empty. Where you came in at street level purports to be an international patent agency, but we think that's a cover for another part of our organisation. This 'need to know' business can be very frustrating at times, especially when they don't seem to think we need to know very much at all. Behind the empty front rooms, the office is very well-equipped and extremely hi-tech. You could call it 'state of the art', but that wouldn't quite describe some of the gizmos that we didn't even know had been invented yet. We leave those to the others who are paid for it. The four of us aren't paid. We all have good jobs in London, and we give our time here because we want to.

By the way, kindred spirits are not ordered to do things. We take actions as a result of requests or suggestions, or sometimes because it is obvious that we should. As to the layers of the organisation, the funding, and the initiators of the requests, as Mike wouldn't say, – at the moment, 'God only knows'. All we really know is that Sorbo must be looked after for as long as it takes. We don't know what he will be doing, but we do know that it is for kindred spirits and therefore, by extension, it has to be for the good of all life on Earth. That is enough for us until, hopefully, we learn more. Glad you're staying with us. Any problems, however small, call us anytime. You'll be seeing Sorbo on Friday afternoon, but now you'd better get yourselves ready to move into Owl Barn. No, Kate ... please!"

CHAPTER 7

Wednesday 7ᵗʰ May 2014 – 08.30

Sorbo, you have just been looking at some of the more positive minded people on Earth. I say more positive, because as you will learn throughout this week there is no aspect of human personality which can be defined as exactly one thing or exactly the opposite. To give you just three simple examples, nobody is either totally selfish or unselfish, totally intelligent or completely stupid, or one hundred percent either heterosexual or homosexual. They may consider themselves, and be perceived by others, to be so but this would be inaccurate. Every human characteristic lies somewhere between the two extremes. So it is with attitudes to life. Generally positive or negative minded people, or those who usually tend to be optimistic or pessimistic, react to events differently, believing respectively that in the future their lives will either get better or worse, as the case may be. The optimists are the more fortunate souls. These positive types have faith and trust that they are alive on Earth for a good reason. They don't need any more proof that God exists and that God is always there to guide them. On the other hand the pessimists mostly don't believe in God. They much prefer not to believe in anything that can't be proved to their entire satisfaction, and many are unable accept even the existence of their own soul. But as you have just realised, these people are not kindred spirits. Kindred spirits are by nature the more positive thinkers. Anyway, you asked me earlier about men wearing frocks, so now we'll talk about clothes. There is no logical order, so we'll start at the top, – I mean the top of the human body of course. And I don't need to tell you what God has commanded. Nothing. No, nothing. You might choose to wear, or not to wear, a hat, or any other form of head covering. This should depend only on the climate and your preference. Wearing a hat or head covering is traditional in many societies. However some cultures and religions demand or expect covering of the head to show to yourself, or to other humans, that you respect, or worship, God. But this is unnecessary and irrelevant. It shows nothing to God. God knows. The wearing of hats, or any other forms of head covering, either as a sign of respect to God, or acceptance of subservience to other humans, is not God's wish. And it should not be considered as such. It is a matter for culture or convention, but it is not a matter for religion. But there is absolutely nothing wrong in the wearing of head coverings for other reasons. And the male tradition of removing hats as a greeting or as a sign of equality or camaraderie, or when entering a covered building, is also very acceptable. But not essential.

While we're talking about hats and heads, I'd better mention hair. And the rules observed by some cultures and religions. These may be quite sensible for a variety of reasons, – with one exception. None of them is in any way a wish, desire or requirement of God. You may live in a society, or adhere to a religion, which dictates that you should not cut your hair or shave your face, and there may be good historical reasons for such beliefs. But it is wrong for any person or religion to say that their rules came from their God. God does not make rules or commandments, and God has no preference as to the manner in which humans display or wear, or keep or cut their bodily hair.

So next it's faces. And yes, you're right – this is a contentious matter for many religions. So we should think about religions, and cultures, and traditions. And how, in many ways, they have become so intertwined that it can be difficult to understand the difference. In fact, in many cases humans do not perceive any differences, – but they do exist, and they should be recognised. We'd better get back, for a moment, to what religion should mean, and how it should be observed. And here, there is no room for semantics. Sorbo, I know we haven't discussed that yet, but we will, – so please be patient for a little longer.

For a religion to be acceptable to God it must be based on a simple belief. Belief in God. God, the original creator of human existence. God who asks for, but does not demand, faith, love, trust and respect. God who will commune with any soul at any time, and give whatever guidance that soul is seeking. And God who is the way for souls to reach towards the understanding of Universal truth and purpose. That, Sorbo, is what religion should mean, and most of Earth's major religions understand that. But how religion should be observed is where difficulties arise, and where humans have created problems for themselves.

Each of the major world religions has a different interpretation of God's wishes for mankind. Many of them developed codes of conduct, and incorporated them into their cultures and traditions. The only problem with this is that they based these codes on what they called God's law. There are innumerable lists of commandments and of sins, all purporting to define God's laws. And there are prescribed or implied punishments for disobeying God's laws. But this could not be further from the truth. God does not make laws or demands. God only guides souls as to what is right or wrong, and then only when asked. And God does not punish souls for transgressions. Any punishment for transgression is totally self-inflicted, as it leads souls away from Universal truth, and consigns them to long periods of lost direction and purpose. As I said, you might call that purgatory, limbo, tartarus, or whatever you wish. But it is not a punishment from God. It is the consequence of the soul not seeking the truth, or not wishing to seek or understand the truth. It is indeed a form of punishment, but it is not God punishing the soul. It is the soul punishing itself. The torment and darkness which the soul will inevitably experience as a result will have been entirely self-inflicted. And the time spent in that state will depend on the soul's willingness to learn.

How then should religion be observed? And in your twenty-first century CE? Sorbo, it won't be easy, but you knew that already. Humans must learn to separate God's wishes from their historical cultures and traditions. All of your bibles set out at least some rules for human behaviour. Many of these were, and still are, valid rules and very acceptable to God. But many are not. In the early days of human development, we were quite prepared to allow God's name and authority to be given to various codes of conduct. And we still are, but only in matters in which we have given our guidance. As I said about head covering, that was, and is, a human interpretation and a human rule, sometimes derived from a human interpretation of God's guidance. But it was not God's guidance. And the same applies to the covering of the female face. Yes, in some cultures and religions it does have its roots in the attempted prevention or reduction of carnal lust in the male of the species. But it is not a God-given direction, and it should not be taken as such. Humans, – of any age or sex, – should not be directed to cover their faces in the name of God. And they should not be given the blame for any human consequences of not doing so. Indeed, at this stage of human development, there are still times when it could be important that the face is uncovered for recognition and identification, and religious or cultural belief is not a valid reason for refusal to do so. It may be so in the eyes of various religions, but it is not in the eyes of God.

We will talk about lust and temptation, but for the moment I'll carry on with clothing. You asked me about men wearing frocks, so I'd better deal with that. Actually, God doesn't regard any particular types of human clothing as being specific to any sex. There is nothing wrong with women wearing trousers, or men as you say wearing frocks, – but I know what you mean. Leaders of most religions traditionally wear robes to show their status or authority. You could call it religious uniform. And humans have historically respected uniforms, and they have traditionally expected leaders, religious or otherwise, to wear uniforms. But their leaders are also humans, and therefore of course, like all humans, they are not perfect. Yes Sorbo, they make mistakes.

In the past, many leaders have made serious errors, often with tragic consequences. Some of these were apparent at the time, some became obvious later. And, of course, many have been carefully covered up, and will only be revealed on Earth in time, – if at all. But globalisation of communication and information on Earth, is leading to widespread distrust of leaders, and their actions and motives. In some cases this is both right and necessary, but in others it is quite undesirable. At this point in time in Earth's development, humans still require leadership. But it must be the right sort of leadership, – and this is where there is a problem. At the moment, there are different opinions about every aspect of human life. And each of these opinions has a leader or leaders. But the aspects of human life are not as simple as just being about human existence. The facts of existence are quite different from the reasons for existence. And it is quite wrong to put them all into the same melting pot. Humans need to be able to quite clearly understand the differences, and to be able consider them separately from each other.

We'll talk a little about some facts, before we come back again to reasons. Yes, I did say you could choose whatever subject you wished, and sex is highly important, so we'll deal with that. And don't forget that we will always have to start every topic with basics, and in many cases I will have to generalise. At the moment, and in most animal life forms on Earth, reproduction is mostly by sexual conjugation between the male and female of the species. That's about the only easy bit, as from here on it starts to get complicated, particularly with humans. So for the moment I will only deal with humans, although there are many similarities with other animal life forms. To ensure the continuation of the species, the sex act has to be a high priority, – almost, if not equal to, day to day survival itself. To give it this importance, sex must be highly desirable. And to make it highly desirable, it must give pleasure and satisfaction to at least one of the partners. This pleasure and satisfaction must be memorable, but fairly short-lived, as it is necessary that it is sought after very regularly.

Historically, the human male has generally appeared to demonstrate the higher obvious sex drive, whilst the female has had the consequent multiple responsibilities of pregnancy, giving birth to, and mostly looking after, the young children. As you know many cultures did, and still do, regard children as an insurance policy for their old age. Large families usually mean a bigger struggle to find enough food and shelter while the children are young, but more young and middle-aged adults to care for the parents when they become less able to look after themselves. And since many children do not survive to adulthood, parents historically tended to produce additional numbers to counteract the potential deficit. But this is changing, so attitudes must also change. Medical developments mean that the mortality rate of the young is being reduced, and the elderly have an increasing lifespan, so the population of Earth is both growing and ageing rapidly. Your scientists may disagree about the numbers, but they all accept that there is a limit to the population which Earth will be able to sustain. Some countries have already recognised this, and tried to limit their own population growth by various means, but some have not. Before it is too late, a global consensus needs to be reached, – not only as to the sensible maximum population, – but more importantly, how limiting it is going to be achieved and how Earth's resources are going to be shared by that population. Remember, Sorbo, – in God's eyes all humans are equal, so they are all entitled to an equal share of Earth's assets.

No, Sorbo, – I am not talking about utopia. I'm talking about fairness, or equity, – something which, at the moment, many humans would prefer to ignore. Or think that while it is a noble idea, 'I can't help the fact that everybody else seems to be taking as much as they can get, so I'm going to do the same until someone changes the rules.' Yes Sorbo, – human rules, or the lack of them. But you can't pass human laws to force everybody to share Earth's resources equally, – they simply would not work. Populations have got to want fairness, and they need to tell their leaders that they want it before it is too late. Individuals cannot act alone, but kindred spirits can express their collective wishes. To put it very simply, – humans need to work together now to become less selfish, and kindred spirits can be the powerful voice which can start to bring this about.

I am not going to leave the subject of children just yet. As you know, the human body and mind have developed in such a way that it is quite normal for the female to want to have children. Actually it is quite normal in males too, and animals of both sexes, but I'll just talk about female humans. This desire is sometimes almost overwhelming, sometimes less so, but nevertheless still quite strong. But it is also quite common for females to have little or no such longing at all, or in some cases actively reject the idea. This is often considered strange or unusual. But it isn't. It is quite normal, and no individual of either sex, and no nation, society or culture should expect or say otherwise. All single females should be perfectly free to make their own choice as to whether and when they either try to have children, or prefer not to do so. And those who are in relationships should reach a mutual agreement with their partner. Of course this means that all females, with or without partners, should have ready access to a suitable and reliable method of contraception. In your 21st Century CE, the human race is not in any danger of becoming extinct because some females decide not to procreate, but it is if the population of Earth continues to increase at the present rate because contraception is either not freely available, or not widely used because of perceived prejudice by cultures or religions.

Anyway. I'll get back to the act of sex after we've briefly talked about love. Love is what humans would call an emotion. But a lot of the time when humans talk about love, and particularly when they talk about being in love, they are really referring to passion, – a passionate feeling towards another human, quite often linked with sexual desire, mutual or otherwise. That is indeed an emotion. When we were talking earlier about jealousy being a human emotion, I said that God does not have emotions, but I did not talk about God's love of the Universe and all of the souls in it. The love of God is not an emotion in the human sense of the word, but it is the spiritual love or agape. A part of this is a wish for all souls to strive towards Universal understanding, peace and harmony, and to offer God's unconditional help and guidance at all times find their way towards it. Yes, Sorbo, – I did say unconditional. God's love is always there, – unchanging, selfless, and unconditional. It is a part of God's covenant with the Universe.

Now we will come back again to the physical aspect of sex. And whether it is necessarily a sin to enjoy it for reasons other than reproduction. Historically, sexual intercourse between male and female has been necessary to ensure reproduction. But this is rapidly changing, and before very long, your scientists will be able to reproduce any desired life form without the need for any heterosexual physical conjugation. This will become a fact. Whether or not this is desirable development for life on Earth is a different matter, but ultimately only humans will decide this. As you know, any soul can pray to God for guidance about anything, but whether this guidance is followed is a decision that can be taken only by the individual, whether alone or in groups, societies or nations.

So eventually sexual intercourse will generally not be essential for reproduction. But it can be very enjoyable for other reasons, in the right circumstances. Two humans may have a strong sexual desire for each other. But this desire does not necessarily have to be heterosexual. For an innumerable variety of reasons, many people find that homosexual relationships are preferable to heterosexual ones. And there is no reason why anyone should not enjoy the physical pleasure of sex, whether together with someone else of either sex, or on their own. In itself there is nothing wrong with this, provided it does not disadvantage any other people and it does not involve any form of coercion or exploitation. Both of these are more than unreasonable behaviour – they are sins. Why did I mention sex on one's own? Because despite many people's thoughts and beliefs, there is nothing wrong or sinful about sexually exciting oneself in private and in the right circumstances. There is nothing wrong with eating or drinking alone to satisfy your hunger or thirst, and few people would criticise you for it. And despite any common perceived taboo, there is nothing wrong with self-stimulation to satisfy your own sexual appetite. Although it might not be quite such an erotic event when performed alone, it is better to do that than to persuade or cajole or force an unwilling partner to join in what may well be a satisfying experience for you, but not for them. Of course there are exceptions. One would be if masturbation caused such a reduction in your sexual appetite that you were subsequently unable to take part in sexual intercourse with a willing and eager long-term partner. Depriving them in such a way would be selfish, and therefore a sin.

But we'll go back to male and female and heterosexual sexual intercourse as it is today. They want sex now, but they don't want a child at this time. If the male sperm penetrates and fertilises the female egg, there is a probability that the female will become pregnant. But they don't want this to happen, so they use some type of contraception to prevent the formation of a viable embryo. This may be wrong in the eyes of some cultures and religions, but it is in fact neither wrong, nor a sin. Yes, the ingredients for the creation of a new life form are indeed present, but the act of fusion does not take place, so the life form is not created. You might consider this to be a waste of a perfectly good egg and countless virile and energetic sperms, but the female and male bodies do this very regularly on their own anyway, without any outside influence.

Sorbo, at this point in human development some religions and some nations consider that any form of contraception is wrong. Of course they are entitled to their belief, but they are not entitled to claim that it is in any way derived from God's guidance. Planned contraception before sexual intercourse is not a sin in the eyes of God. A willing couple who wish to enjoy sexual intercourse are free to choose beforehand whether or not they mutually wish the female to become pregnant. Lack of this prior consideration would be thoughtless and irresponsible, which are sins of omission. But we are going to consider what might happen if the sex act does indeed lead to successful fertilisation of the egg. And we must consider the exact point at which a new life begins. For thousands of years scientists and theologians have put forward and debated many theories, but they have never reached a consensus. And they will not be able to, as they are looking for a method of calculating an exact date on which they can all agree. But there is no such date. Each different fertilised egg in each different female body develops at a different rate, so the point at which the potential life form is ready to receive its soul and thus actually become a living being, is also different. And it can be at any time between the successful fertilisation of the egg and the first foetal heartbeat. Ensoulment does not involve any physical change to the receiving body detectable by humans, so although of course God knows, humans cannot.

Nations and religions will have to decide themselves how to formulate their laws and rules. But we will talk about deliberate human intervention from the time of fertilisation of the egg, which prevents further development of the potential life form. And we are going to call it termination. Yes, there are many other words you could use, all effectively with the same or a similar meaning, but we haven't got round to semantics yet, so we'll just say 'termination'. Can it ever be right, or is it always a sin? As you have guessed, there is no single simple answer. But, as you have also guessed, if there was a simple answer to any human question about any of God's guidance, your visit here would not have been necessary in the first place. Actually, since your question is in two parts, the answers are yes and no, but the explanations are just a little bit more complicated than that.

God's wish is that humans do not deliberately extinguish any non-threatening life form. But as we are talking about life on Earth, there have to be exceptions in almost everything, whether it be reproduction and sexual proclivity, – as we're discussing at the moment, – or consumption of animal flesh, or any other topic we'll talk about later. One of the many things that the soul will learn in its Earthly body is that compromise is essential, again in almost everything. No, Sorbo. The love of God needs no compromise or exception but deep in your soul you already knew that. So does every other soul, – but at the moment only kindred spirits are able to come to terms with it.

As usual, I am digressing again, so we'll get back to termination, and I will firstly give you a fairly simple example. An adult male and female, both with full normal mental capacity, knowingly and willingly have sexual intercourse without any form of contraception, and the female becomes pregnant. As far as any medical tests can show, both the expectant mother and foetus are healthy, and there should be a normal pregnancy and birth. There are no other significant changes in their lives or their circumstances, but both prospective parents decide to change their minds, and that neither now wishes the pregnancy to continue. The female willingly undergoes a termination. That is wrong. They are both committing a sin. In some countries and cultures the decisions may be based on the sex of the unborn child. That may be acceptable to them, but not to God. Termination for such reason does not in any way mitigate the fact of the sin. But of course you are right. Even in this seemingly simple case there could be other relevant considerations. What if only one party changes their mind? The male willingly gave his sperm in the expectancy that the female would or might become pregnant, but he subsequently had a change of mind. Although in human law terms he might have some rights over his potential progeny, it would be a sin for him to ask or insist that the female has a termination, and for her even reluctantly to agree to it. However, if it was only the female who had second thoughts and unilaterally proceeded with a termination against his wishes, then she alone would be the sinner.

But that is a straightforward case which does not involve any external factors, and as such it is unusual. Normally, there are other factors to be taken into account, and some, or all, of the humans involved have to consider these before they make their own decisions. I'll give you a few more examples, and you will have to remember that, as in everything we discuss in your short time here, I will only be giving you guidance, – not an exhaustive list of God's wishes. And we will not talk about present rules and laws of cultures, religions or nations, as those are matters for their consideration and prayer.

Firstly, we will take situations where a normal adult male and female both willingly have sexual intercourse. She has tests, and is advised that she is pregnant. Medical screening then reveals that the foetus has severe abnormality. In many instances, as you know, the female body will itself abort the pregnancy without any external intervention. But not always, – and this is where human decisions have to be made. How serious is the abnormality? On best medical advice, is the pregnancy likely to continue to a successful birth? Is there an unusual risk to the health or life of the foetus or the expectant mother? What sort of quality of life could the child expect? And many more questions. Depending on the answers, the expectant mother, and father, and any other people involved, should reach a responsible mutual decision, and prayer for guidance will help them with this. If this is the case, then termination would not be against God's wishes. However, if a decision was reached without proper consideration of all the factors, or purely as a matter of convenience, this would indeed be wrong. Yes, it would be a sin. As I said just now, a sin of omission can often be just as bad as a sin committed deliberately.

We'd better talk now about the female. What if she is not yet mature enough, or not of sufficient mental capacity, either permanently or temporarily, to properly and willingly consent to sexual intercourse? Or, if the intercourse is forced upon her either by physical or mental coercion? Yes, Sorbo, – however you want to look at it, that is rape. A particularly nasty sin in itself, which we will discuss later, – but for the moment we will stay with termination. If, after an established rape, the female becomes pregnant, and she is mentally capable of making a rational decision, then she should freely be given the option of termination of the pregnancy. And the choice should be made by her, without undue external influence or expectation of her decision. In this case the sin is the rape, but not the termination, – and no, not both.

However, if the female is not capable of making her own decision, this should be taken by others on her behalf, considering only her best mental and physical interests. And the people involved in that decision should not include anyone who is opposed to termination in any circumstances. They do not yet properly understand God's guidance. Deliberate termination of a pregnancy, without proper consideration of all of the factors involved, is indeed wrong. However, there can be many instances where the pregnancy should be terminated, and in some of these it would be just as wrong not to do so. Yes, sometimes it can be a sin not to terminate a pregnancy. You've quite rightly noticed that I haven't said anything about at what stage a pregnancy should or should not be terminated. Because that is not a matter in which humans need God's guidance. The medical profession should debate this rationally and objectively, and try to reach a consensus. But in doing so they need to understand that while it is preferable not to terminate a pregnancy, their decision should depend entirely on clinical circumstances, and not on any pre-conceived attitudes. And while it is a sin to terminate for the wrong reasons, it can also be a sin not to do so in other circumstances.

You are right, – now we should talk about homosexuality. Yes, we will call it homosexuality, because that it is what it is, in the case of both males and females. Human heterosexual conjugation was historically essential for the continuation of the species. As I said, this will change in time, but until it does it is God's guidance is that the majority of humans should be born and raised in nuclear heterosexual family units. The differences between male and female physical strengths and weaknesses in the adult members of a family tend to lead to the allocation of day-to-day tasks to those who are better able to carry them out. But at least as important are the mental aspects. Just as it is God's responsibility to guide humans, so it is the older humans' duty to give care, nurture and spiritual guidance to their younger members. The physical differences between the sexes are usually so obvious that it is often all too easy to ignore the mental differences. But at this stage of human evolution, parts of the male and female brains function very differently and have different priorities, so to try to guide children in a balanced way it is preferable to have input from the brains and emotions of both sexes. Leaving aside adoption, which we will discuss separately, same sex couples can contrive to have children, but their upbringing would be different from those reared by heterosexual partnerships. Not necessarily either better or worse, but different.

Anyway as I said the heterosexual preference is a part of God's guidance for the majority of humans. But of course God knows that there is a significant minority who do not feel at all comfortable with heterosexuality, and who for whatever reason choose same sex relationships, whether mental or physical or both. Your historical records of the Greek island of Lesbos gives female homosexuals the term lesbians, but there is no convenient male equivalent. However, it will not surprise you to learn that God is not at all concerned with labels, so any word which is used to describe male or female homosexuality is perfectly acceptable, as long as the meaning is quite clear and unambiguous and not used or considered in any derogatory way. But of course it often is. Because homosexuality is a controversial subject to humans, and many of them hold entrenched views. But God doesn't. No Sorbo, although God would prefer the majority of humans to have heterosexual relationships, and reproduce and rear children in heterosexual nuclear family units, there are some people who this does not suit. And while God has given this clear heterosexual preference to many of the prophets and spiritual and cultural leaders who prayed for guidance, this preference has been interpreted by many people as a command of God. But of course, as you now know God does not make commands or issue orders.

Is homosexuality in itself a sin? No Sorbo. Homosexuality of either sex is a minority but not abnormal part of life, and the latent tendency is present in every animal, not just humans. You might think that all animals are either completely male or female. But as I said when I was talking about positive and negative attitudes, you would be wrong. OK Sorbo, you can read as much as you like about the sex life of snails when you get back to Earth, but while you're here we're only going to talk about humans. Most humans are fairly easily physically identifiable as either male or female, but this is actually a simplistic description and of course it does not give the full picture. All animals, even those which are apparently obviously of one sex, have some physical or mental characteristics which could equally apply to the other. No Sorbo, gender is not purely a matter of physical make-up. The hunter-gatherer instincts which are usually considered as largely male territory, are also present to some extent in all females. And the caring and tender side of humans, generally thought to be more of a feminine characteristic, is present to an extent in all males, regardless of whether or not they acknowledge or accept it.

I have only given you two fairly obvious examples, but in fact every mental attribute of humans exists to a degree in both sexes. The only difference is the extent of the feeling, and the emphasis placed on it by the human concerned, and by the society in which they live. But that's not all of the mental side of gender distinction. As I said, the majority of humans are physically identifiable as either female or male. However some are not, either obviously at birth, or in some cases recognised only during childhood or in their early adult life. They may be of no determinable gender, or sometimes a combination of both. And there are others who are physically born as male or female but who, at any stage of their life, have an overwhelming conviction that their minds actually belong in a body of the opposite sex.

So no life form is uniquely either heterosexual or homosexual. Even the most apparently totally heterosexual people have a degree of mental affinity or rapport with, and physical attraction to, other members of their own sex. Just as many homosexuals do with members of the opposite sex. And as I said this is quite normal. The only difference between what you might classify as either homosexual or heterosexual behaviour is the degree to which this manifests itself. God's preference is that heterosexuality should be the majority choice, but that does not mean that homosexuality in itself is a sin, because it is not. Cultures and religions may take whatever view they choose, but they cannot truthfully claim any authority from God. So, homosexuality, of either sex, is a normal part of life And so is bi-sexuality. The great majority of humans do not choose or prefer or identify with either, but a significant minority can and do. And as it is a normal part of life, they are perfectly free to make that decision.

Actually in a lot of cases it is not considered to be a decision, but a question of who or what the person really is, and many people feel that they are naturally homosexual. But there are also many people who are confused about their sexuality, particularly when they are growing up from childhood to become young adults, when same sex relations can often seem easier or even preferable. They should not be influenced by minority groups or popular trends, but freely allowed to reach their own decision. There are some who will decide that they are naturally homosexual. Others may feel that their soul is trapped in a body of the opposite sex, or even that they feel gender-neutral, and that medical intervention to change or correct their gender may be a solution. Prayer to God will help to give all of these people answers. And when they have the answers, they should lead their lives accordingly. And seek human help if or when they need it. A minority will follow a homosexual or bisexual lifestyle, whether or not in any sort of relationship. And, because the enjoyment of sex is not confined just to reproduction, homosexual physical pleasure is also quite acceptable.

However of course, as in all human life, there must be constraints. Although homosexuality and bi-sexuality are not in any way abnormal in humans, heterosexual feelings and relationships, and the raising of children within heterosexual nuclear families, are the majority and God's preferred choice. Of course God understands and accepts the homosexual and other communities which are not in the mainstream of sexual orientation. And because God accepts them, the human majority should do likewise. They should not be condemned for their differences and they should enjoy the same rights and freedoms, and be treated with the same respect as any other minority groups. But on their part, all minority groups, whether in terms of sexual orientation or anything else which sets them apart from the majority, also need to understand that they are indeed minorities, and that those same rights and freedoms also belong to the majority. Minorities should be allowed to live their lives according to their values, and they are entitled to equal consideration and respect, but they are not entitled to claim any form of preferential or special treatment over the majority, or to try to impose their values on them. Neither should they flaunt their minority beliefs in such a manner that they appear to consider that it sets them apart in any way as superior to, or have more rights than, the majority.

Whether in majorities or minorities, all humans have souls and in God's eyes all souls are equal and have equal rights to their existence. Caring individuals and societies and nations will try to understand the additional problems often faced by those people who are in minority groups. And instead of condemning them as second class or inferior citizens, they will give them the extra support which some will need, whether physically or mentally or spiritually. Don't forget that one of the reasons why souls have a short time in an Earthly body, is to try to show selflessness in what often seems to humans to be a totally selfish world. And that includes accepting and respecting the rights of minority groups, provided only that the minority groups do not themselves deliberately disadvantage the majority.

Just before we leave sexual preferences and sexual identities, we'll come back to bibles and their relevance to life as it is today. When most bibles were written, humans were only identified as either male or female or something else. There were no proper alternatives recognised then. In those days most humans considered that homosexuality and bi-sexuality were sins, and many bibles record this. But these were intolerant human rules, and not part of God's guidance. This guidance did not inspire the therapies or punishments intended by humans over the ages to 'cure' homosexuality. Humans of uncertain or undeterminable sex, were often considered unnatural, or freaks of nature in modern terms, and treated accordingly. But they are not freaks. They may be in a very small minority, but they are still human beings with souls. And God's guidance is that such minorities should be treated with understanding and respect. As I said, bibles and religions should evolve to take into account those things which were not understood or recognised when the bibles were written.

God's guidance evolves as humans evolve, and God will always give guidance relevant to the time of asking, and to the extent which humans are able to comprehend. Yes Sorbo, I've already said many times that God regards all souls as being equal, – and I'll be saying it many more times, – especially when we get round to talking about leaders of religions and nations, and powerful or well-known people in business or sport or entertainment. A lot of them think they are superior to everyone else, and a lot more don't even realise that they have a soul, but they will all eventually learn the truth.

But for the moment it's back to sex. Is it wrong to buy or sell sex? We must go back to basics again, as I said we would for many topics. The way most peaceful human activities are currently carried out often involves the buying and selling of goods and services, usually in exchange for money or other mutually acceptable means of reward. You need somewhere to live. If you are fortunate, you may have a number of choices. If you are in a town or city, you may be able to buy or rent somewhere. If you are in a small village, there may not be anywhere to buy or rent, so the elders or leaders may give or sell you a small piece of land, and you could build your own place to live. Or you may find a job of work which provides accommodation as well as money. Apart from very unusual and exceptional cases, you have to offer something in exchange. And so it is with all of your other human needs, wishes or desires.

But what can you offer? Unless you are one of the few humans born into a wealthy family, or you otherwise inherit money or property, you must offer something which other people need. No, Sorbo. Right now I'm not talking about those people who are either unable or feel unwilling to offer anything, or those who consider that the world owes them a living regardless of whether they contribute something in return. I am talking about the average reasonable human being in normal circumstances, as they are by far in the majority. And usually they can offer to carry out some sort of work, in return for reward, either on a temporary or longer-term basis. And this work will inevitably involve the use of both their body and their brain, in different degrees, depending on the task required and the reward offered. You cannot separate the brain and the body in any human activity, as they are both involved at all times.

A labourer on a farm or building site is probably using slightly more body than brain, whereas an astrophysicist is almost certainly the other way around. But what about a supermarket cashier, a bus driver, a cleaner in a hotel, or a chef in a restaurant kitchen? Actually, nobody bothers to think about the proportion of use of the brain and body in most work activities. And nobody thinks that there is anything wrong with willingly and freely buying or selling the use of either, in any proportion. Except in the case of prostitution, which has always been considered to be completely different. But it isn't. A prostitute is not just selling the temporary use of a body, but her or his brain as well, as the two are inseparable. The historical taboo about this sort of work for reward is that it involves sex. But sex is a normal part of human life, although unlike many other activities it is usually, and preferably, carried out in private. There are many reasons why two consenting adults would wish to have sex, but not to have the sort of relationship which involves any other commitment by either party. Just because you might decide to eat at a particular restaurant on one occasion, it does not mean that you are in any way obligated to go there again. They have sold, and you have bought, food. Food is a commodity. Sex can also be a commodity, if it is freely accepted to be so by both parties.

In itself, there is nothing wrong or sinful about the buying and selling of sex, any more than there is about the buying and selling of any other goods or services. No, Sorbo. Nothing I have said about sex should be taken out of context, and nothing can be taken to mean that there are no constraints. There are many reasons why people may become sex workers, but even more reasons why they should not. In countries where it is, or may become, a legitimate paid occupation, it should be undertaken completely willingly and voluntarily by the sex worker, and in properly designated and regulated premises, or otherwise by direct and confidential negotiation between client and worker and all carried out in private. But this occupation will not suit many people, and it is currently much the minority form of the buying and selling of sexual services. In the vast majority of cases the seller is not acting entirely voluntarily, but more in desperation, as their only perceived means of getting access to their needs, such as providing food or shelter for themselves or their dependants, or often to buy alcohol or drugs to satisfy an addiction. Of course this is highly undesirable, and such people need considerable help to try to change their lifestyle. In many other cases the seller is entrapped into prostitution by criminal means, often by enslavement after thinking that they have been offered a genuine employment opportunity. In any country this should be a crime. In any event it is of course a sin. And, of course, this does not just apply to sex, but to all other similar human behaviour.

We will talk more about slavery, and as I promised we will also talk about semantics, but for the moment we will stay with sex. And free will. It is wrong for any sexual activity to take place without the full, knowing, and willingly given consent of all of the parties involved. Yes, it seems obvious, – it must be rape. It is indeed rape, sometimes also incestuous rape, and any rape is both wrong and a sin. But rape and incest are both very common occurrences in the animal world, so why is it a sin for humans but not for other animals? Yes, Sorbo, – all animals have souls, and for their very survival, all animals need instinct and some reasoning ability, but the soul in its human incarnation is different from that of other animals. Humans have evolved with a mental capacity far greater than that needed just for continuation of the species. Most of them have the ability to differentiate between right and wrong, at least in groups or societies, even if not individually. God cannot force an individual to act in a particular way, but it is God's wish that humans try to act, as selflessly as they are able, in the best interests of their fellow humans, and ultimately, therefore, for the good of the Universe. And the act of rape of a fellow human is certainly not normally in their best interests. OK, yes. Some devious wranglers could construct hypothetical situations where rape might be a preferable alternative to other possible worse consequences, but these would be so rare and exceptional that they are not relevant to our discussions at the moment.

Just before I continue about rape, I'd better mention incest as it applies to humans. There are many different definitions of incest, but usually it is considered to be sexual intercourse between close blood relatives. Depending on the distance of the relationship, it is nowadays generally taboo and a crime in most societies for various reasons, not least because any offspring of incestuous sex is likely to be impaired in some way either physically or mentally or both. Incest is also usually a sin. However, there could be exceptional circumstances. Consider a brother and sister living in a remote community in which there are few other people who are not in long-term relationships. They love each other. They are both adults and of sound mind, and know that sexual intercourse would constitute incest. However, their desires for sexual pleasure are so strong that they take precautions to ensure that the female does not become pregnant, and then proceed to have sex. In most societies they have committed a crime. But have they committed a sin? Most humans would say yes. God's guidance is that there could be rare, indeed very rare, circumstances in which such incestuous relationships may not be sinful. Unwise, yes, – sinful, not necessarily. As I said this would be very rare, as incest is almost always a sin.

But of course there is also another exception which applies to humans and more importantly to animals. Most human communities will know of any blood relationship between their members and advise them accordingly. However it is quite possible that two closely related people could be separated from their communities and from each other at an early age. If by chance they met again as adults and, without knowing of their relationship, proceeded to have sexual intercourse this would of course be incest. But if they had no way of knowing that they were committing incest it would not be a sin. This also applies more importantly to other animals. At their current evolutionary stage of development, they have little or no knowledge of family relationships and their importance, and no concept of incest as being wrong and a sin.

But now we'll get back to rape. And the key is consent, and what really constitutes consent. We'll start with age. At what age can a person reasonably make a decision to have sexual intercourse? And don't forget that we're not just talking about females. Although it is less common, males can be raped too. The age at which a child can make a decision about sex, or indeed anything else, depends entirely on the circumstances of their existence. It is a matter which should be decided by their culture, religion and nation, and it is to be hoped that they can all eventually reach a consensus. And it is also desirable that whatever they agree on today can be progressively reviewed as human evolution continues.

At the moment humans still need human laws and codes of behaviour, but there should be some flexibility in these laws or rules. For instance, in the case of age, it is unreasonable to consider, of someone who has a birthday today, – 'what they did yesterday was a crime, but today it is not'. It is more important to consider whether someone is, or was, mentally capable of reaching a responsible decision, or whether they suffer from some kind of disability. If this is the case, is the disability permanent as a result of any inherited or birth deformity or illness or accident during their life, or was it temporarily induced by any form of short-term trauma, or alcoholic, narcotic or other drug? Taken willingly by all parties concerned, or introduced without consent? The permutations of circumstances leading to the committing of an alleged rape are almost endless, and therefore the consideration of culpability will rarely be straightforward in terms of human laws. So some flexibility is often needed in the interpretation and administration of these laws and rules. But flexibility is not needed in other cases.

I have already told you that prostitution is not in itself a sin, nor in itself should it be a crime. But it must be entirely voluntary on the part of the person selling the use of his or her body and mind for the sexual pleasure of others. It is a sin, and should also be a crime in any legal system, for anyone to use any mental or physical pressure to coerce someone to have sex for any form of reward, or no reward, or by any threat. Because of the nature of prostitution, and the public perception of it, and the laws of many nations, it is an easy target for criminally minded people, whether individually or in organised groups, to prey on this form of sex. It does not need God to tell you that this is entirely wrong. Of course it is a sin. But one which only humans can prevent. Yes, nations and their leaders could start by looking at their laws, and thinking about what I have said about the buying and selling of services. And they could pray to God for further guidance. Yes, and not just about this. At any time, and about anything. And of course although at the moment I am talking about criminally organised and enforced prostitution, the same applies to all other forms of forced labour, regardless of whether or not the subject is rewarded in any way. It is still slavery, and slavery is always a sin.

Yes, Sorbo. Now we will talk about the eating of animal flesh.

Many cultures and religions have all sorts of rules about eating animals. Some believe that it is wrong in any circumstances. Some believe that you may eat certain animals, but not others. Others believe that you may eat animal flesh but not blood. And there are people who believe that you may not eat land animals, but eating fish or other sea creatures is acceptable. You can think of almost countless other rules, including those of vegetarians and vegans. Many of these originated in early human times, and were laid down by patriarchs, prophets and the like after prayer to God for guidance. Those who didn't believe in God developed their own rules for different reasons, often dictated by the availability of potential food animals and the practicality of preserving carcases in a safely edible condition.

In the early days of the co-existence of humans and wild animals, there were many confrontations between them, and humans were often the losers. This began to change when humans developed tools to use as weapons which they could use to kill or incapacitate the animals, and of course other humans which threatened them. This type of killing could be called killing for survival, and it is the only acceptable reason for killing, but then only if it used to combat a real and current threat. Kindred spirits and other similarly minded people abhor violence, but there are times when they have to use it in defence of themselves or others who are imminently threatened. In these circumstances killing of humans or animals is permissible. But only in these circumstances. Killing in the name of justice, or as retribution or punishment after the event, is wrong and a sin, and nations will eventually start to realise and accept this and amend their laws accordingly.

Killing for survival by humans also historically included killing animals for food or other products. With the exception of killing for cannibalism which has always been a sin, this was acceptable in situations where they could not find any realistic alternatives. But now there are alternatives, and the human race needs to accept this. In the early days on Earth, humans had little choice except to eat any food which they could find. God's guidance to the patriarchs and prophets then, as it still is now, was that unless there is no alternative it is wrong to kill and eat living creatures. And one simple definition for them was creatures which have blood. Some cultures adopted a vegan or vegetarian or semi-vegetarian diet, whether or not they believed in God. Some because they followed our guidance, some because they preferred it, and others because it was more freely available or an easier option. Of necessity some did not, as in those times there was either not sufficient vegetarian food available in their part of Earth, or they didn't believe in God anyway. Those various religions and cultures which did believe in God established many different ways in which they could eat a mixed animal and vegetable diet, while still appearing to be following God's guidance. That was reasonable then, and acceptable to God. Now, it is not.

Humans no longer have any necessity to breed, rear and kill for food, or for any other animal product. And that includes all creatures, whether they live on land, or in the sea or air. In the case of diet, and as in many other aspects of human life, religions have mostly considered their bibles and sacred texts to be immutable. But they are not, and they should not be. God expects human life to evolve, and therefore for human beliefs to evolve accordingly. And that includes religions and religious beliefs. And all of their bibles. Yes, I've started yet another sentence with a preposition or conjunction. And I've used many sentences without verbs. I know, – you've been wondering about that for a while now. And I don't just do that in English, but in all the other thousands of Earth languages. But of course it's against all the rules you were taught at school. Well-written and well-spoken language is very nice and quite desirable, and it should be included in all education. And those people who choose to write and speak correctly, conforming with the rules of their language, should be respected for such belief. But it is not always strictly necessary. The crucial importance of language is that it should be absolutely clear and unambiguous. Unfortunately, human language often fails in that respect, either deliberately or accidentally. But more about that when we get round to semantics. For the moment, we'll go back to diet.

I am not saying that all humans should immediately adopt a vegan or vegetarian diet. It would be impossible for billions of people to want or even be able to change their lifestyle that quickly. And you must also consider the billions of people who are employed in the farming and harvesting and slaughter of animals, and fish and fowl and insects, either as food or for any other product. It would be totally unreasonable to deprive them of their livelihoods without giving them sufficient time both to accept the reasons for change, and then gradually to find alternatives. What I am saying is that humans should start to come to a collective understanding that God's guidance is that animals should not be used for consumption in any form. Of course many humans do already believe this, even though they may not yet believe in God. And many who do believe in God, have either not yet sought, or have not yet understood, God's guidance. And there are many people involved in the existing human food chain, who are not willing to accept or follow God's guidance.

So the change must be very gradual, and like all of God's guidance to humans, there should be no coercion. Only gentle persuasion by reasoned argument, over a period of many years. This may seem too idealistic to become a fact. However, you should consider how human attitudes to cannibalism have changed over time. Thousands of years ago it was common practice not only to eat the flesh of dead humans, but also to kill them for consumption of their bodies. But the human race has evolved, and killing for cannibalism is now considered totally wrong and repulsive by virtually all nations and peoples. In the not too distant future humans will also start to accept that is wrong and equally repulsive to breed and kill animals to consume their flesh. And because humans do not now need to do this for survival, they no longer have any right or justification to continue.

You have noticed that I have only talked about the use of animals to satisfy human needs, and I have given you God's guidance about this. This guidance is all humans need to enable them to make the right decisions. But the sensible human use of the limited resources available on planet Earth is of course also a highly important issue, and it will require humans to have much considered and responsible debate, discussion and resolution. But it is not relevant to God's guidance about the killing of animal life. Yes, Sorbo. You are quite right, – I cannot leave it just like that, without a bit more explanation, as of course there are many exceptions. For a start, it is quite acceptable for humans to eliminate, or try to eliminate, bacterial, viral or other life forms which threaten, harm or damage human or animal wellbeing and Earth's environment. And that necessarily includes some other animal life forms as well, if they are invasive in a pestilent way. They should be eliminated as quickly and as painlessly as possible, and without any form of ritual or ceremony. And never for entertainment.

A few thousand years ago, the killing of humans in an arena was considered to be a desirable form of entertainment. But that was wrong, and over time, humans began to realise it was wrong and largely stopped doing it. But the killing of animals by humans for entertainment still persists in some parts of Earth, as does the human organisation of the killing or maiming of animals by other animals. Yes, of course this is wrong, and humans should all have agreed on this by now. Killing, or the organisation of killing or injuring, for entertainment, is always wrong, even if it is a ritual or ceremonial and traditional part of the extermination of pests. Yes, if committed by humans, it is a sin. As you know, some people get a kind of pleasure or thrill from the killing of animals, or from watching other people doing so. And many of them often call it sport. But it isn't any kind of sport. It is cold-blooded killing, and it is a perversion. A perversion which will disappear when the majority realise that it is both totally wrong and a sin, and persuade all governments to make it a crime. But of course there will still be humans who will ignore any such laws and continue with their sadistic behaviour. And as with all criminals, if present laws and justice properly and fairly carried out do not result in reductions in their criminal activities, governments may wish to consider whether any other form of treatment or education may become necessary.

Now I will go back to your question about animals killing animals, and other life forms. Some animals do indeed appear to derive a form of pleasure or amusement during the killing of their prey, prior to its use for food. However, this is not typical of the majority. Like humans, most animals have evolved with a herbivorous, carnivorous, or omnivorous diet, depending on their species, and the food available in their location. Apart from gradual evolutionary development, and without human intervention, this will continue, as the animals themselves are not capable of effecting change. Those animals which catch and eat other animals, and those which eat dead flesh, will continue to do so for the time being, as they have no other option.

But this is where there is a big difference. Humans do have the option. Globally, they now have the technical expertise to grow enough food to be totally herbivorous, and to ensure that a herbivorous or vegetarian diet can provide all of the required nutrients. They also already have synthetic alternatives to most of the animal products which they have historically required, and before long they will have the ability to produce all of the others. All they now need is the resolve to share this technology with those societies which do not already possess it, and the determination to move gradually towards following God's wishes that they cease breeding, rearing and killing animals, for their consumption as food or for any other purpose. Yes Sorbo, that does include fish, fowl, and birds of the air, and even grubs and insects. But while humans will need time to change to a wholly vegetarian diet, more urgent consideration should be given to the welfare of the animals currently used in the food chain. They should be bred and reared in humane circumstances, and slaughtered without any pain or suffering. Historical methods and rituals used by many religions and cultures in the slaughter of animals for food should be consigned to where they belong. To history. No Sorbo, no culture or religion today can rightfully claim God's approval to continue their traditional practices unless they can prove conclusively that they do not cause any pain or suffering to the animal. Scholars and ministers can study and debate their religious texts for as long as they wish, but they will only be discussing their own human interpretations of God's guidance as it was many years ago. And they should also remember that when they consume animal flesh, it is irrelevant whether that flesh still contains blood. Draining the blood either as part of the slaughtering process or afterwards does not change the fact that the animal did have blood when it was alive, and they are still eating animal flesh. Until that changes, the most important consideration is the welfare of the animal both during its life and at its death.

However, the breeding and rearing of animals for products other than their flesh needs different consideration. You immediately thought of dairy products and eggs, but there are many more. And there are still many parts of Earth where, at this point in time, there is little realistic alternative to using animals as sources of power for needs such as agriculture or transport. But for the moment we'll go back to chickens and eggs. No Sorbo, – this time God will not indulge you in Earthly humour. Consider a little child, anywhere on Earth, who is lucky enough to have a pet chicken. This chicken lays eggs, which are a very valuable source of nourishment for the whole family. But, sometimes just as importantly, the child grows fond of the chicken, gives it a special name, and looks after it as one of the family, as children often do with pets. Now consider a large farm, with thousands of nameless chickens, all looking much the same. The only consideration is how many eggs the farm can produce every day. The welfare of the chickens is usually secondary to that, unless it affects the rate of egg production. Or you could think of a family, perhaps in an under-developed country, who have a cow. The milk it produces is of great value, so the cow is very well cared for, and like the chicken, it often becomes almost one of the family. And then there is the large dairy farm, which produces milk and all of its associated products. To stay in business, it has to try to make a profit, and the welfare of its cows may often become secondary to their milk output.

I also mentioned animal power. Horses, donkeys, oxen and similar animals are still used in many countries to provide motive power for essential day-to-day activities. In other places horses and donkeys are employed in the spheres of leisure and entertainment. And they, and other animals and birds, are often used in competitive sports. There is nothing in itself wrong in the use by humans of any animals for these and any other similar purposes. But the relationship should always be symbiotic. For instance, you could breed hens to provide eggs, or cows and goats to give milk and sheep to produce both milk and wool. But your scientists must first devise a form of selective breeding to give life to only those female animals required to produce the eggs or milk together with sufficient males to continue the species. And this selective breeding should be accomplished without any termination of life even at the embryonic stage. As I said the relationship should be symbiotic.

Humans may want the product which the animals can provide. In return they should give the animals a pleasant and comfortable environment not only from birth and during their productive years, but also after that, as they are entitled to a full natural life-span. Yes Sorbo, that does mean that these products will become more expensive for humans. But humans should accept that all animals, including themselves, deserve to be treated fairly and compassionately and with respect. If humans decide that they still want these products, they should accept the increased costs of truly symbiotic relationships with the animals which provide them. And in this as in all matters concerning animals, God's approval can only be given if humans respect the welfare and sanctity of all animal life. Any form of mistreatment causing mental or physical suffering to any animals, whether accidental or deliberate, and whether by commission or omission, is totally unacceptable. It is a sin.

When we talked about the creation of life by sexual intercourse, we also said that it is now increasingly possible for humans to create life forms in other ways. Humans will also have to decide whether this is a desirable alternative form of reproduction, but in doing so they will need to consider carefully many aspects of this. The question of termination of a viable human or other animal embryo is still the same. If it was created for any other reason than to lead eventually to a properly formed adult of the species, then both the creation and the termination are sins. This is something which scientists need to accept and act on now, regardless of whether they believe in God during their Earthly life. No Sorbo, – despite what they may think today, humans do not have any right to create life forms for any other purpose, regardless of how much benefit they might derive from it. Neither do they have the right to carry out experiments on any animals, unless they can demonstrate unequivocally that death, or physical or mental suffering is not involved. And yes this applies to mice, rabbits, pigs and every other animal used or considered to be used for human benefit.

The only exceptions are creatures such as insects or vermin which threaten human or animal life or food production. It doesn't matter how much humans might gain from the breeding or use of any other animals for experimental purposes or for the harvesting of any of their body parts, it is still wrong for them to do so. There is a fundamental difference between having the ability to do something, and having the right to do it. In this case humans do not have that right. Unless they are a positive threat to human or animal wellbeing or livelihood, or to your own planet, all life forms are sacrosanct and should be respected. To do otherwise may be legal and acceptable to nations and cultures, but it is not only wrong but also a sin. A sin of commission by those directly involved, and a sin of omission by the leaders and lawmakers of their nations if they do not start to realise it and eventually legislate against it.

Yes Sorbo, I will repeat that a sin of omission is still a sin, and it is wrong to regard it as being in a different category from a sin of commission. No, they are not exactly the same, but they are still both sins. And I will also repeat that genuine remorse or repentance after committing a sin is at least a sign that the sin has been acknowledged, but it can never fully atone for the sin. God knows of the temptations facing the soul while it is in a physical Earthly body, and God is both patient and forgiving. But the soul should also try to act in such a way that it does not commit a sin in the first place and that such forgiveness will not be necessary. The short time during which the soul is in a human body is one of the most difficult stages in its eternal journey, but God is always there to give guidance to any soul which seeks it. It is far better to pray for guidance before you act, than to pray for forgiveness after.

When I talked about reproduction and the creation of life forms, I did not include artificial intelligence, as it is not a true life form. Scientists are creating machines which will be increasingly more powerful than the human brain in calculations and analysis, and they will be useful tools for performing complex tasks. As you know, they are already outperforming humans in many things such as playing chess, simultaneous translation of language, and facial recognition. But scientists will need to be extremely careful to ensure that their creations must adhere to precise sets of rules and limitations pre-determined by humans. They must not ever be allowed to have the extent of free will that humans do. The crucial difference between these machines and humans is that the machines will not have souls. Scientists cannot create souls. And creatures without a soul will not be responsible to God or the Universe for any of their actions. And your scientists and philosophers should all realise that the creation of artificial creatures with unfettered free will but without souls is both dangerous and irresponsible. Such machines would very quickly decide that humans are inferior to them in every way, and therefore an unnecessary waste of resources, and this would inevitably lead to the extinction of life on Earth by the very machines which humans themselves created.

Of course one of the problems with scientists and inventors is that if something seems even remotely possible, some of them will always try to find a way to do it. And if they succeed, they will then usually try to absolve themselves from their responsibility for any untoward consequences. Firearms and nuclear weapons are just two very simple examples of their familiar claim 'yes we made them, but we didn't tell you to use them'. So before scientists create machines with free will, all nations will need to find a way to restrict their use and capability only to actions beneficial to the peaceful continuation and evolution of life on Earth. It will be very difficult to reach a global consensus on this, but acting after such machines have been created will be too late.

Sorbo, justice does not logically follow on from diet, killing, animal husbandry or artificial intelligence, but I did say that you could ask for topics in any order, so we'll talk about justice. Or the lack of justice in many parts of the Earth. Back to basics again to start with. Humans have always had, and for the foreseeable future always will have, differences of opinion. Sometimes these are relatively minor, and can be sorted out by discussion or with family or friends. Slightly more important issues can be resolved by some form of mediation or conciliation, or advice from community or tribal leaders. But many problems go beyond this, so other people have to become involved. I'm not going to complicate things by being specific, so I'm going to call all of these people lawyers. No, Sorbo. God does not mind what these people call themselves. We are going to call them all lawyers, and we'll talk about their legal profession.

And here we immediately have a problem. Universal law decrees that ultimately all differences should be resolved by consensus. But most humans and human societies are not yet capable of reaching this, so on Earth, and as far back as recorded human history, you have had lawyers. You could call it the oldest profession, but of course others may disagree, so we'll leave them to debate that. Without consensus or other mutual agreement, all differences have to be resolved by lawyers acting for the conflicting parties and bringing forward evidence to whoever will make a decision. And the most important part of the process should not be the decision itself, but how accurately that decision represents the truth in the case. All too often it doesn't. All too often it depends on the relative skills, eloquence and semantic manipulations of the advocates acting for the disputing parties. In the adversarial system of justice which exists in many countries, the prime consideration is usually the end result, – the decision or verdict of the arbiter or arbiters. Truth is often considered to be secondary, or even inconvenient or irrelevant.

The inquisitorial system should be more likely to get nearer to the truth, but for various reasons it often doesn't. Your lawyers take great delight in making the whole process as complicated as possible, often with the result that the only beneficiaries in any legal action are the lawyers themselves. Yes Sorbo, the legal systems on Earth have been developed over thousands of years, but that doesn't mean that they have to be right. And as you know, all too often the outcome of a legal action may be correct in judicial law, but not in common sense terms or natural law.

However, God is not interested in the specific legal systems adopted by various nations, or the difference between civil and criminal proceedings, or in points of law, or in the learned pronouncements of very clever people, or in the sometimes quite arcane legal paraphernalia which has grown over the centuries. But God is interested in justice, and justice means also fairness. And truth. And these should not depend on who can afford to pay for the most expensive lawyers, or bribe officials in corrupt governments or members of judiciaries. And it also means that many countries and religions should re-examine their laws and rules to make sure that they do not unjustly penalise people who are innocent of sin. Sorbo, remember what I said about contraception and termination. At the moment, these are always crimes to many nations and religions, but not always sins in God's eyes. And the same consideration applies to many other human activities No, of course Earth's legal systems will not change overnight, but they should constantly be reviewed to see how they can be improved. Improved primarily for the benefit of the user, not for the extra financial reward or self-aggrandisement of lawyers. And if the legal profession will not accept that change is reasonable and necessary, and willingly work towards it, then such change should be carried out by people who are not lawyers.

Don't forget that God doesn't make rules or issue commands for humans to follow, so I am just giving you God's guidance. And as I have already said, and I will be saying again, whether or not humans decide to follow God's guidance has to be their decision. But they should always know that choosing to ignore God's guidance is at least a mistake, and often a sin, and the consequence will be a punishment which is inflicted not by God, but by the soul punishing itself. Such souls will spend unnecessary time in ignorance of Universal truth, and therefore in a state of torment, for far longer than God wishes for them. It is not always easy for souls, while they are in a physical body, to follow God's guidance, but they should try. As I said earlier, the soul's progress through other Universal planes is of relative simplicity, as it consists of spheres of contemplation and striving towards Universal truth. But each soul, during its journey, must also have at least one physical incarnation. This incarnation is where the soul reveals its true nature, by its reaction to the temptations and vagaries of life in a physical form.

We have created Earth, and other planets, specifically for this incarnation of souls. On Earth, it is in the form of humans. On other planets there are different life forms, depending on the different conditions. But in each case the soul is exposed to extreme temptations, and it is its reaction to these which determines its progress towards Universal truth. But we'll get back to life on Earth, which is the only planet causing us problems at the moment, and which is why you are here. You noticed that when I said Earth, I only mentioned humans. Yes, animals and other life forms also have souls. But the difference is that, at this stage of Earth's evolution, only humans really have the ability to make decisions about how to live their lives. And at the moment, many humans are not listening to God's guidance. Or, if they are, they are choosing not to follow it, or deciding that it is not relevant to them. Or, that God really doesn't exist, except in other people's imaginations. Or even that what they do in their human lives doesn't matter, because God won't know or care anyway. Sorbo, they are very wrong. Every action of every soul during its entire journey is known to God. There are many things which humans can do, which will never be revealed to other humans. But nothing which humans can do can ever be hidden from God. God knows.

Now we should talk a little more about religion. Eventually, all souls will accept and believe in the existence and meaning of God. But this will not happen to every soul while it is in an Earthly body. Some souls will resist the Universal truth during their short time on Earth, and consequently spend prolonged periods of turmoil on different planes. That is their choice. God will always give guidance to any soul, but as I have said, the soul can accept or reject that guidance. Yes, I will give you some of God's guidance about the different religions observed by humans at the moment. But I will only mention the twenty or so major religions. Each of these has similarities with others, but each also has many differences. I did say that you could choose what we talk about, so we will start with God's commandments. How many do you think there are? You would have guessed at anywhere between a few and more than a thousand. But of course you'd have been wrong, because as I've already told you, there are none.

All sorts of religions have all sorts of commandments, but they were all laid down by humans. Of course, a great majority of them are good and sensible rules for living, and a lot of them came from leaders and patriarchs who had prayed to God for guidance. But they are not God's commandments. As I have said many times, God does not command humans to act in any way. God gives guidance, and human free will chooses whether to follow that guidance, or continue on a path of darkness. And the one over-riding guidance which God has always given to anyone who genuinely prays for enlightenment, is that if they behave selfishly, they are committing a sin. Yes Sorbo, it is that simple. Simple to understand, but not simple to do. God knows that humans will always give way to some temptations to be selfish, quite often without realising it, so it is not a question of whether a human is or has been selfish, but how often and to what extent. Incidentally, any soul who prays to God for guidance will eventually know whether an action is selfish, so there is no justification for not realising it.

Anyway, I'll get back to human commandments, and as I said many of them are quite acceptable to God. But there are some exceptions. I've already told you about blasphemy, and how it can upset humans but not God. But I haven't mentioned some other things about God. You can make an image of God, or an effigy or idol. Of course it won't be very realistic, because God doesn't exist in a physical form visible to or discernible by humans. Over thousands of years creating such images has given some comfort or reassurance, but it is actually both unnecessary and unwanted. However it is not a sin, and the people who do this are not sinners, they are just people who have not yet understood the reality of God. And the same goes for the folklore about God being jealous. As I said before, God does not have human emotions, but even if I did jealousy would be irrelevant as there is no other God anyway.

We've already talked about working for six days, then having a day of rest. An early human rule or command which, although not inspired by God's guidance, still has a certain merit. Human bodies do get tired, so of course they need time for rest and relaxation, appropriate to their occupation and circumstance. Races, cultures and religions can and do observe their own rules for resting and abstention days, and fasting and feasting days according to their traditions. But you should always remember that they are all human rules, and made entirely by humans without any guidance from God. God did not invent the calendars used by humans nor did God name the days of the week or give guidance about any significance often ascribed to these particular days by humans.

I'm not going to leave religion quite yet, because when we were talking earlier you asked about the devil, and I said that had no place there. Well it didn't then and there, but it does now and here. Do you remember that night in the pub when your friends were talking about how many other names like satan and beelzebub there were to describe the devil? You thought it was probably a hundred or so, while others thought more. Of course you were all right, – except for one little detail. Hundreds of names, yes. But for something that does not exist. Yes Sorbo, – the devil, or any other word you care to use to signify the concept, is a figment of human imagination. A very convenient one, too. It can explain away many reasons why humans ignore God's guidance. 'It wasn't their fault that the devil had got into them.' Or a multitude of different expressions all amounting to the same thing. Disregard of God and fellow human beings.

For thousands of years the devil has been blamed for leading people astray. As you know, until quite recently many people who had serious mental defects were often thought of as being possessed by the devil. Fortunately, most of these conditions have now been identified and the true explanation given. Leaving aside people with mental disabilities, many cultures and societies also practised all sorts of ways to get the devil out of any other people who they considered possessed. And some of these rites and rituals are still practised, and even today. exorcism is a recognised part of many religions. But you can't eliminate something which does not exist, and therefore cannot be held responsible for sinful or otherwise undesirable behaviour. That sort of behaviour can only be changed by the person or people themselves recognising that what they do is not acceptable, either to other humans, or in the eyes of God. Whether consciously or unwittingly, they are being selfish, and selfishness is the greatest sin of all. It is actually the only sin, as all of the others which you are familiar with are consequences of selfishness.

The devil does not make a person selfish. That is the soul putting itself before others and choosing not to listen to God. And as I said before, one of the reasons for God putting the soul into a physical body for a brief time on a planet such as Earth, is to see how the soul responds to the difficulties it faces. Yes Sorbo, – every soul in a physical body faces many difficulties. Some far more than others, some less so. But the important thing to remember is that being in an Earthly life is only a very short part of the soul's journey, and that however difficult that part seems to be at the time, the next phases will be easier for those souls who have tried to be selfless. Those who have not, will suffer prolonged anguish and torment inflicted not by God, but entirely by their own selfish actions. What they do in their Earthly life will not vanish when their souls leave their human bodies, but will remain with them eternally.

You are quite right Sorbo. I've mentioned semantics many times, and we've finally got round to it. I've left it until nearly the end of your visit, as it will affect everything you write, and it will be the key to whether God's message is really properly understood. And semantics will also include context. And translation. But first we will talk about the meaning of words. Sounds easy, but it isn't. It doesn't matter which of the many thousands of human languages you consider, as they all have words which have more than one meaning. The meaning of these words will often depend on the other words used with them, and the context in which they are all used. And context is often the way in which humans distort other people's messages.

Sorbo, let me take you back to that concert at the Royal Festival Hall. The first part of the programme included Beethoven's Violin Concerto. The soloist, conductor and orchestra were all among the best on Earth, so the performance should have been really outstanding. However, as is so often the case with Beethoven's compositions, even top-class artistes disagree on the tempo at which he intended his works to be played, and this night was no exception. The conductor favoured a more majestic and flowing style, but the solo violinist increased the pace each time he took the lead, so the result was a little reminiscent of the slow, slow, quick, quick, slow of a foxtrot dance. Thus the performance was little short of a disaster, and you said as much in your review. Or did you? I'll just quote from your article. 'If they had all melded sympathetically together, the combination of these two supreme musicians, and this world-famous orchestra, should have made this probably the best performance of Beethoven's Violin Concerto this year, instead of which it was arguably one of the worst.' Now I'll remind you of what the critic from the 'Musicians Daily' quoted you as writing. '... probably the best performance of Beethoven's Violin Concerto this year ...'. Yes Sorbo, your exact words, – but with almost exactly the opposite meaning.

It is unfortunately a common habit of some humans to deliberately take other people's words or phrases out of context to further their own, usually erroneous, views. In that critic's case, he was being paid a great deal of money by the agent of one of the musicians. So, when you are writing your books, you must try to avoid using phrases which can be given this treatment, although you will not be able to prevent it completely.

You will remember that when we talked about sex, we also discussed incest. I said that there are a very few exceptional and extenuating circumstances in which incest is not a sin. If you write it just like that, you will give some rather undesirable people the opportunity to take your words out of context and proclaim that God has said 'incest is not a sin'. And when I mentioned images of God, I said that they would be unrealistic because God does not exist in a physical form visible to or discernible by humans. Out of context, you noticed I said the four words 'God does not exist'. So, context is highly important, and you should emphasise again and again that to misrepresent God's words by taking them out of context is a sin. Yes, Sorbo, – a sin.

I told you earlier that the traditional understanding of blasphemy against God is not in fact a sin. However, deliberate misrepresentation of God's word is. Accidental misrepresentation may not be, but it is less common and mostly not accidental at all, but just used as a pretext by those people who do not wish God's guidance to be properly understood. Re-phrasing purely to distort the message. So blasphemy of God's name is not a sin but misrepresentation of God's word is. Yes, this can confuse many people, but that's only because they do not properly understand the meaning of taking the word or the name of the lord in vain. And don't forget that God is not a lord, or The Lord, in the sense that most people think of it. God is a guide and teacher.

And now is the time for this teacher to talk a little about translation, because we would like your book to be published in as many languages as necessary for the entire world population to have access to it. Sounds easy, – but it won't be. And it will give you a great deal of extra work. You know that many languages have words which have multiple meanings. And many have words with no exact or sometimes even no approximate equivalent in other languages. And you are also familiar with the common problem that when, say, a sentence in one language is translated into another, and then re-translated back again into the original, it often has a different meaning, or no meaning at all, or is complete nonsense. So you need to do your best to avoid this. Firstly, you should use a different translator for each language. And they should be chosen very carefully, as there will be some people who do not want your book to be published at all. Then you should get another independent person to translate your words back into English. And that is where your extra work will start, as you will need to read each version extremely carefully to make absolutely certain that it is still exactly as you wrote it. Yes Sorbo, – a lot of extra work.

But you will have some help. Although you saw her on Wednesday, you haven't really met her, but you will do shortly after you wake up on Friday afternoon. Her name's Kate Gurley and she's a doctor, – actually one of the Air Ambulance crew who took you to St. George's, so she's already met you. She doesn't know it yet, but she will offer to help you with the production of your book in any way you wish. Yes, she and her partner will be with you for another five years. Both of them are completely trustworthy, so you'll have no worries on that account. Unlike some other people who you'll meet. Yes, I'd better explain that. At the moment, only a very few people on Earth know how and why you are here. They are the kindred spirits who prayed to God for better understanding of the reasons for human life, and how humans should try to lead it. And they are the kindred spirits who acted on God's guidance and arranged for everything leading up to the 'accident' which was necessary to get you here. And when you get back to your Earthly existence, they will be the people who will help you to publish the book to convey what you learn here to the entire world population. But some of the truths you take back to Earth will be difficult for many people to understand or accept, so some of them will go to great lengths to stop you.

There will be leaders of countries or religions, because they will feel that their authority is being challenged, but there will be many others, including zealots and extremists of all persuasions who currently have misconceived ideas about the nature and meaning of God. It may seem a little strange, but you will find that some atheists, agnostics and other non-believers are also hostile to a book about God and human life. But whilst all of these people need to learn by reading your book, it will not be written for them. It is for the vast majority of the human population, most of whom are, or could be, kindred spirits. Yes Sorbo, most human beings are decent, well-meaning and considerate people who would like to live their lives peacefully and to the best of their ability without aggression or interference. You could call them the silent majority, because that is what they usually are. They know within themselves when something is right or wrong, but for a number of reasons they rarely shout about it to others. The extremists and the minority groups make their voices loud and insistent, but the silent majority usually stay silent. Some because they prefer a quiet life, but many more because they think that they are so insignificant that they can't do anything about it. But they are wrong. No soul is insignificant in God's eyes, and they need to be told this. And your book will tell them.

But first you will need to get it published. And you will need kindred spirits to help you. How will you find them? You won't, – they will find you. But others who are not kindred spirits will also find you, and for all the wrong reasons. So how will you know whether to trust someone or not? Yes, I've already said that kindred spirits are not an organisation, club or society, and that they have no shibboleths or secret codes or passwords or anything else by which they could be identified or which sets them apart from others, – in other words they just seem to be like ordinary people. That is because they are ordinary people, – but with a difference. They are the ordinary people, and that includes the majority of humans, who have an inner sense of moral decency and most of whom, at least by the time when they reach adulthood, do not any longer need to be told the difference between right and wrong. They come from all walks of life, from every race, colour and creed, and rich or poor. But what they have in common is a belief in God and a desire to lead decent lives. Sorbo, you cannot see moral decency, any more than you can see God or your own soul, but you will be able to recognise it in others. And in many people you will see kindred spirits. Kindred spirits who will be there to help you when you need it. Sometimes so unexpectedly that it will seem like fortunate coincidence. Of course you will make some mistakes and be disappointed, and at other times you will not be sure. But mostly you will just know. And when it involves the book, you will get an inner feeling of uneasiness if someone seems to be just a bit too interested in helping you. Yes it will happen, but you will be ready for it.

But I was talking about semantics. Actually we could discuss words and their use and the subtleties and nuances, accents and stresses employed by clever people in many forms of rhetoric, – sometimes to clarify what they are saying, sometimes to conceal an underlying meaning or hidden agenda, and at other times to disguise the fact that what they are saying really means very little, if anything at all. But here we don't need to talk any more about that, because you won't use any of these undesirable tactics. You will need to keep the book as straightforward as possible, using simple words wherever you can, and trying to avoid anything which could give rise to any ambiguity of meaning. There should be no room for human semantics in the understanding of God's message. And although God's message is the same to all souls throughout the Universe, you should keep to just those parts of God's guidance relevant to life on Earth. Because it is simple. And because it doesn't involve all of the rules, codes and rituals developed by humans over thousands of years, which have only served to make the understanding of God and human existence complicated and confusing. But it isn't. And it shouldn't seem to be. Human life on Earth is not a rehearsal for another life. Nor is it the beginning and end of the soul's existence. It is the small part of the soul's journey when God assesses the soul's reaction to selfish temptation. And it is this reaction alone which determines the soul's next destination.

Sorbo, it is nearly time for you to make your decision, but before you do there is something else which we should discuss. And that is human leaders. All nations have a leader or leaders. Some are born into the position or inherit it. Some are elected by their countrymen, whether democratically or not through fair and free elections. Some seize power by either peaceful or violent means. Some are honest and straightforward, but some are corrupt, whether financially for themselves or their friends or family, or by using dishonest means of holding on to their power. Some really want to do the best for their populations but others are only interested in using any method to keep their positions. And it doesn't matter whether they are leading small countries or nations of many millions, these leaders are all completely different from each other. Except for one thing. They are all humans, and they all have souls, and they will all be judged by their actions. Many of them may not yet realise or believe this, but in due time they will have to learn the truth and accept the inevitable consequences which follow. And the time to start to seek and act upon God's guidance is now. Not in a few years or weeks. Not tomorrow. But now.

If leaders pray for guidance, God will give it. Guidance on how to act, not in their own selfish interest, but in the best interests of their own group or nation of people, at the same time as in the best interests of the whole world population, both now and in the future. And yes, this must include the halting and reversal of the damage which humans are causing to their own planet. There is a limit to how large a population Earth will be able to sustain. This will not be dictated by God, but it does need all nations to reach a consensus very quickly, both on numbers and how to persuade people to accept and act on these numbers. And how to convince billions of people that they should very gradually change to a vegetarian diet, as they no longer have the need to kill animals for food, and a as a result they no longer have the right to do so. And how to change consumption of energy to that solely derived from renewable sources. How to re-cycle all natural resources, and stop contaminating the planet with waste material. These may all seem almost impossible, but if they are not tackled without delay, humans will eventually give God little choice but the undesirable option of deletion.

As you know, there have been some attempts at dealing with a few of Earth's sustainability problems, but these have been less than adequate. You are familiar with the story of the Roman Emperor Nero who reputedly 'fiddled while Rome burned'. With their normal zeal, scores of scholars have spent countless hours debating what 'fiddling' actually means, since Nero lived many hundreds of years before the violin types of instruments had been invented. And, as usual, the academics have completely missed the point. It is irrelevant what instrument Nero used, or if he actually used one, or even if the story has nothing at all to do with Nero. As you know the phrase means to do something trivial or inconsequential, when there are far more important things which you should be addressing as a matter of urgency.

Most of today's major world leaders are indeed 'fiddling while Rome burns', while the few who are actually trying to do something are either not trying hard enough, or are not being listened to by the others. Leaders are looking at the short-term view of what they consider right for themselves or their country. Leaders who are trying to achieve world dominance or at least increasing global importance for their countries and putting this far ahead of what is right for planet Earth and all humans. And in those countries which have democracies, their populations are doing exactly the same, selfishly considering themselves, their consumerism and their own livelihoods before the welfare of the rest of humanity.

Unless this changes quickly, planet Earth and your solar system are inexorably heading towards deletion. And this can only be prevented if the great majority of your leaders act in consensus. They need to understand the urgency of this, and kindred spirits need to impress this message on them. In the early days of humans on Earth, virtually nothing which they did had any impact on the planet. But this started to change a few hundred years ago, and has accelerated so rapidly that unless action is started immediately to reverse this deterioration of your environment, Earth will become uninhabitable. And if humans are unable to act together, God will have no alternative.

Sorbo, you have just given me your decision, although we still have a little time before you go back to Earth. Yes, it is the right decision but as you realise it will be very difficult for you. You will receive no thanks on Earth for your efforts, – in fact just the opposite. And it will be the people who really need to listen to God's message who will be the last ones to believe it. Many of these will consider themselves to be devout worshippers of God through whichever religion they claim to follow. And they will not accept that any part of that religion is mistakenly interpreting God's guidance. Of course religion has always been a contentious subject for humans, and as a result it has always attracted a large following of the less desirable elements in society, often more so than other topics of discussion. But there should be no place in the mainstream of any religion for extremists, zealots, bigots, or anyone else who pervertedly distorts the true message of that religion. And all ministers of all religions should say very loudly and say very clearly that there is no place in their religion for violence or aggression, whether physical or mental. And anyone who does not accept this is misunderstanding and misrepresenting that religion. If they are not prepared to say this, and say it now and keep on saying it, then either they are not fit to hold their position, or their religion is not one acceptable to God.

Violence and aggression in the past, whether between religions or between different sections of a religion, was both wrong and regrettable and a misunderstanding of God's guidance. Violence and aggression between religions today is a sin. However, religious strife is only a part of human disagreement. Wars, and other forms of violence and aggression, are caused by a multitude of other factors. Territorial disputes between or within countries, either regarding boundaries or natural resources or distribution of wealth. Criminal organisations or gangs fighting each other for dominance, or fighting law enforcement agencies to try to ensure their survival. Tribal or cultural differences within countries or regions. Nations trying to preserve or gain or enhance perceived world dominance, either politically or economically or both. Nations claiming to use military force to eliminate threats to world peace, either real or potential. Revolutions against corrupt or despotic or totalitarian regimes. The list is almost endless, but the result is the same. Needless and futile misery and suffering. No Sorbo, I am not saying that aggression and wars can be stopped immediately. What I am saying is that, in your twenty-first century CE, world leaders need to understand that differences between nations or groups within nations must be resolved quickly and peacefully whenever possible, and that world ascendency or world domination by their countries are pointless aspirations in a world which is rapidly heading towards its own self-destruction. They must stop fiddling while Rome burns. The future of humans and planet Earth depends on it.

Before we leave leaders, we should talk about how and why people become leaders. And I am not just talking about leaders of groups or tribes or countries, as there are leaders in every aspect of life, including criminal activities of all kinds. I have already said that at the moment humans still need leaders. This will change, but the change will happen only very gradually, so we will talk about today. Some leaders inherit their position, some seize it by force either singly or in groups, and others are elected, sometimes fairly and democratically, although at other times corruptly. Leaving aside regimes which rule by virtue of criminal ascendency, God does not have any particular guidance as to what system of government is practised in any particular country, or who leads it.

But there are two important exceptions. Firstly, the current inability of religions to reach agreement on their understanding of God and God's guidance means that at the moment the only fit way to govern a country is by secular rule. This will change, but until it does no religion has the right to try to impose its values on anyone else.

Secondly, and just as important, is that the leadership of any country should have at heart the best interests, not only of their population but also of the whole human race, and planet Earth. It may not seem obvious, but in the long term all of these interests are in fact identical.

At present many leaders do not understand this, and consider that their own country and its population is more important than others. These leaders are wrong, both in their own understanding of life, and in the false message they give to their populations. It is time for all humans to realise that struggles between themselves should be relegated to history, and concentrate their energies on preserving planet Earth in a state which is properly fit for habitation by both human and other life forms for the many generations yet to come. And it is time for all leaders to realise that they too are human beings with souls, and that they will also eventually have to accept full responsibility for all of their actions during their Earthly life. Yes Sorbo, all leaders are humans, and all humans have souls, and all souls are accountable. There are no exceptions.

There are some other aspects of leadership which we haven't discussed. In an increasingly materialistic consumer oriented world, with increasingly sophisticated global communications, there is a tendency for populations to expect that they should immediately have any material thing which other people have, and which they desire. And many leaders, or aspiring leaders, are too ready to promise that they will provide such things. It is quite right that all humans should share equally both the fruits of their industry and Earth's natural resources, but it is also quite right that all humans should share the effort involved, in proportion to their ability to contribute. And above this, they should not expect today anything that has not been earned today.

A promise by leaders, or an expectation by populations, of wealth or opportunity which has not yet been created, or which cannot be reliably expected to be created within a short space of time, means irresponsibly borrowing against the future. A future which humans cannot accurately predict. Although the majority of people either do not realise it, or do not wish to accept it, such borrowing is actually stealing from future generations. Yes Sorbo, stealing from unborn children. And while most leaders recognise this harsh fact, there are still some who refuse to accept it, and very few who have the courage to tell their populations. These people are being dishonest, not only to themselves, but also to all of those who believe them. Self-promotion is often one of their many motives, but all too frequently the best interests of the entire human race is not. They are not kindred spirits.

Sorbo, it is 3.29 p.m. in London, and you will wake up in one minute in St. George's Hospital. What will happen after that is up to you, but always remember that you are not alone, as there are billions of kindred spirits who also want to improve life on Earth for all its inhabitants and not just themselves. Of course there are many things which we haven't discussed here, and on which humans will need future guidance. But now you know how to communicate with God at any time. Pray for the right reasons, and you will get the right answers. One last thing before you go. Your body has been unconscious for nearly a week, so when you wake up you won't immediately seem to be completely lucid and rational, but slightly disorientated and rambling for a short while. And now I won't say 'goodbye', but 'au revoir', as we'll meet again when your soul is finally released from its Earthly commitment."

CHAPTER 8

Friday 9th May 2014 – 15.30

The wonderful light. It's gone. Gone! Of course, – He told me it would. Must be a bit groggy.

"Welcome back, Mr. Grundy."

"Where am I? ... No, – please don't answer that, it's just a silly human question. But why do you call me Mr. Grundy? ... He called me Sorbo. And what's happened to the light?"

"Easy now, Mr. Grundy. You had a bit of an accident last Friday, and you are in the Neuro Intensive Care Unit at St. George's hospital in Tooting, in Southwest London. I'm Professor Drayton and I and my team operated on you. You have been asleep for about a week, but I'm pleased to say you are doing very well and we are confident that you will eventually make a full recovery. Can you tell me a bit about what happened?"

"There was this lovely light, and the man in the white coat said I must remember everything as I couldn't have a pen and paper. You must know him because he's been here all the time, and he only went a minute or so ago. He said he had so many names that I could call him by whichever one I liked, but he called me Sorbo and he just said au revoir and he'd see me again one day."

"Yes, yes Mr. Grundy, we'll talk about him in a minute. But first, can you remember when you were born?"

"Oh no, doctor. No, – I was much too young to remember anything then."

"Sorry, Mr. Grundy. My mistake, – I really meant to ask you the day you were born?"

"Wednesday, – no it must have been Friday, as mum said the sun was out and we had fish and chips for supper."

"Yes, er – thank you. And please would you tell me your home telephone number?"

"Well I could, though I don't usually give it out to people I've just met. But there's no point in me telling you anyway, because I can't answer it when I'm not there, can I?"

"No, er – quite so, Mr. Grundy, – silly of me not to think of that. I don't want to overtire you, so just one last question. Could you tell me the name of our Prime Minister?"

"Mrs – er, – Heath. No, – let me think. They got rid of them and now it's Gordon Blair. I'm very thirsty, doctor – do you think someone could get me a glass of waterloo?"

"Of course, Mr. Grundy. I'll ask Sister straight away, and then I'll be going. I'll see you again tomorrow."

***

"Sister Flanagan, you're Sister McCreedy's sister aren't you?"

"Yes sir, I'm the married one of us twins. Aileen would've been too, – she's far better looking than me and she had all the boys running after her, – but she frightened them off with her ways, if you know what I mean."

"Yes, Sister – I really believe I do. I'm away now, and I'll be back at ten tomorrow. Mr. Grundy would like a jug of water, if you would be so kind. And please keep an extra special eye on him. He's still very confused at the moment, but hopefully that should start to wear off soon."

15.40

"Good afternoon, I'm Professor Drayton. Haven't we met before?"

"Don't think so, – David Graveney, and my wife Sue."

"But surely you were with the Air Ambulance team last Friday?"

"Afraid not. We're property agents. Just got back from a couple of weeks looking at apartments in Sardinia. Wonderful island, and there's some really great deals going at the moment. Could we interest you in a few?"

"No, – no thank you. Sorry, my mistake. You looked a bit like someone else, and your voice sounded familiar too. Oh, you're friends of Mr. Grundy. He's still quite weak and very confused, so please don't stay too long, and try not to tire him too much. Good afternoon."

15.45

"I'm not half as confused as that Professor Whatnot thinks. Anyway, who are you, because I don't have any friends answering to the name of Mr. and Mrs. David Graveney that you so unconvincingly gave him?"

"Is that all the thanks we get for chasing you all over the place for two years, and then saving your life?"

"Oh, so you're the paramedics, who were really doctors, but who didn't exist, in the Air Ambulance that wasn't, and anyway didn't ever go to Wrotham, and actually never came here either. Except that I was at Wrotham, and you were there too, and I did get here in your helicopter. And I've read all about it in the local papers."

"But you can't have read about it Sorbo. You've been unconscious for a week, and the papers only came out yesterday. And yes, we've known your nickname ever since we started the job."

"David and Sue, – I think I'll call you Charles and Kate, if you don't mind, because that's who He told me you were. Not only did I read yesterday's papers last Friday night, about half an hour after you brought me in here, but I've also seen the video taken from your helicopter. Not bad, – but I wish you'd stayed there a little bit longer, so I could have seen myself being loaded into the ambulance. Mind you, probably better not, as I guess it wouldn't have been a pretty sight. And, while you all thought I was in a coma, we've been working flat out for nearly a week for kindred spirits. Ah, I see you know the name. Yes, one hundred and sixty-two hours, and no sleep and nothing to eat, – and all for kindred spirits.

No wonder I'm tired and hungry. And don't look at me like that. I haven't completely lost my marbles, but it's a long story and I'll tell you about it later, – as He would have said if I hadn't kept interrupting him. Meanwhile I, or rather we, owe you big time for a first-class job and we are very grateful. Thank you. And that goes for the ground ambulance crew too, if you would be good enough to pass on our thanks to them. Now, since you're here, I guess it must be for a reason."

"Well, it seems that our job didn't finish last Friday, and we're going to be with you for as long as it takes, whatever it is. Don't know if they've said anything to you yet, but we've been asked to move into Owl Barn Annexe and look after you – whatever and whenever."

"Strange as it may seem I can't say I'm very surprised at that. And I think I'd call it a fortunate coincidence, as I will need help with housekeeping and shopping and getting about and things. They didn't tell you about this book I'm supposed to be writing? No, it was news to me too. Never written a book, and I don't even know how to start, – but He said all I had to do was write down everything He told me – said I'd remember it word for word, all one hundred and sixty-two hours of it. And I think He was being serious, although with that God I could never be sure, – He had an unearthly sense of humour. Anyway, they probably didn't tell you about my book because they hadn't been told themselves, – something about need to know, whatever that is. But wait a minute, – you're not married and surely you both have partners, – and I may be old-fashioned, but I couldn't go along with you living together in my house. And I'm not sure I could afford to pay you either."

"That's our long story Sorbo, so we'll tell you about it later too. But briefly, neither of us has a partner so we are both free agents, although you're right, we're not married yet. As to money, whoever has been employing us up to now, is going to continue for at least another five years, and don't worry, we're well looked after. We must go now, but we'll be back tomorrow afternoon, after the professor's well out of the way. OK if we move into Owl Barn, – probably Monday by the time we've sorted ourselves out?"

"Yes, and thank you again. See you tomorrow. Don't suppose they'll give me anything to eat, but at least I'll be allowed to get some sleep now, for a change."

***

"Charles, you took a bit of a chance with Professor Drayton didn't you? What were you going to do if he was interested in Sardinia, or even if he knew it? I've never been there and I don't suppose you have either."

"No problem. Travel agents in Sevenoaks tried to get me to buy me a place there a couple of weeks ago and I've still got the DVD. It's quite hard-sell stuff and he'd have gone off the idea as soon as he looked at it."

"And what did you mean telling Sorbo that we're not married – yet?"

"And I thought I was just a dumb male of the species, and women had all the intuition. Hasn't it been obvious ever since we first met. Let's go back to my place and talk about it in the morning, if we've still … OK, sorry."

"Where to now? Yeah, why not? Only ever seen it from the air before. Just wait until I tell my friends about our new address – Owl Barn – they'll think it's a … no, they won't, honestly. It's just because I'm so excited about our new life, us and together. Of course, – I'd forgotten they don't know about us, I mean you, yet. I've absolutely no idea how I'm going to explain getting hitched up to such an old bozo like you. Probably never live it down."

Saturday 10th May 2014 – 11.00

"Good morning, Mr. Grundy. Professor Drayton again, – do you remember I saw you yesterday afternoon? Well you were a bit drowsy then, so I thought I'd come back today to tell you about your accident and what we've done in the way of treatment."

"That's very kind of you, professor. Thank you. Shall I guess at acute left-sided subdural haematoma, – sorry, I forgot the 'large' bit. You sorted that with a craniotomy, I think. Total left hip arthroplasty. That would have been Mr. Greenwood, and his famous Superglue. Cracking joke, if you get me, although I was told he really uses Palacos. Oh, and last but not least, my new liver. Was that Mr. Hallibury? Yes, I thought that's what He said. So now I'm all mended, when can I go home?"

"Mr. Grundy, – has someone been reading your notes to you?"

"Well I'm entitled to see them, – but no, professor. You see, although we've been working non-stop for the whole week, He's still kept me up to the minute with my treatment and everything. Even offered me a bit of a look a couple of times, but I was too squeamish."

"Mr. Grundy, ... er, ... I think I'll leave you to have a little rest now, and I'll be back tomorrow."

***

"Sister Flanagan, please would you ask Miss Blakelock to organise a conference call in my office, with Mr. Greenwood and Mr. Hallibury. Yes please, – urgent, even though it is the weekend. Thank you, Sister."

13.00

"Simon, Warwick, – glad I caught you both on this lovely Saturday afternoon. Yes, – Mr. Grundy. His physical recovery is remarkable, – or I should say staggering. I would have expected at least another two to three weeks, but seeing him just now, I think he'll be fit enough in days. God knows, because I certainly don't. Could you both have a look at him soonest, – yes, next hour or so if you can make it, – and let me know what you think? Also spend a few minutes chatting with him if you can. He's not running a temperature, but he seems to be hallucinating quite badly, and I'd appreciate your opinions. But I'm not sure hallucinating is quite the right word, because there's something weird about his ramblings. For a start, his speech is clear and lucid and not at all slurred. Then he told me all about his injuries and our treatment.

Yes, of course he could have got that from his notes, – but Simon, – how would he have known about you and Superglue? Yes, yes, – I know that orthopod joke's as old as Superglue itself, – but he's not a medical man, and he's been out for a week, so who on earth could have told him about Palacos? Oh, and it gets worse.

He thinks that all the time he's been unconscious, he's actually been talking to one of our doctors, – the man in the white coat, he said. And, wait for it, – one hundred and sixty-two hours, he claims. I've worked back from three-thirty yesterday, and I get to nine-thirty last Friday night, just fifteen minutes after we got him here. No, odd isn't the right word for that either. At the moment I'm a bit lost as to what to do. Do either of you know any trick cyclists I could get hold of over the weekend? Of course, – The Priory, don't know why I didn't think of that – thanks, I'll give Tim Weatherford a call. When you've seen Mr. Grundy, I'll be here or on my mobile. Sorry Warwick, I missed that. Well, yes. Archie Prescott got a strange e-mail at two last Friday afternoon, and when he queried it with his man at the Department, he was asked to do exactly as instructed, and no questions. That's why we were all in A&E on Friday evening, waiting for someone special. Even now, all we know is that his name is Andrew Grundy, and he's hardly a VIP, to put it mildly. To be honest, I was more than a little surprised that you two, and Pete Da Silva, were all happy to work through a Bank Holiday Friday night. I thought Archie must have nearly twisted your arms off. Yes, Simon."

"Archie didn't persuade me or Warwick, Huw. We both also got e-mails at two on Friday, so when Archie rang us we already knew. Neither of us had ever heard of the sender, so I had it checked with the CEO at Guy's and Warwick with his at the Royal Free, and we both got the same answer as Archie, although ours were more like requests than orders. But they were put in such a way that we really felt obligated, otherwise you wouldn't have seen hide nor hair of either of us anywhere near any theatre, let alone St. George's in Tooting. And if you want to talk of surprises, we were amazed to see Lord Cortex himself. We thought the only theatres you went to on Friday nights were in London's West End. Seriously though, Huw, as you say, it does seem there's something a bit weird about our Mr. Grundy. I think Warwick and I had better go and see him pronto and meet in your office, say five-thirty. OK with you ,Warwick? And Huw, don't call The Priory just yet, – right now I've got a funny feeling we might just get something from our patient."

15.00

"Good afternoon Mr. Grundy. Nice to see you, – awake this time. I'm Simon Greenwood and this is Warwick Hallibury. We both did a bit of patching you up after your accident."

"Ah, yes, Mr. Bones and Mr. Swapsie. He said you were the best, so thank you for working on your weekend off. But please call me Sorbo, everyone does except Professor Whatnot. I was going to say even the doctor in the white coat called me Sorbo. Then I was going to tell you that He was talking to me about life on Earth for the whole week, but somehow I feel you'd find that a bit difficult to believe."

"Quite so, Sorbo. But we are interested in this doctor. Could you tell us about him?"

"Well actually He has been talking to me non-stop since last Friday, but he's not really a doctor at all, – I just made that up for the professor's benefit. Yes, He told me that the prof's real name is Hubert Drayton, but He said I should try to appear groggy and rambling for a day or so. Thought I did pretty well, even if I have to say it myself. Thank you, – maybe I should have had a career on the stage after all. And Simon, I know that the Superglue thing is meant to be a bit of a laugh, – He said you were still using Palacos. But when I told the professor I thought it was a really cracking joke, all I got was a po-faced stare. Don't think he's got much of the sort of sense of humour I've been used to for the past week. But I think now is the time I should tell you about what has really happened, or at least what you need to know, – I think that's the buzzword of the moment. It starts with something I will describe as the temporary separation of the human body and soul, – and here I must stress temporary. This is a very complex, precise, and indeed highly unusual procedure, and ...."

"Thank you for putting our minds at rest, Sorbo. We're seeing Huw Drayton in a minute and we'll tell him the whole story, and that there's nothing to worry about. Yes, he thought you might be a bit confused, but now you've cleared it all up for us. We'll pop in again tomorrow to see how you're doing. Goodbye for now."

17.15

"Huw, – Simon. On our way up. Just seen Sorbo ... yes, that's what he's asked us to call him. Any chance of getting Archie right now? Thought we saw his car downstairs."

"Archie said five minutes, so I think we should wait. This had better be good. Tea or coffee?

"Come in, Archie. You know their names of course, but I don't think you've met Simon Greenwood or Warwick Hallibury until now. They've just seen Mr. Grundy, – I should say Sorbo, because apparently he's asked us to call him that. God knows, – funny nickname, but that's what he wants. Anyway, over to you Simon."

"Thanks, Huw. As you say, just seen Sorbo. First impressions, both of us, – classic OBE. Oh, Archie, – for Pete's sake leave it out. Huw told us you were near to retirement, and you're bound to get a gong, but for the moment we're talking about Sorbo, not your earthly medal, no matter how important that might seem. What he was describing, to start with, was a classic Out of Body Experience. Not at all uncommon, particularly with the sort of trauma he went through. However, we have to say to start with, as after a few minutes things didn't really all add up. Huw, could Sorbo possibly have seen those Kent local papers you showed us?"

"No way. Neither of them publishes online, and in the end I had to send a courier to Maidstone. Why?"

"Because he quoted both articles in their entirety, and absolutely word for word. And there were a couple of paragraphs both Warwick and I had forgotten, one being the bit about the Air Ambulance being a Bell 429, which isn't a type in the KSS, or anyone else's, fleet at the moment. How on earth could he possibly have known about that? But much more interesting was his detailed description of the mechanics of temporary separation of the human soul from the body. Yes, temporary. I think most of us believe that the soul is indeed separated from the body on death, and goes to God knows where, but he very nearly convinced me that it could happen on a temporary basis. Only nearly though, because I'm a battle-hardened cynic, – but what a story – and I think Warwick felt the same."

"Indeed, – so plausible it nearly got me going too. We did learn something else though, whether relevant or otherwise I've absolutely no idea. He talked about working for something called kindred spirits, and they had set up his accident, and privately organised and funded his treatment here. And as soon as we told him our names he knew who we were and what we did, because before we said anything else he called us Bones and Swapsie, – I won't tell you what he said about you, Huw. Yes Archie, as long as it's about Sorbo."

"Did you say kindred spirits, as with a K and an S? Thought so. And where did our last Friday's e-mails come from? Yes, all from KS 1419. And did it then occur to us that there might be a very good reason why we had three of the country's top specialist surgeons all waiting around for hours on a bank holiday Friday evening to operate on a nearly-dead Sorbo Nobody? No, of course it didn't – then. And did I tell you that since noon that day we've had some new 'volunteer porters' working in specific areas of this hospital, – porters whose shifts cover twenty-four hours a day? No, it didn't seem worth mentioning at the time, – actually, until two minutes ago I didn't think much about it myself. I'd had a call from my man at the DH, who said they were working with the Met Police Protection Command to give some of their new chaps real-time experience in large public buildings, and St. George's would be an ideal place. We're always a bit short of porters, so it seemed a great idea, – but now I think we can all smell a rat, – or more likely a bloody great kangaroo. Bet none of you can guess where they wanted them posted. Yes, they said the area around A&E was always busy, with loads of people about, so it was a good place to start. I think we should e-mail this KS 1419, whoever they are, and try and get some answers, – see if they like working on their weekends off. Can you all keep your phones on, please. Sorry, Warwick, you'll have to tell your wife that Nobody is more important than her, – that'll keep her guessing. No, I will not pay for your divorce. Be in touch, hopefully tonight – although somehow I don't think so."

***

"Huw, we might as well e-mail from here, – save me going back to my place. Just 'KS 1419', no dotcom or codot, etc... Don't know, but it works. Just ask for a meeting, and sign it from me. Strong black coffee, please. Need a bit of caffeine before I doze off. No, only joking, – when I ring the wife and tell her I'm coming home very late, her language will more than keep me awake. Probably ought to have a double brandy before I call.

Don't tell me, Huw. 'Mail delivery failed, etc.' You are joking, aren't you? Already? Come to think of it, that's how it was last week. Immediate. They're coming here at eight tonight? Better call Simon and Warwick before they go too far. They don't have to be here, but I've a feeling they're as curious as we are. Huw, I might be a bit odd, but I didn't mean curious in that sense. Yes, I'm pedantic about semantics. Actually that might make the start of a good poem, – one of my hobbies, you know. No, not exactly my most riveting piece of news is it? Anyway, what are we going to say? No, Huw, we can't just say 'what's it all about?' – we might just as well add the Alfie bit too, so they'll know we really are mad, instead of only thinking it. I think we must explain Mr. Grundy's, – Sorbo's, accident and treatment, – no mention of anything he's said – and ask whether we can be of any further service. Full stop. Then see their reaction. If we do it like that, one way or another I reckon we'll at least get something out of them."

20.00

"Good evening, Mr. Prescott. Sorry, – Professor Drayton. Roxy told me I should believe what it says on the door. I'm Alan Bululough and this is my wife Roxanne. Yes, it's a bit of a mouthful, so we pronounce it Bulow. And Roxanne prefers Roxy, as you probably gathered. Ah, Mr. Prescott, – good to meet you. And Mr. Greenwood and Mr. Hallibury, – very nice to meet you too. Yes, we've certainly heard about you both, although we gather that our mutual friend addresses you somewhat less respectfully than I do. No, we haven't met him yet, but we're told he's only playing games. Apparently he's a really nice chap, but his sense of humour can seem a bit out of this world at times.

This meeting won't be at all formal, so I guess we're happy with first names, and we won't need a Chairman. But I'd better kick off, as we know a bit more than you, or you wouldn't have asked us here in the first place. Andrew Sebastian Grundy. Better known as Sorbo, but probably only he and God know why. In his early seventies, by all accounts. Apparently used to own quite a few successful businesses in a variety of fields, but he was never comfortable about making money. In fact, he really felt quite guilty about it, as he didn't think he should be materially better off than anyone else. A bit strange for a businessman, I suppose. Anyway, he's retired now, although he's an ardent Beethoven fan and sometimes does concert reviews for Classical Composer magazine. He lives at a place called Owl Barn in Wrotham, Kent, and being eco-conscious he drives a small hybrid car. That much we do know. The rest is part fact and part guesswork, as we're only told what we need to know at any particular time. But firstly I'd better tell you about kindred spirits, which so far you only know as KS, because it's something that's going to become part of all of our lives. And I don't mean just us here tonight.

Kindred spirits is a grouping of like-minded people from all over the world, regardless of their race, religion or circumstance. The essential common factors are the knowledge that there is a reason for our existence, and the belief that this is for the good of the Universe. Although not yet widely understood by them or almost anyone else, kindred spirits will be an important part of Universal development, no matter how small or insignificant they may feel themselves to be at the moment. There is nothing particularly new about kindred spirits. Deep down within themselves, anyone who has ever had the chance to think about anything except just day to day survival, has realised that there must be a reason why the human race exists on our planet. And countless people have come up with countless theories, but nobody has provided an answer which is acceptable to the majority of thinkers, let alone to the whole of humankind. So humans are stumbling forward with little sense of purpose and making mistake after mistake, but not learning how to improve either themselves or others. And with scientific knowledge and technological development mushrooming in recent years, particularly in terms of global communications, human error has become significantly more blatant and widely recognised.

It doesn't really matter whether present human behaviour is accidental or deliberate or malicious. What does matter is that it must change, and kindred spirits is the way to that change. But kindred spirits is not a club or an organisation or a religion, or anything else which you can join. There are not, and never will be, things like badges or uniforms, rule books, codes, passwords or secret recognitions. Anyone not totally accepting this is, quite simply, not a kindred spirit. We haven't been told a lot about the structure of kindred spirits, as apparently we don't need to know much, except that it is working for the good of all mankind and will eventually become a standard of moral behaviour to which all decent humans will aspire. The funding is a complete mystery, but we assume that it is provided by a number of wealthy anonymous philanthropic donors, as money seems to be freely available for anything required at any time. For instance we, and our colleagues Christine Arberry and Michael Raine, have been given a state-of-the-art office in Whitehall Mews, staffed by five highly skilled full-time technicians. We've no idea what they do, but they always seem to be extremely busy. However, we only use the office occasionally, and that's just for interviews, – because all of our other work is done on our iPads, tablets or smartphones. If we need anything we just go out and buy it, and the money is transferred to our bank accounts the same day. We've never traced the paying authority, but we think it's offshore, although somehow connected with or through a number of Central Banks.

At this point you might well wonder how we got involved with kindred spirits in the first place. About three years ago we were asked by a highly respectable friend whether we would consider doing some voluntary work for an essential humanitarian project. She outlined kindred spirits to us, and we needed no persuasion, as we've both always felt that we should put something back into life, – not just take whatever we could. Christine and Mike got into it much the same way. So we were given the office, and asked to recruit teams of drivers and pilots for ground and air ambulances, and two doctors for each ambulance. Oh, and we were asked to find home security teams as well. At that time they didn't tell us why, but they just said that all operatives had to be both highly qualified and experienced. Here, I'd better tell you that the four of us all have very good jobs in London, so we're all voluntary and unpaid. But the people we needed were not in the same happy position as us, so they are all paid for what they do. To start with, we could not find people who were both available and had the right qualifications and backgrounds, so we used a bit of subterfuge, by identifying who we wanted, and arranging for them to be dismissed from their current employments. Their interviews with us were merely a formality, as we already knew everything we wanted to know, – except of course, whether they would accept our offers. Fortunately for us, they all did. Yes, I know what you're thinking. We did bend the rules a little. We're not allowed to break the law in any serious way, but we can sometimes turn a bit of a blind eye, if it's for the right reasons. Like our ambulances. They're all borrowed from various sources, but they're all liveried as belonging to genuine local emergency services. I'm pretty sure Huw will remember the paramedics Charles West and Kate Gurley from the apparently KSS Air Ambulance which brought Sorbo here last Friday. Actually, they're both exceptionally skilled doctors, although sometimes they may appear to have double lives as property agents. You do remember David and Sue Graveney from yesterday afternoon, Huw?"

"Well, I'm damned. I could have sworn I'd met them before, but they acted so innocently. Just goes to show."

"Anyway folks, time's getting on so I'd better get back to Sorbo for a moment, and then I can tell you something Roxy and I only learnt a few hours ago. A little over two years ago, we had all of our ambulance and home security teams in place, and as requested, – kindred spirits only ever requests, never orders, – we started watching over

Sorbo twenty-four hours a day. Six weeks ago, we were asked to find a driver to deliberately run into Sorbo, causing life-threatening injuries to his left side, but on no account to kill him outright. What a request! And no reason given. And we couldn't find one anywhere in Europe skilled enough to guarantee the required injuries at the same time as guaranteeing not to kill him. Then, thank God, we had an inspiration. We found Chopsticks Sanford, – Hollywood's megastar stunt driver, – you've probably heard of him. Blank looks all round. Never mind, I'll continue. Everything was set up for just after eight last Friday evening, when as usual Sorbo would leave the Rose and Crown in Wrotham and walk home. You all know the rest of that. But now I will tell you what Roxy and I learnt this afternoon, and we're still struggling to make sense of it. Yes, although Sorbo didn't know it then of course, we had planned his 'accident' for kindred spirits. But why? Because, – and I'm only repeating precisely what we've just been told, – Sorbo had to have a communion with God! Simon, – are you alright?"

"No, I really don't think I am. We've all been talking about Sorbo's post-trauma out-of-body experience, but what you've just said is giving me an out-of-mind one. Have any of you any idea what Sorbo told me and Warwick this afternoon? No? I'm not surprised. He told us that he'd had a meeting with God, and that they'd been talking together non-stop for a week. Actually, he was more specific. He said exactly one hundred and sixty-two hours – 9.30 last Friday evening until 3.30 yesterday afternoon. Yes, you work it out. And he told us all sorts of facts that he didn't have an earthly chance of knowing. Unless …? No. No, – I'm not going for that."

"Right. I said we didn't need a chairman, and we don't, – I'm just making suggestions. And we're all in this for the same reason, so we should be able to reach a consensus. It's late, so I think we should call it a night and go home. Tomorrow's another day. I've no idea how you're all going to explain to your wives that you've got to work on Sunday, – for Nobody. I'm lucky enough to work with Roxy, so I don't have that problem. Would anyone care for a note saying 'we must meet urgently'? From Roxanne, of course. No takers? No spirit of adventure, I'd say. OK, my idea for a plan. Simon, you and Warwick got quite a lot out of Sorbo this afternoon, so you'd probably be the best person to see him again. Say ten o'clock, to give you a couple of hours or so. Not with Huw, though. Sorbo thinks he's the old-fashioned sort of surgeon, – you know, God of the hospital, – Sergeant Major whose haemorrhoids are playing up. No, take Charles West, – he talked to Sorbo yesterday. He's on call 24/7, and he's seen a lot of trauma in his Army job. Huw, why don't you and Warwick go and see Tim Weatherford at The Priory. Probably the leading expert on OBE, and he's one of us, so he won't mind working on a Sunday either. Archie, – here as coordinator, if that's alright. Not sure how, but Huw seems to have wangled a bigger office than yours. If you're bored you can get the coffee ready for when we get back. No, Archie. Supposed to be a joke. Even kindred spirits are allowed a bit of humour occasionally. Roxy and I will be working on logistics. Simon, don't be so cynical, – anyway crudeness doesn't become a man of your standing. All meet back here about twelve-thirty, I would think. Everybody agreed? Good. That's how it's supposed to be, apparently. Consensus, – according to Sorbo."

Sunday 11th May 2014 – 10.00

"Good morning Mr. er, – sorry, Sorbo."

"Ah, – Mr. Bones and Dr. West. No, please don't apologise. I'm the one who should be sorry. Now I no longer have to do the 'confused patient' bit I'd be very happy to call you Simon and Charles, if that's OK with you. Of course I remembered. Actually, I was half expecting to see Alan, too. You know, – he with the unpronounceable surname. The man who's going to help me get the book published. Well, I hope he is anyway, because he's the one who organised my 'accident', and got me into this mess in the first place. And all the work I've had to do with 'Him up there'. Or is it down there? Just playing, really, because God's everywhere, – although I hadn't thought much about that until last week. And talking about last week, He said I wouldn't get tired there. And He was quite right. But it's a very different story back here, – like I could sleep forever. But I can't, – I've got work to do that won't wait. And first, I've got to convince you all that I haven't gone completely mad, and that what you've got yourselves involved in is actually both essential and urgent. Simple really. Well, that's what God said. And God knows."

"Hold on a moment Sorbo, – how do you know about Alan?"

"Easy. On Sunday, – no Monday, He showed me the CCTV footage of Alan and all of the others at the interviews at the Whitehall Mews office. I didn't see you there in any of them Simon, but Charles and Kate have been there more than once. The last time was just before 8 o'clock last Wednesday morning, and I've seen that too. Just to remind you Charles, towards the end of the meeting Alan asked whether you could cope with Kate's ridiculous sense of humour for another five years, then complimented you on your mental stamina. Yes, I was sure you'd remember that. Do you also remember him telling you that you arrived five minutes early, too? Shall I continue? I could repeat it all exactly word for word if you'd like, and I'd probably remind you of things you'd already forgotten."

"No, no thank you, Sorbo. You've already said quite enough to convince me, but how on earth you know it completely beats me. After all, you've been in here unconscious for a week until you woke up on Friday afternoon, and it's only Sunday now."

"Sorry to interrupt you, Charles. I know He kept telling me not to be so picky, but I can't let you get away with that. It wasn't quite a week, – only one hundred and sixty-two hours, – and anyway it was only my Earthly body that was here, and that everyone was operating on and fussing about. I was there talking to Him for the whole time at the processing centre, or the pearly gates or whatever you want to call it. Actually, I only really said a few words, as He did nearly all of it by thought transference, – but I won't go into that at the moment as it might just confuse you, and we wouldn't want that."

"No, of course not, Sorbo. Confusion is the last thing we would want, – right, Simon?"

"What? Confusion? No, we really wouldn't want to be confused. Let's keep things as simple as … they are. But, Sorbo, I would be interested to know who told you about Palacos bone cement."

"I was sort of hoping you wouldn't ask that, Simon. But here goes. He did. And He showed me some of the papers you'd been reading about the comparisons between Palacos and Refobacin. He seemed to understand it all, but it was way over my head. But then that's not really surprising, as I can't speak ten thousand languages, and I certainly don't understand four thousand religions either. Anyway, He said that you felt more studies were needed, and for the time being you were going to stick with Palacos. Oh yes, I got quite used to that sort of sense of humour, – I'll tell you about it later, – as He would say.

So, you see, everything I've already told you, and a lot more I'll tell you when the time is right, has come directly from Him. My task is to remember it all and write it all down in a book, and then get it published. Sounds easy, doesn't it? But He said it wouldn't be. But He also said that there were billions of people who needed to read this book, and there were millions of kindred spirits who would help me get it published and distributed. I wouldn't necessarily know who they were to begin with, but they would be there when they were needed. And by the way, Charles, the reason that you and Kate will be around for another five years, is because apparently there will also be millions of not-so-kindred spirits who won't want my book to be published, or even written, and they will try anything to stop it. And that includes people who will appear to offer genuine help, but who will actually be intent on sabotage."

"OK Sorbo. For the moment, let's say we believe you. But what's so special about this book, – which you haven't even started to write yet?"

"Mmm, – how shall I put it? During their eternal journey towards Universal understanding and enlightenment, all souls have at least one physical incarnation, – if you'll excuse the tautology. In our case, and at this time in Universal evolution, it is as human beings on planet Earth. God has the Universal responsibility to be our guide and mentor. But, for a number of reasons, we are failing to follow God's guidance. Some of us because we don't believe in God, or because we consider that God is irrelevant. Some, because they are following what their forefathers wrongly laid down as God's commands. And some who don't care, as they don't yet understand that what they do in this life will affect their entire eternal journey. There are many others, with many other reasons, but these will do for the time being. Anyhow, God is concerned that humans are increasingly losing their way, and that the time has come for more explanation and enlightenment. My book will just be the start of this, as others will follow. Simple really, – as long as I just write down everything He told me. Well, – that's what He said, anyway. Simple but not easy, if that's not too confusing."

"Ye...s. Don't know about confusing, but it'll surely be controversial. Sorbo, we've got to meet the others in a minute, but we'll come back later if that's OK with you. Bye, for now."

10.30

"I've not been to The Priory before, Huw, – where should I park?"

"Right there in front of the '**STAFF ONLY**' sign. Tim says I qualify as an honorary member. No, not that often, but every now and again I help them out a bit. Very much as a last resort though, as they're not too keen to ask, and they really only call me if they think they have diagnosed a physical problem requiring surgery, which is fairly unusual.

Morning Tim, – nice to see you again. Yes, they tell me she's getting along fine now. I didn't do a lot really, but it's always nice to show you that I can sometimes perform the miracles that you can't. Probably do you out of a job altogether one day. Tim, I don't think you've met Warwick Hallibury. No, I suppose you wouldn't have. He'll transplant almost anything, but I'm very glad to say that he hasn't got round to brains, – yet.

Tim, we have a problem. We've got a patient like neither of us has ever seen before. No Tim, – this is serious. RTA last Friday, nine days ago. Very severe trauma, – we had to try of course, but we really didn't expect him to make it. Left hip total wreck, subdural haematoma, liver beyond repair. And a couple of other very odd things, before I forget. A&E theatre fully staffed, and three surgeons including me, all ready for hours for an anonymous important patient. Three hours before, yes before, his accident, Tim. And Warwick was staggered to find a fully tissue-matched liver waiting on standby. Before he asked for it. But back to the patient. Out for a week, – woke up Friday, two days ago. Physical recovery quite remarkable. But here's the problem. Seemed to be hallucinating for a few hours, but now apparently lucid, except that what he's saying is impossible. He claims that his soul was temporarily separated from his body for nearly a week, and while his body was unconscious in St. George's, his soul was awake and talking non-stop with God for the whole time. And, – wait for it, – he has told us too many things which happened during the week he was unconscious, all of which are true but none of which he has absolutely any earthly chance of knowing. We'll tell you more later, – as he keeps saying, – but before we do, have you come across anything like this before?"

"Hmm. Not exactly as you describe it. Obviously we have patients who come in here with the weirdest stories, but they are usually easily disprovable straightaway. Occasionally we get the more persuasive type, and we have to dig a bit deeper to find out what it's all about. It's very rare indeed, although not entirely unheard of, to draw a complete blank. But I don't think that's the case here. What you are telling me rings a bell in my mind. A bell which I have been expecting. Before I go any further, could you repeat what he said about the temporary separation of the soul and body. Did he describe the method? Mmm, – in graphic detail? Yes, I had a feeling you were going to say that. And, in his apparent ramblings, did he go on to tell you the reason? And what he learnt? And what he said God asked him to do? But you were convinced that he was hallucinating so you didn't believe any of it, did you? No, of course not, – otherwise you wouldn't be here. Now, I'm going to tell you something else that you'll find just as difficult to believe. What you've got is something many of us have been hoping, praying, waiting for, – for quite some time. Right now the human race has lost, – or I really mean never found, – its intended sense of direction, and what their souls should be looking for and aspiring to during their brief time here on Earth.

In His infinite wisdom, God has decided that in today's world there was little point in sending another prophet, messiah, saviour or whatever you want to call him or her. So instead, He has done it another way. He has temporarily borrowed a soul from its Earthly body, and explained some of the Universal truth which we have all either missed or ignored or deliberately rejected. That soul is in the person you know as Sorbo Grundy, – your patient, – who you all think of as a nobody. Well, you've got that bit right. Forget Sorbo Grundy the person. He is not important. He is a nobody. But for God's sake listen to what he says, – and believe it, more than you've ever believed anything before. Why was such a nobody chosen? Good question. Well, for a start he is fairly honest, upright and straightforward, and he thinks a lot about the meaning of life. But there are millions of people just like that, so that's obviously not the real reason. What is, then? He has an absolutely prodigious memory, which will shortly be put to the test when he starts to write his book. And, God knows, he will pass with flying colours. Why so important? Oh ... just a little matter of remembering in precise detail the million or so words which God spoke to him in the week he was there!

Well, Huw, Warwick, can I tell you anything more, or is that too much already? Or are you going to suggest that I immediately commit myself within these walls as yet another patient? No, no, – I was only joking, I hope. I've told you what you came here to find out, so it's up to you to take it from here. You, and all the other kindred spirits, of course. Yes. Kindred spirits. Yes, yes, I know. Just like the scientists you are, you surgeons only deal with physical bodies. I deal with minds and souls."

"Thank you, Tim. We'd better get back to St. George's, – but before we go I will say just one thing. Strange as it might seem, we both actually believe you, but God only knows what's going to happen when we tell the others what you've just told us. Or even more, what's going to happen when word of this gets out."

12.55

"Sorry we're a bit late, Alan. Tim had a bit more to say than we expected, to put it mildly."

"No problem, Huw. Simon and Charles haven't been back for more than a few minutes, and they're still trying to get their heads around what Sorbo told them. And that goes for the rest of us.

Huw, let's try to get this straight. Give or take a few words, what Tim told you is exactly the same as Sorbo recounted to Charles and Simon, right? Well, nearly right I think. Because Tim has been expecting something like this for quite a while now, but Sorbo had absolutely no idea of what was coming, – least of all to him. Apart from that the stories are the same? Yes, I thought so.

Well, what have we got? Sorbo says he's been asked to write a book. And that we've been asked to help. Sounds simple, as Sorbo would say. But now that we have an idea about the purpose of this book, it isn't simple at all, is it? Many people have written books in which, deliberately or inadvertently, there are passages which could be taken as questioning some aspects of religious or cultural beliefs. And many religions and cultures have reacted violently to these books and their authors.

But can you all imagine the uproar that will follow the publication of a book which will say that absolutely every culture and religion will need to accept some changes, however small they might be? Especially as what might be small changes to other people, will be considered as absolutely fundamental changes by the followers of any particular system of beliefs. Just think about the reaction of Christians when you tell them that Jesus did not perform miracles. Or Muslims when you tell them that there are no angels. Or would you prefer to tell a fisherman or butcher that it is a sin in God's eyes to kill any creature which has blood? And from what little Sorbo has told us so far, these are just the tiniest bits of the tip of the iceberg.

So, we all need to think very carefully about where we go from here. Roxy and I have been in this from the beginning. Well, the beginning of this phase of the operation anyway, if you'll excuse the terminology. Charles and Kate are a team and they've been working for us for a little over two years, so they're in as well. No, apart from Huw, none of you has really met Kate yet, although you all saw her very briefly ten days ago, when she and Charles brought Sorbo in. But I promise you won't forget her when you've had a taste of her somewhat unusual sense of humour. Right, Charles?

Anyway. back to business. Archie and all of you medics got into this totally unwittingly, apart from having a suspicion that it was quite important. Whether you would have acted as you did, if you'd known then what you know now, is a different matter, but it's irrelevant because it's history, and like it or not you can't change history. What is relevant is whether or not you wish to have any further part in what happens from now. You probably need to talk it over with your partners and families, so I'll obviously give you all some time to think about it. We could do with all of the help we can get, but there is absolutely no pressure on you either way. You must be completely at rest with whatever decision you make. By the way, very shortly after Huw and Warwick left The Priory, I had a call from Tim Weatherford. I'm not sure whether he sounded excited or happy or apprehensive or what. He said 'It's been a long time coming, and it's just the beginning, but it's started at last, and this time I believe it's going to work. I'll help in any way I can'. That's all. Don't know. Doesn't make a lot of sense to me. Anyway, I've been doing all the talking, and I'm not the Chairman, so somebody else should have a go. With pleasure, Archie."

"Firstly, I think I should say that I believe in God, but I'm not religious. OK Simon, you're being pedantic as usual, but you're right. I'll re-phrase that. I believe that some sort of God exists, and whilst I agree with many of the beliefs of a number of recognised religions, I cannot accept all of those of any particular one. OK now? Thanks. I don't go to religious services of any kind, except when asked and as a token of respect to those people involved. You know, things like weddings and funerals. Then, it doesn't matter to me what religion it is, or where it takes place. Those things are not relevant to me. God is. And my God is the same as everyone else's God, regardless of what they might think. Well, now I've got that off my chest, I'll tell you what I think about Sorbo. He's convinced he's been talking to God for a week, and that God's asked him to write a book about it. He could be a complete nutter, but Tim doesn't think so, and Tim should know. One way or another, I think we all agree that Sorbo has had some sort of transcendental experience, and that he is determined to write about it. I, that is this hospital, and I think I also speak for Huw and the whole surgical team now, have done our bit in resuscitating a near corpse, but apart from continuing medical care. I'm not sure how we can be of any further help. As you gather, I don't know much about religion, and I know less than nothing about publishing books. Much as I'd like to, I can't see that I could contribute anything more. Sorry Alan, but it's back to you."

"OK thanks, Archie. Of course you're absolutely right, but I don't think you realise quite the importance of what you've already done. Eventually you will come to realise the key role you've all played in this, but in the meantime you'll have to be content with the thanks from us mere mortals, – or in this room I think I should say kindred spirits, as there's very little doubt that you all are, even if you didn't already know it. We'll move Sorbo out of here as soon as he's fit enough to go home, and you can get the hospital back to normal, although you'll lose a few 'porters'. Yes, we were all thinking an absolute minimum of two to three weeks, but now it will be this week, hopefully Tuesday. Of course it's far, far quicker than any of you would have thought possible, but you have seen just how fast he is recovering. Actually we were told to expect that, so we've already done some modifications to his house. No Simon. It's not a miracle. It might seem incredible or even almost impossible, but that's just because we can't find a rational explanation for it. But it's not a miracle, – it's just something which we can't understand at the moment. Anyway, thank you all again for everything you've done and are doing. Now we'll leave you to enjoy what little's left of the weekend. Goodbye for now."

"Charles, – OK with you if you join Roxy and me for a few minutes to run through what we've got to do tomorrow? Great. Our car's parked right next to yours. Need to talk to Archie before we go, but I won't be very long. See you downstairs."

"Well, I must say that the last ten days has been an experience that none of them will likely forget in a hurry. Us too of course, but we're starting to get used to expecting the unexpected. Right, then. Plan of action. Starting early yesterday morning the home security team's been flat out getting Owl Barn ready for Sorbo. Should finish in a few hours. Stair rails, loo seats, ramps, you name it. Oh, and a state-of-the-art voice-activated intercom, with mics and speakers in every room. Yes Charles, including the annexe, so you'd better make sure Kate remembers that. The only room they haven't sorted out so far is the sitting room, which we think ought to double up as a bedroom and office as well, subject to your and Kate's agreement. If so, they'll come back tomorrow to give you a hand with the furniture. Dr. Katto has very kindly volunteered to come in every day to start with, not as a surgery visit but in her own time, and of course we have gratefully accepted. She has also arranged for a practice nurse and a physio to call as necessary, and she's liaising with St. George's to agree a schedule. Domestic stuff is all down to you and Kate, as you know. That's fairly straightforward so far, but now we get to the book. All we really know is what Sorbo told us in St. George's. Anyway, it's not our job to worry about what he writes, but it is up to us to make sure that he can write it. Yes Charles, but have you looked at what passes for his computer? He may not like it at first, but he's going to have a new one. Tomorrow, again. I'd like you and Kate to buy him a suitable desktop. Nothing fancy, as he'll only use it for word processing and a bit of Internet access. He hasn't even got an e-mail address yet, – says he doesn't need it. No, I know, and I found it a bit difficult to believe as well, but that's up to him. Buy it anywhere you like, but please don't spend too much, – and don't forget it's not our money. Since you were about to ask, we have absolutely no idea whose money it is, or where it comes from, but we have been told that we can spend whatever we need to.

And talking about money, here's a couple of debit cards. Hope you don't mind, but I've had them issued in the names of David and Sue Graveney. Quite original, don't you think? Pin numbers are both 2345 at the moment, so change them to whatever you like. There's no limit on them, and you can use them for anything, as long as it's for Sorbo. Don't worry about billing and payment, – already taken care of. No, I can't read your mind, but actually

I was wondering when you were going to get round to asking. Kate will set up the new computer, and transfer all of Sorbo's files from the old one. It'll be child's play to her, as she's been used to far more sophisticated stuff. Yes, in Scotland. I guess you know her pretty well, but she obviously hasn't mentioned that when she was working at Glasgow Royal Infirmary she was seconded for a while to their IT team, and she helped them tailor their new system to become more doctor-friendly, to coin a phrase. OK, I think that's about it for now. So, first thing tomorrow you and Kate start moving all your stuff into the annexe, then buy and set up the computer. Don't really mind, – I suppose latest Windows would probably be the easiest for someone who hasn't quite got out of the twentieth century. Or you could always try some A4 pads and lots of pencils instead. No Charles, it really was supposed to be a joke, – sorry if it wasn't up to Kate's amazing standards. Call me latish p.m. tomorrow and we can arrange Sorbo's homecoming. Genuine ambulance this time, by the way. Bye. OK Roxy, let's go and get some lunch. No, I reckon it's your turn, – I'm sure I paid last week."

15.30

"How much more to do Kate? No hurry, but I thought we could probably take a couple of carloads over later this afternoon. Alan's given me two sets of keys. Here, you might as well have yours now, – it's the one with the owl on the fob, just in case you were likely to forget. Mine? A pussycat of course. Goes nicely with the owl, and anyway it suits my gentle nature. Ow, that hurt. No, not really, but any more and it might just give me an excuse to get my claws out. About five would be fine, and we could take both cars. Won't take very long, and it would be nice to get some of it out of the way, because tomorrow's going to be rather busy. Unless you can think of somewhere better, I'll reserve a computer at Argos in Maidstone, and we can pick it up first thing. Drop you off at Wrotham, so you can get going with it, while I come back here for more stuff. Two or maybe three runs should just about do it, but then we've got all the unpacking. OK yeah, I've got all the unpacking, – you'll still be playing computer games. Ow, don't do that again, or this pussycat might turn into a sabre-toothed tiger. No problem for me, – I'll just turn the clock back twenty thousand years and un-extinct one. Bet you didn't know that time can go backwards as well, did you? I'll tell you about it later, as Sorbo would say. When we drop this lot off, I'll have a look to see if we need anything to make the place more habitable, and I can get that in Maidstone too. Can I start taking some of the boxes down now? OK, which ones first then?"

18.30

"That's the first lot done. I really hate moving, but at least we'll be able to stay put here for five years. Have you ordered the computer yet? Why? Because we'll probably need some other bits and pieces after I've had a look. Right. First, I guess we should put the old stuff in the garage. But not the printer, – amazingly for him it's almost new. More paper though. And ink. Mostly black, but I suppose you'd better get a few more colour in case he feels a bit arty. And a new router, – this one's well past its use-by date. I think that's about it. Can we go and get something to eat now?"

"Same Westerham takeaway, if that's OK with you. By the way, did you notice his shopping list in the kitchen? No, only corn flakes. But next to it is a very neat little book with all his receipts from the Village Store. Shouldn't be surprised really, because even though he's getting on a bit, just looking round the house tells me he's obviously extremely well-organised. He gets the main stuff delivered from Sevenoaks, but he still spent over a hundred pounds at the shop in April, so I'll go in tomorrow and settle up. I can park across the road at the Rose and Crown, have a quick drink, and introduce myself. Don't know if pubs run tabs nowadays, but if he owes anything I'll pay that too. OK Mrs. Graveney, we can both go in and introduce ourselves before I drop you off. Don't dooo that when I'm driving. Later would be different. Much later, though."

"Charles, when you were checking Sorbo's septic tank or whatever you called it, I was thinking. Yes, I do sometimes. Daddy said it was a very good thing to do, – even for girls. Well, I was just thinking back to my time in Africa. Do you realise that in loads of countries there virtually nobody can get to even a basic toilet, let alone a proper sewage system. And clean water. What clean water? It wasn't very funny watching women and children walking miles every day with buckets on their heads to get to the nearest well. Specially when the well had dried up. You must have seen much the same in some of the places you've been. And that estate agents blurb about Sorbo's neighbour's house they're trying to sell. Local GP surgery and 'great choice of excellent local schools'. Well, doesn't it make you realise how lucky we are to live here? Yeah, I know lots of places in England didn't have things like that fifty or a hundred years ago, but I'm talking about today. Here and now. And that what we take for granted as basic necessities to us are things that millions, or in some cases even billions, of people in other parts of the world can only dream of as unreachable luxuries. Food, shelter, water, toilets, healthcare, education, – and that's just for starters. Places I've been to, even if they existed, most people couldn't afford to pay for them. No, don't start me on poverty. Getting on for half the world's population struggle to live on about two US dollars a day, that's not a lot more than a quid, and if that's not poverty I reckon somebody needs to find another word for it. Yeah, injustice isn't too far off the mark. OK, OK, I'll get off my high horse now, but I'm beginning to wish I hadn't got on it in the first place as it's going to make me feel guilty again the moment we start eating the takeaway. I wonder if Sorbo's book will talk about this sort of thing. That's if he ever writes it of course."

"Just for a change, darling Kate, I'm a bit ahead of you. Don't forget that I've had the advantage of talking to Sorbo for quite a few hours now. Yes, he will write the book. Actually it'll be at least two books as there's too much to get into the first one. And yes, I know it will include injustice because he mentioned it when he was telling me some of the things he has to write about. That's one of the reasons I suggested it to you instead of poverty. Say that again. Oh, sorry if darling's a bit twee for you Ms. Gurley. It was only meant to be a term of affection. How about Poppadumchickpea or Honeysucklesugarplum. Or we could go for some of the really silly names that all the film superstars and sports heroes seem to be choosing these days. Can you imagine being a five-year-old going to school on the first day? "My name's Butterbean Candytuft Bacon, but everybody calls me Butty." No, if we ever have kids I wouldn't want to put them through anything like that. Seriously though, I'm OK with Kate and Charles if you don't like pet names. No, definitely not Kitty and Chas. You can't have a snuggle-bunny called Chas, and obviously we can't have a Kitty in Owl Barn or the bird people would be down on us like a ton of bricks. There it is. Dragon Palace. Over there, – same place as it was last time, oddly enough. I'll stay in the car if you don't mind getting it. Oh, and take my credit card. No, not those, use my personal one, – can't spend the firm's money on us. Don't worry, I changed the PIN numbers on the way back from the hospital, so it's the same on all three now. Rather fancy chilli garlic prawns, Jalfrezi chicken, and mushroom fried rice, but I'm OK sharing if you'd rather get one of their set meals. Pretty good last time. And see if you can hurry them up as I really shouldn't wait here. If I do have to move, stay put and I'll be back soon as I can."

20.00

"Don't know about you, Charles, but I thought that was great. And amazing value. I'd always regarded Westerham as a bit up-market and pricey. Well the food's quite up-market, but it certainly isn't pricey. Can't see how they can make a profit, but that's their problem. And talking about our problems, we've got to do something about Sorbo's bed. Yes, that's the conclusion I came to. Not sure you can have a consensus with only two people, so we could just call it an agreement. Agreed? Good, that's how it's supposed to be apparently. So we take the sofa out of the sitting room, – OK, lounge if you must, – and put the bed in there instead, by the armchair. Good job it's a big room, because we need to move the computer desk in too, – next to the table. Combined bedroom, sitting room, office and dining room. TV's there as well, but I don't think he'll be using that a lot. And the loo and shower room are right next door. Did you say home security are coming to give you a hand? Good, because you're going to need it, – I'll be installing Windows. No, you fool, Windows as in computer. Didn't dare change to Apple as it's going to be difficult enough explaining to him that XP belongs in the Ark, so now he's got Windows 8. At least it's in the same family, so the change won't be too traumatic, even for him. No, I didn't say he belongs in the Ark too. It might be in our minds, but hopefully Sorbo isn't into thought transference. Early-ish night I think. Tomorrow's going to be just a little bit busy. Forecast's wet and windy, but you've only got to bring the rest of our stuff over so it shouldn't be too much of a problem. Me? Soon as we've done the shopping and been to the pub, I'll be in the warm and dry. Apart from a few more clothes, my things can stay in Croydon for a while. No hurry at all. I've given them a month's paid notice and I don't have to be out until early June."

Monday 12th May 2014 – 08.00

"Thanks for making the coffee. Reminds me I didn't tell you I'd ordered a new machine for the Annexe. Argos too, so we can pick it up when we get the computer. Same as this. Nowhere near top of the range, but it makes coffee exactly how we like it, so there's no point in paying any more. No. Sorbo's happy with his old cafetiere so we can't go spending his money on something just for us. Same goes for the set of cooks' knives I'm getting for the Annexe kitchen. One of them is so bad I can hardly work out which is supposed to be the sharp side. OK, so it's a bit of an exaggeration, but you get the point. Sorry, shouldn't have said that should I? Almost forgot I was talking to the comedienne."

"I should think so too. Two people making corny jokes in one house is one too many, so kindly leave it to me in future. Anyway, what time do you think we should leave? The computer shouldn't take me more than three or four hours max, so as long as I can start by about one that'll be fine. If we go out about nine we should get to Wrotham easily by twelve. Village shop should be open, but I don't know about the Rose and Crown, – lots of country pubs don't open on Mondays. Well yes. We can park there anyway, pay the shop, and even if the pub's closed there'll probably still be someone around. We may not get a drink, but we should be able to say hello and find out if Sorbo owes them any money. OK, – nine o'clock. Another consensus, – or did we agree agreement?

12.15

"I thought the lady in the shop was lovely. And so friendly. Sorbo's obviously highly thought of round here. You were right about the pub on both counts, Kate. Closed Monday lunchtime, but someone in there clearing up, or is she re-stocking? Doesn't matter, – see if she'll talk to us. I guess her opening the door is a good start."

"Hello, – sorry to interrupt your work. I'm Charles West and this is Kate Gurley. We're friends of Sorbo Grundy. Are you by any chance Sue? ... Whoa, – slow down a bit Sue, and we'll tell you. Yes, he is indeed alive. A bit battered to put it mildly, but surprisingly well in the circumstances. Most people would have written him off for dead but thank God St. George's Hospital and its doctors didn't. How do we know your name? Well, Sorbo told me about this lovely young lady who worked at the Rose and Crown, and he said her name was Sue. So we put two and two together. Yes, he's been very chatty since he woke up on Friday, and he's remarkably cheerful. And much to everyone's surprise he'll be coming home tomorrow. No, he won't be fit enough to get out for a while yet, but judging from the way he's recovering it won't be too long. Actually, that's one of the reasons we came here today. We've just paid his April bill at the Village Store, and we wondered if he had a tab here and whether he owed anything. Also we wanted to introduce ourselves. We're moving in to Owl Barn Annexe for a little while to look after Sorbo, so we'll be regular customers here. Sorbo says the Rose and Crown is good enough for him, so it's bound to be good enough for us. Yes, we've known Sorbo for a little over two years now, although we only actually met him on the day of his accident. Don't worry, – Sorbo will explain that later. We've got to go and sort out Owl Barn now, but we'll be back in a couple of days. And next time we'll make sure it's during opening hours. Bye for now."

***

"Charles, did you notice Sue blushing a bit when you mentioned Sorbo?"
"Blushing a bit? Is that what you call it? To me it was more like someone had poured a can of red paint over her face. But why? Sorbo's ancient, and Sue's probably only in her late twenties, if that."

"And I thought you were kidding when you said you didn't understand women. But you really don't know anything about us at all, do you? Or much about men either, come to that. Or blushing Lots of people blush for loads of different reasons. They can't help it because it's totally involuntary, and usually the more they feel embarrassed about it the redder they get. No, not everybody by any means, but quite a few, – particularly when they're young.

And you're wrong about colour too, Charles. It's not just pink skinned people who blush. As it happens, judging by the way she acts when you go to the surgery, I think Dr. Iwu actually finds you quite attractive. And she may blush at times when the two of you meet, although you and I probably wouldn't notice it because of her dark skin. But to anybody who knows her well it's a different matter. To them it would be obvious straight away. Yes Charles, if you blush, you blush, – regardless of your skin colour. And there's always a trigger for blushing. In Sue's case I could see it wasn't guilt or embarrassment. It was right at the moment you said Sorbo's name. She obviously finds him very attractive. Strangely enough attraction is often mutual, so maybe Sorbo feels the same way too. Blushing tends to fade as people get older, so Sorbo didn't blush when he talked about Sue. Or far more likely he did, but anybody as dim as you wouldn't have noticed anyway.

No, Charles. Age has nothing at all to do with attraction. Anybody of any age can be very strongly attracted to anyone else, totally regardless of any age difference. Totally regardless of sex too, for that matter. What do you mean? Charles, I think it's about time you started living in the real world for a change. It may go against your ideas and all sorts of religious and cultural beliefs but yes, same sex attraction is very common and quite normal. Of course I'm not talking about you and me, but we're not exactly the only people in the world. Other people have views too, you know. They may be in a minority, but they're still entitled to their opinions. And their feelings. Oh, and before you start confusing attraction with looks, I'd better tell you that you don't have to be what people might consider to be good-looking or beautiful to be attractive. It all depends on what you could call chemistry, or magnetism if you like. So Sue blushed when you talked about Sorbo. I can understand why she finds him attractive, – a lot of women would. And it could be, probably is, mutual. Nothing wrong in that. In fact I think it's rather nice that an old man and a young woman could be attracted to each other, and care about each other. Or an older lady and a younger man, – it's just the same. But, – if you stop interrupting, I'll tell you, – this is where age does come into it. Age and circumstances. Both Sue and Sorbo are sufficiently mature to acknowledge their own feelings, – maybe even tell each other, – but also recognise the realities of their situations and accept the fact that things might have been different in a different world at a different time, but not in this one.

No Charles, I have no idea whether their souls could meet in a future life, but it would be great to think that they might. Meanwhile in this life they can continue to care about and want the best for each other, and be grateful for the good fortune they've had in being able to meet each other at all, regardless of when and where they did. Most people are not so lucky. So Doctor West, please do not worry about an old man and a young woman. They understand both each other, and the facts of human life, and they are not about to do anything stupid. Let them enjoy just knowing each other. By the way, if I don't finish you off before that, one day you might just get to Sorbo's age. And although I'm so much younger, I might even find you attractive. No, only joking. Of course I find you attractive, in a funny sort of way I can't really explain. I've already told you attraction's nothing to do with having good looks, so it must be the chemistry, I suppose. Ow, don't do that."

13.00

"OK, I'm off now I reckon three trips, so probably finish about six. Much the same for you I guess. Yeah, seems a good idea. Mustn't make a habit of takeaways, but I haven't done a food shop yet. Anyway, there's not really enough time for proper cooking tonight. I'll get one on the last run. Bye. Don't I get a kiss? Because I might have an accident and finish up in a wooden box. How would you feel then, if the only goodbye kiss you gave me was in the mortuary? That's better. Don't worry, I'll be extra careful. See you later."

19.15

"Just as good as the last one. Still don't know how they do it for the money. Did you say the intercom was voice activated? And in every room? Even in here? So if I want to make any noise in the bedroom, I'd better do it tonight, because Sorbo comes home tomorrow? I don't know really. Sort of bedroom noises I suppose. Well, not cooking or eating or bathroom noises. You know, – bedroom noises. Alright Charles, you know perfectly well that I don't, so I was only teasing. Actually I was really only checking, as from now on we're going to have to be very careful anywhere in the house whenever we're talking to each other, or on the phone for instance. Not so much worried about Sorbo overhearing anything, but there will be a lot of visitors in the next few weeks, and probably not many of them will have any sort of security clearance. Alan's expecting all sorts of problems if or when anyone finds out what Sorbo is writing, and since that could be any time now, we've just got to be ready. Yes, computer's all set up and working perfectly, thanks. Went like a dream, and much quicker than I thought. They've got these programmes down to a fine art nowadays, so they almost install themselves. No, Sorbo couldn't have done it himself without some help, but it was quite simple compared with what I was expecting. And though he will notice some slight differences, he won't have any trouble just using it for word processing. Which after all is about the only thing he knows. Internet's connected too, but I'm not sure whether he uses it. I might try to talk him into e-mail. Some older people aren't too keen on the idea. Not until they try it, that is. Then wow, – it's a completely different story. How did they ever manage without it?"

Tuesday 13th May 2014 – 12.30

"Welcome home, Sorbo. No, don't worry about the neighbours. We guessed they'd see the ambulance, so we've already told them you were on the way. Yes, they're a really nice couple, and very concerned about you. Hope it's alright, but we said we'd invite them over for a drink as soon as you'd settled in. Looking at your drinks cupboard, we figured you weren't exactly teetotal. Sorbo, I know

Alan's already told you we've had to alter the house a bit, but I hope you won't be too horrified. Yes, until you're completely recovered, all four rooms in what used to be your one lounge. Didn't think you'd need a commode though, as you've got the bathroom right next door, and Simon reckoned you could manage that. Said he wasn't quite sure how, – or other words to that effect, – if you know what I mean."

"Yes Charles, – I believe I do. Thank you, both of you, for everything. All looks pretty good to me. You've obviously put a lot of thought and hard work into it. It'll do extremely well for a few days before we can move my bed back upstairs again. Yes, a few days Kate, – I'm not exactly an invalid you know. You said you'd seen Deirdre and Paul. Yes, I would love them to come round for a drink. Why don't you ask if six this evening suits them? Of course I won't get tired, – according to the doctors I've only just woken up from nearly a week's sleep. Better to get these homecoming sort of things out of the way as soon as we can, as I've got some serious work to do. Talking about work, what's happened to my computer? I know I needed a new monitor and that looks fine, but where's the tower? Oh, don't they? I didn't know that, – guess I'm a bit too old to keep up with this modern stuff. But no, I didn't quite know Noah actually, just in case you were wondering. Not that either of you would dream of being so rude as to think that, of course."

17.00

"Now you've tried the new computer Sorbo, what do you think? No, it's not that much different from the old one, especially for Word. And now you know you didn't need to worry about losing your old files, because I just saw you having a look through them. I knew they were all there, – I was very careful about that. Can't upset an important client on the first day. Have you thought any more about e-mail? Very useful if you need to send proofs or things to anybody. No paper, no postage. Just a click of a button. Yes I can, – all we have to do is think of an address for you. Something original or you won't get it registered. And we must choose an ISP. Sorry, I should have realised. It's a company that sends and receives all your messages through what's called your mailbox. That's a bit like an electronic form of letter box, except that this postman also collects your outgoing mail and sends it for you. I think we'll use the same ISP as mine if that's OK with you, as they've always been very good. Address? Yes, I think that's great. Even Charles is nodding, or maybe he's just falling asleep, – difficult to tell sometimes. I'll start setting it up straight away, – pussycatowl, – I really like it. Sorbo, I was wondering. Have you given your book got a title yet?"

"God Knows, Kate. No. I mean yes, – "God Knows" is the title. Why? Well for a start I could hardly call it Sorbo Grundy. It's not an autobiography, – it's about human beings and their races, cultures and religions. And like most people I don't really know much about any of that, except what He told me. And He knows everything. So I'm calling it "God Knows". And when they read it, people will begin to realise that those two short words actually signify a lot more than they think at the moment. What they really mean is that God's knowledge is infinite. At all times God knows exactly not only what all living creatures are doing, but also what they are thinking. Yes Kate. What they are all doing. And what they are all thinking. At all times. God knows."

"But Sorbo, how can God possibly know what seven billion people are doing and thinking at every moment?"

"Yes Kate, that's exactly what I was thinking when He said it, but of course He already knew that, so He started explaining before I could even ask. The trouble was I couldn't really understand what He was saying. But He knew that too. You see it's all to do with infinity, and He said that humans can't fully understand infinity, or eternity either, come to that. And He said that in all the more than ten thousand human languages, there weren't yet the proper words to describe the real meanings of infinity or eternity. And He should know because He speaks them all. Then He told me that it wasn't only seven billion souls that He knew all about, because that was just our human population, and I hadn't taken into account all of the other living creatures on Earth. And that's still only a tiny bit of it, as there are billions of other planets with billions of souls in the life forms on them as well. No Kate, – I can't quite read your mind, – but it was all far too much for me too. But of course He already knew that, so He gave me the answer. There are many things which souls in their short human life will not be able to understand. But that doesn't mean that there's no explanation, – it just means that we can't understand the explanation at the moment. So the answer is that we must have trust. And faith. Faith in God. Faith that if we lead our human lives to the best of our abilities, and as selflessly as possible, God will guide us towards Universal truth and eventual eternal happiness. I'll tell you more about it later, as He kept saying. Yes, later. But I think you'll agree it might just take a little bit more than a few minutes, and Deirdre and Paul are due any time now. No, I won't forget, – He wouldn't let me. Well actually He would, but my conscience wouldn't. Tell you about that later, too."

20.45

"Lovely couple, and they obviously think a lot of you Sorbo. They stayed so long I was getting embarrassed we hadn't got any nibbles to go with the drinks. Sorbo, you were going to tell Kate what you learnt when you were away with the angels, and I'd like to listen in too if that's alright with you both. You sure you're not too tired tonight, or would you rather leave it till tomorrow?"

"Charles, for a start I might be old, but I'm not feeble. And I'm not sick. Of course I got a few little scratches in my 'accident', but I'm nearly back to being as right as rain. Mind you, I've never known why rain should be right, or wrong come to that. Anyway, I'm not tired. And I wasn't with the angels, as you put it. They don't exist. Yes Kate, I know it's going to be difficult telling that to the millions of people who still think they do. Wait till I tell them that the devil doesn't exist either. That it's just an excuse used by people who know they've done wrong. Blame it on the devil, they say. But no, they can't blame it on the devil. They have given way to temptation, and that's selfish. And selfishness is the biggest sin of all. Actually He told me that selfishness is really the only sin, because one way or another all sins come from selfishness. Yes, – I had to think about that one too. But He's right of course, – well He would be, wouldn't He? Hey, – slow down a bit, both of you. I can't tell you everything He said all at once. I mean, we were talking non-stop for nearly a week. No, I didn't get tired, – Gods and souls don't need rest. I'd better start with God, and then if it's not too late we can go on to other things. Firstly, there is only one God. But God is made up of an infinite number of … Don't be so picky, Charles. I know perfectly well that numbers can't be infinite, and infinity can't be numbered, – I was just saying that to try and keep it simple for you, and anyway you knew exactly what I meant. May I continue? Thank you. God is made up of an infinite number parts, each of which is also a God. So God is one, and God is infinite at the same time. The one infinite singularity. Each part of God is slightly …………………"

23.35

"You two look tired and you've both had a long day, so why don't you get some sleep. We can carry on in the morning. I'll be alright, so I shouldn't need to disturb you. Yes, I know about the intercom thanks. So sophisticated it's almost spooky. Me? I'm going to start on the book now, if I can get the hang of this new computer. Well it's going to take a while, so the sooner I get cracking the better. Don't really know. I'm aiming for not much more than a couple of weeks. Then the real work starts when I try to find a publisher, because I reckon most of them will run a mile when they know what I've written. Anyway, I hope Alan will take care of most of that. Oh by the way Kate, before you go. Would you be able to do some proofreading for me as I go along? Of course I'm sure you're up to it, – as long as you don't try to put in any of your jokes. Thank you Kate, that's very kind of you. Did I say jokes? I must be getting senile. Goodnight to you both."

Wednesday 14th May – 08.00

"Morning Sorbo. Up with the lark this morning. Nearer six by my watch. This your usual time?. Haven't talked about meals yet, so we might as well start with breakfast. What do you like? Is that it? Just toast? Brown or white? Charles has bought a new filter machine for the Annexe, but he reckons you'd rather stick to your old cafetiere. Don't blame you. No point in changing if you're happy with what you're used to. No, both of us just have coffee and toast as well, so breakfast won't exactly take a great deal of effort by anybody. Better think about lunch and dinner. Much the same as us.

We really only have proper cooked lunches if we're out and about, and that's not very often. Charles is doing a shop today, so I'll put cold meats and salad on the list, – oh, and some cheese and decent crusty bread. Dinner? Sorbo, you know very well you're not fit enough to go there yet, so we've got to eat here until you are. Yes, I do understand, – better than you think. A lot of people at the Rose and Crown are looking forward to seeing you too, and we've told Sue we'll take you down there as soon as you're better. Yes, Sue. We popped in on Monday when we paid the Village Store, and told her you'd be coming home yesterday. She was very relieved, as they'd all thought the worst after your accident. Yes, she's fine. You were right when you told Charles she's an attractive young lady. Sorbo, would you like me to open a window? Me? – no, I'm fine, but you seemed a bit uncomfortable and you looked as though you might be a little too warm. Anyway, it's back to dinners. We can all eat at the pub most evenings as soon as we can get you there, but for the moment it's Owl Barn home cooking. Charles and me. Yeah, we're both OK. Not Cordon Bleu standard, but it's usually edible and we haven't poisoned anybody – yet. Between us we can cook just about anything you like, so if you make a list of some of your favourites I'll add what we need to Charles's list. Yes he does most of it, – he's much better at shopping than me. For food, I mean. You can tell it's not for clothes, just by looking at him. Coffee alright for you the way I made it, Sorbo? Tell me if you want it stronger or weaker next time. I'm going back to the Annexe to sort out today's programme with Charles, so I'll leave you to get on with your work ... Oh, and just call out if you need us. Please not too loud though. This new-fangled intercom's so sensitive and we haven't worked out how to turn the speakers down yet. Bye for now."

08.45

"Charles, I thought you said Sorbo doesn't blush. Well in that case I'd like to know who poured the red paint all over his face. When? Just now, when I told him we'd seen Sue at the pub, of course. Knew it was mutual. Women's intuition. Men just haven't got it. Even clever ex-Army doctors, – except the lady ones of course. OK, apart from you doing the food shopping, what's on for the rest of the day? No, we cannot. We've got to get lunch for Sorbo, – here. Anyway, what's the great attraction of the Rose and Crown? Don't tell me that you want to see Sue so desperately. You're almost old enough to be her father, Doctor West, and let me remind you what you said about age difference, – dirty old men and young women, you were thinking then. Of course I knew what you were thinking. I can read your mind like an open book. Yes I can. But this is one chapter that's closed before you even start reading. Sorbo's a free agent, but you're not. You're stuck with me, don't forget. For eternity, – and a bit more too, just in case eternity's not long enough for you. So you'd better take this list and go and buy us some food. And no stopping on the way back. Me? Sorbo should have done a few pages by now, so I'll start proof-reading, – see if I can put a bit of humour in without him noticing. No, only joking, – even I wouldn't dare ruin a serious book. It is going to be serious, isn't it? OK, see you later, – after you've given me a kiss, of course. Take care. And don't even think about going anywhere near the pub. Yes, the Rose and Crown!"

13.30

"Another glass of wine, Sorbo? No, Charles and I don't drink a lot either. If today's lunch was OK, we'll do much the same for the next few days, and then we'll think about getting you out and about. Have you made a start on the book? Yes, but the title's only two words, and you've already told us that. Well, if you can't think of anything else, just do what He asked you to do. Write down everything He said. Yes, – starting with when you woke up and saw the light."

"Of course I'll write it all down, but what do I do then? I've never tried to write a book before, and I've no idea how I can get anyone to publish it. Actually, I don't even really know if I'm up to the job. It all seems a lot more difficult now than it did when He asked me to do it."

"Faith Sorbo. That's what you said He told you. And trust. Trust that you will find all the help you need to write the book and get it published and distributed. Charles and I are here for a start, and between the three of us we'll find anyone else we need. And you'll need discipline. From the little I've read, most writers have to work very hard to get things on paper. They have to push themselves to do certain hours every day, even if they don't feel like it. And some days they may spend ages just looking at a blank piece of paper. That shouldn't happen to you as you'll be writing what He told you, but you will need to set a routine and stick to it. I reckon nine till twelve in the morning and three to five in the afternoon should do it Yes, every day, – well six days a week anyway, – I suppose everyone's entitled to a day of rest. No, maybe He doesn't, – but you're only human. See you later."

20.00

"Very nice meal thanks. Kate said neither of you were up to Cordon Bleu standard, but I reckon she was being more than a bit modest. This afternoon? Well, of course I did what I was told. Yes, I started writing, and would you believe what happened? Everything He said to me came back so fast I couldn't keep up on the keyboard. And after a couple of hours I got so tired I had a little nap. But now I've got the urge to do a bit more this evening. Just hope my typing speed gets better. Anyway, thanks again for the meal, and I'll say goodnight. I've got work to do."

Thursday 15th May 2014 – 07.30

"Good morning Dr. Katto. Very kind of you to come in before Surgery starts. Yes, he's doing so well that he almost seems to have forgotten that he's got an artificial hip and someone else's liver. Oh, he's been up for over an hour and he's already at his computer, so I'll show you in. Coffee, or tea? Sorbo, you have a visitor."

"Good morning to you too Sorbo. You know, when I told you that you might try to cut down on your alcohol intake, it wasn't because I thought that going to the pub might be quite so dangerous. No, only teasing, although we had agreed that you would probably need a hip replacement sometime soon, so it was lucky that the driver picked the right side. No, you know perfectly well that I meant your left hip, so I suppose I should have said the worn out side. Your accident hasn't dulled your wits at all, I see. What do you mean it wasn't an accident? Say that again Sorbo, – slowly. Well, if that's what you told them at St. George's, I'm not surprised they wanted you out so quickly. Anyway, I called in to tell you what I've arranged. You know our practice nurse, Rachael Hetherington? Good. She'll come in tomorrow to take the clips out of your hip and put on a new dressing. Also, starting this afternoon, a physiotherapist will visit twice a week to get you fully mobile again. Mondays and Thursdays, for the time being. Yes I know, but you'll be surprised at just how much better it will be if you do the exercises their way. And now I know you're an early bird, I'll pop round most mornings before Surgery. No, it really isn't any bother, as I have to come through Borough Green on my way to work, so it's only an extra couple of miles. See you in the morning."

***

"Kitty's very nice, Sorbo. Sorry, – Karen. It's just with a surname like Katto, I really can't help it. How's the book coming along? Good, I'll start proof-reading this afternoon. Lunch at the usual time? OK, see you then."

12.30

"I've been thinking, Sorbo. I'm not trying to be rude, but you've been around quite a long time, and sort of been there, seen it, done it. So did God really tell you anything you didn't already know?"

"Oh yes. So much that I'm struggling to remember it all. But the most amazing thing is that almost everything He told me is so obvious when you think about it carefully that I just don't understand why we hadn't worked it out for ourselves years ago."

"Like what, for instance?"

"Like despite all the bad news about people that you constantly read or see or hear in the press, television, radio and social media, the vast majority of human beings are fairly decent, honest and hard-working. Yes, of course there are shirkers, small and big-time crooks, murderers, dictators, despots, tyrants and other generally nasty people, but they are very much in the minority. The bad guys get all the publicity, and it tends to make people think that everyone's the same. But they're not, and it's about time the decent people made their voices heard. He called them kindred spirits and he said that they are by far the majority of humans. And all of the media should remember that and put more emphasis on the many good things that these people do."

"Is that it?"

"Of course not. I've already told you that He said that there is only one sin. The sin of selfishness. All the other sins we think about come from our being selfish. And you don't even need to pray to God to know whether you are sinning. If what you do is selfish, – it's a sin. It's as simple as that. The only question is how bad the sin is.

And then He talked about free lunch. No, I am not joking. Well, everybody knows that there's no such thing as a free lunch. Let's say a business acquaintance rings you up and offers to take you out to lunch at their expense. It's a nice restaurant and you have an excellent meal. Then they put an attractive proposition to you and you agree a deal. Or maybe your accountant calls and invites you to a boardroom lunch to discuss the annual audit. In either case, who do you think is paying for the meal? Yes, God did talk about this. Why? Why, because life on Earth is not a free lunch either. It has to be paid for one way or another. Each soul is in a human body for a purpose. That is to learn as much as possible about the reasons for its existence, and to do whatever it can to help others, either in a practical or spiritual way. Those who genuinely try to do this are making a positive contribution now. Those negative souls who don't are just making things more difficult for themselves later. And later is a very, very long time.

And there's another thing which should have been obvious, but I have to admit I'd never really thought about. Despite all of our clever scientists, humans have so far discovered only the tiniest fraction of knowledge about the Universe. And the one thing they haven't got anywhere near to is the reality and importance of God. Yes, I know that many people dismiss God as a fiction, – but they're so wrong. And so are the people who think that humans don't have souls. Souls which are the only things which are the difference between living things and machines. Souls which will go on to other places in the Universe. Bodies and machines will perish and disappear, but souls are eternal. And every human and animal has one. You can't see it or even detect it, but it's there inside each of us. And everything that we do and think is indelibly recorded in our souls.

But anyhow I must get on with the writing. It's a bit odd really, as I haven't got to think about anything, but just to try to remember what God told me and not leave anything out. But I can't put down a million or so words in one book, so I'll just have to work out the more important things in some sort of logical order and call it the first instalment or something. Oh no, – I've just remembered something else He said. There is no logical order."

CHAPTER 9

Tuesday 20th May 2014 – 07.30

"Morning Kate. Stayed up late night last night, as I wanted to finish it. Yes, all done. Computer reckons it's about eighty-five thousand words. Oh, and you remember I sent a synopsis and some sample paragraphs to that publisher? Well, they want me to go in today to talk about it. They said they really like my style. Sounds promising. Would you or Charles give me a lift to the station? Thanks, about eleven would be fine."

14.00

"Dr. Manitoba Heppingstal, – how very nice to meet you. I'm Richard Grimsley, old chap, but please call me Dickie. Thank you so much for coming so far just to see us at little old Wort, Huggins and Grimsley. Traditional outfit you know, but we like to think we keep up with the times. When did you get in from Canada? Sorry, my mistake. Yes, I know Worthing quite well, lovely town. Wrotham? – can't say I've heard of that. Must get a new battery for this ear trumpet. But I thought Miss Pertwee said you must be from Canada, – you know with a name like Manitoba. Oh, – well I'd never have imagined anything like that. In that case it's a jolly good job my parents didn't have their honeymoon in Massachusetts in September, I'd say. Anyhow old chap, now you're here we can talk about your scribblings. Yes, yes, Davey, Norm and me, – yes we've read it all from cover to cover. Lovely style. But we can't publish. Oh no old chap, – can't publish."

"But Mr. Grimsley, – sorry, Dickie, – I thought you asked me to come in to discuss publication."

"Oh yes, Manny, we did. But not this book. Won't sell. But we loved your writing style so much that we thought if you can give us something a bit more interesting, say a bit spicy, we'll do it in a flash and it'll sell like hot cakes. Sure as eggs are eggs. And that's what we wanted to talk about, and see if we can give you some ideas. But this one's just not up to scratch, – won't cut the mustard, and all that. Can't publish a book about God. The other two already think I'm getting a bit senile, but if I even try to run this past them again they'd know I'd completely lost it. You see, nobody wants to read about God any more. It's old hat, passé, so twentieth century. Just look in the churches on a Sunday if you don't believe me. Nobody there, – well nobody except old fogeys like me. Of course everybody needed God in the good old days, but that was before the boffins had worked out all about the Big Bang and everything else in the Universe that's worth knowing. So now they have, and we've got all the answers, who needs God any more, eh? Anyhow I blame it on bibles really, old chap. Too many millions in print, – outsold all the other books put together, but everybody's got fed up with them. Doesn't matter what language they're in, they're all the same. Boring stuff. And old as the ark, most of it. So not another one Manny, – not this one. Yes, I can see you're dead keen on it. And I'd like to do you a favour, but we're not a charity, and you can take it from an old hand like me that this one definitely won't sell. But you just use that great style of yours and come up with something a bit different. Something that nobody else is doing. You know, like a spy story set in America or somewhere on a Pacific island, – and throw in some rumpy-pumpy. Now that does sell, even to the fair sex nowadays, – some of them even write it, I'm told. And I caught young Miss Peckwith having a sneaky read of one last week, too. But keep it straight. Lot of our readers are a bit old-fashioned and they wouldn't take to reading about those domineering French women – you know les bosses, or whatever they are, – doing their thing on Greek islands. Or is it Greek women in France? Doesn't matter. Actually quite like a bit of that sort of stuff myself, but we've got to put the public first, eh? Anyhow, spies, lots of sex and exotic locations, – now you mention it, America sounds quite good. Never been there myself, but I reckon it must be exciting. Do it all in your great style and you're on to a dead-cert winner. Make ourselves a lot of money. And it would keep Davey and Norm off my back for a while longer, come to think of it. Take my advice, Manny, and forget about the God thing. Waste of time. Go back to Canada or Worthing or wherever it was, and start bashing out a humdinger. For both of us. Goodbye, Manny. Hope to see you soon, manuscript in hand of course, – and don't forget the sex. Now where on earth does Miss Perkins hide those batteries?"

18.00

"Thanks for coming to meet me. I really used to enjoy the walk from the station before the accident and I guess I will again as soon as this hip's better, thanks to Simon, or God, – or both, I suppose. Train was pretty much on time. Often is actually, despite what you read in the papers. No, that's the trouble with a lot of people nowadays. They never remember all the days when the train's on time, but goodness me how they shout when it's ten minutes late. I know some train companies are a mess, but not all of them by any means. But it doesn't just go for trains. Almost everything else as well. People can be so negative. Never shout out praise for all of the good things in life, but always pick on any fault you can find. And then make a big noise about it, because everybody likes to moan about all sorts of things, and the louder their voices the better. And of course the media love it. And live on it, because good news doesn't sell papers, they say. But I'd better get off my high horse, because you didn't pick me up just to hear all of that. Are we going to the Rose and Crown for their Tuesday special?"

"Yes Sorbo, in a way. In the sort of way, Sorbo, that we're going for their Tuesday special evening menu, not their Tuesday special evening bar lady, of course. Well, at least two of us are. Anyhow, before we get there, you haven't told us how you got on."

"Amazing, Kate. Can't think of another word to describe it. No, the wrong sort of amazing. They're not going to publish my scribblings, as they call the book. Can't publish anything about God. Won't sell. Yes Charles, – the exact words. But, wait for it. They wanted to see me because they're really keen for me to write something different that would appeal to today's readers. Yes, different. And what do they think would be different? A spy story set in America, with lots of sex thrown in. Only straight sex, mind you, because anything else might upset their more sensitive public. I kid you not. Different, Dickie Grimsley said. Might have been when Charles Dickens was still in short pants, I guess. Oh, and another little riveting snippet, before I forget, – although of course you know I'm only saying that for you, because I can't forget. He's never read the bible. Well he wouldn't have, would he? Why? Reckons it can't be worth wasting the effort if Wort, Huggins and Grimsley didn't publish it! The man's living in a time warp."

"I think we've got the gist of it thank you, Sorbo. So what next? Kate said you'd got a few other hopefuls."

"Don't want to go through anything like that again. I think I should ask Alan to weed them out before I go any further. I mean he got me into this in the first place, – well, him and kindred spirits. And surely there must be a kindred spirit somewhere in the world who's into book publishing? Yes, as you know I'm hardly into modern technology, but I did think about the electronic idea when He was talking to me, but of course He knew anyway. He said it should be a proper book in paper form, because people would need to read it again and again, or get somebody else to read it to them. And most of the people He really wants it to get to wouldn't have computers or mobile phones."

"So, Sorbo, – you wanna be a paperback writer, yeah?"

"Kate! Did you have to?"

"Really sorry Charles, but honestly it just slipped out before I could stop it. Sometimes does that when I'm thinking about other things, – like food for instance, then. Anyway, you must both admit it was the first time for ages, so I must be getting a bit better. Shall I get your crutches out of the boot, Sorbo?"

"No, thank you very much. Never mind what Simon said. People may know I'm old but I'm not having them see I'm crippled as well. If you can squeeze into that space near the gate it's not far for me to walk and there's plenty to hold on to on the way."

"Apart from seeing you know who Sorbo, I can understand why you like the Rose and Crown. The food's good value, and it makes a very pleasant change to find a country pub that puts on a different special every night. By the way, I forgot to ask what name you gave them at the Grimsley outfit. No, not really, – just a bit puzzled that you weren't Grundy."

"Heppingstal. He said I should use that for the book. Apparently, Dr. Manitoba J. Heppingstal is an Emeritus Professor of Cell Toxicology, and his hobby is ancient Shinto philosophy. Should be obscure enough to avoid too many people trying to engage me in small talk. Oh, and according to the girl at Grimsley's office I'm Canadian. Yes, and you wouldn't believe the story I gave them. I'll tell you about it later, as He would say. No pudding thanks, – nice idea but it would just send me to sleep when I should be working. But there's no great hurry, so don't let me stop you. I'm quite happy sitting here people-watching, if you know what I mean."

"Yes Sorbo, I really believe we do."

CHAPTER 10

Saturday 3rd May 2014 – 08.00

"Morning Sorbo. Excuse me coming up to your room, but I thought I'd better see how you were this morning as you're usually down in the kitchen well before now."

"I'm feeling fine thanks Kate. Should be, with all the attention I've been getting for the last few weeks. But I'm puzzled. How on earth did you and Charles get my bed upstairs again?"

"Sorry Sorbo, – I'm not sure I understand."

"Well, since I got home from the hospital I've been sleeping in the lounge as we decided that the stairs were a bit too much for my new hip. And working there on my new computer. But now I'm suddenly back in my old bedroom. So that's why I'm puzzled."

"Sorbo, I think I'd better get Charles to come up. Between us we've got some sorting out to do."

***

"So you see Sorbo that after we picked you up from Sevenoaks the three of us had dinner at the Rose and Crown. Kate and I were going home in the car, but you decided the walk would do you good. We left just after eight. As you were crossing the road, a car came speeding along and in your hurry to get out of the way you tripped on the kerb and hit your head on the wall of the house opposite the pub. Quite a bump and you were out for half a minute or so, but after you came round we gave you the once over and decided that it was safe to drive you home. So you didn't need to go to hospital. But you will have to take it easy for a day or so."

"What about all the other things? You know, the haematoma, liver transplant and hip replacement."

"Very pleased to say that the only things you suffered were a nasty graze on your forehead, and these after effects of mild concussion."

"So I haven't written a book at all?

"Not unless you've done it in twelve hours."

"No it's been almost three weeks. Let me see. What's the date today? No, it can't be the 3rd May. I didn't finish writing until Monday 19th, and I went up to London to see that idiot of a publisher yesterday – the 20th. So anyway, if it's not the 21st May and if you're not the Charles and Kate who were the paramedics who were really doctors in the Air Ambulance which took me to St. George's on the 2nd May, who on earth are you and what are you doing here?"

"It's OK Sorbo. Yes we are Kate and Charles and we are both doctors. But not with any Air Ambulance. We're both GPs attached to your surgery in Sevenoaks. We needed somewhere to live locally, so we've been renting your annexe for the last six months. And we often join you for dinner at the Rose and Crown, as we did last night. You've had quite a shock, so we'll leave you to rest for a while and we'll see you later. Might get a Chinese takeaway for this evening if you'd like that. OK, you're on."

19.00 Saturday

"Mmm. This is really excellent. Where did you get it?"

"When he lived in New Addington Charles used to go to super place in Westerham, but that's a bit far from here, so recently I've tried a couple in Borough Green. Both very good, but this is my favourite. And great value too. How's the head?"

"OK now, thanks. I dozed on and off for most of the day and I feel a lot better. And I'm pleased to say that I've got my memory back, so I do know who you both are. But I'm still a bit puzzled. Are you both seriously telling me that in the brief moment I blacked out, I actually lived every second of every day for nearly three weeks? It's unbelievable."

"Well it certainly doesn't happen very often to the extent that you've experienced. But it's not unbelievable, Sorbo. Not if you realise how fast the human brain can work when it's in a subconscious state, – a sort of dreamlike mode if you like. Years are condensed into seconds. But the power of the human brain is nothing compared with the speed of recall of the soul at the moment you die. Everything you have ever thought or said or done right from the time your soul enters its temporary Earthly body until the moment it leaves, will be replayed to you in a fraction of a second. Yes, your whole life, – in detail, – in a fraction of a second. There can be no escape as it is all indelibly recorded in your soul. All of the good bits, but also all of your selfish transgressions. You are accountable for all of them, and how well or badly you have reacted to temptation will determine your soul's next destination. Some people don't think they have a soul. These people will learn, but for many it will be an unpleasant awakening. Anyhow, enough of that. Are you going to try to recreate the book you thought you'd already written? Because if so, we really will have to get you a new computer."

"I've thought a lot about that and somehow I've got a sort of weird feeling that it's already been started. No idea yet, but I should know more in a couple of days. Oh, and by the way I've found out my real family name after all these years. From now on I am Andrew Sebastian Brandon. Yes, Brandon, not Grundy. Don't worry, you can still call me Sorbo, and now I even know where that nickname comes from as well. They say God moves in mysterious ways, but I've never properly understood that. Until now. Goodnight to you both. See you in the morning."

"Can't say I know what he was talking about, Charles. You?"

"No, but he's obviously up to something. He wants to go to London on Monday, but this time not to a publisher. If anything, I think I'd say that it was Sorbo Gru ... er ... Brandon who moves in mysterious ways."

CHAPTER 11

Monday 5th May 2014 – 15.00

The British Library is an awesome place. At least, that's how it felt to Sorbo as he entered. Even more so when he was ushered in to the Chief Executive's large and impressive office. Something of almost nineteenth century grandeur about it, he mused. Wouldn't like to be a staff member called into here for a carpeting.

"Good afternoon, Mr. Brandon. Please be seated. Yes, that will be fine."

Sorbo sat facing Roger Instone. An imposing figure of a man, in his early sixties he thought. Sparkling blue eyes behind designer frames, well-groomed silver-grey hair, and an immaculately tailored suit to match.

"Mr. Brandon, you gave one of my assistants the ISBN, – sorry, International Standard Book Number, – of a publication you were enquiring about, but her search showed nothing. The number does have the modern thirteen digits, but could you possibly have made a mistake somewhere?

"No, sir. I wrote them down very carefully and re-checked them."

"Well, I have to tell you that the search did not in fact draw a blank. It flagged up 'Access Restricted', which meant that she had immediately to alert me. My computer has a mass of information which is not available to any other staff members, and I keyed in your ISBN. To find that a number has not yet been issued is quite commonplace, as you might imagine, but what my screen shows isn't that at all.

To start with, the ISBN is that of a book which has apparently already been written and filed, but will not be published for over five years. That, in itself, is something I have never heard of before, – to call it odd would be an understatement. What my computer is showing is this Title – GOD KNOWS (Or Sorbo Grundy), Author – Manitoba Heppingstal, Publication date – 15th August 2019. That is all I can tell you as, for some unknown reason, the entire contents of the book have a Government security classification of 'Top Secret', and I am not cleared to that level. But even if were I wouldn't be able to divulge anything to you. I've been working in libraries for the whole of my life, but I've never come across anything even remotely like this. Maybe you know a little more than I do Mr. Gru ... er ... Brandon?"

Sorbo suppressed the slightest trace of a smile as he replied ... "Maybe." ?

18.15

"Thanks for coming to meet me. Actually it's only about a mile and a half and it's quite a nice walk in decent weather, but not in this sort of wind and rain though.

Dinner at the Rose and Crown? Absolutely fine by me, but this time I will accept a lift home afterwards. I always seem to get into trouble in Wrotham High Street. Kate, you remember you mentioned a new computer? Yes, the one you didn't buy for me when I wasn't in St. George's Hospital. Well, I will need it now. Nothing fancy, just for word processing basically. I don't have a clue what to look for, so is it possible that either of you could come with me to Maidstone and tell me what I need."

"Yes, of course. I will. Charles is on duty tomorrow afternoon but I've got a couple of hours off and we can go then. So you really are going to start writing after all?"

"I must. I promised Him that I would try to reach out to the billions of kindred spirits worldwide and get His entire message across to them. And that would fill about four thousand pages, so the first book is just the briefest outline of a few of the things he told me. Although only God knows how that's already been written, because I certainly don't. Anyway, that's just the beginning and it's now up to me to carry on and get the rest of it on paper.

What am I going to call it? God knows, Kate – **GOD KNOWS**."

The author

Manitoba July Heppingstal was born in Yorkshire in April 1956 to Gladys, chartered accountant wife of research chemist Thomas Heppingstal. From an early age Manitoba showed a fascination for all things scientific. He excelled in physics and biology and after high school in Hull he studied at universities in Scotland and Canada where he was awarded first-class degrees in both subjects. He is an emeritus professor of cell toxicology.

Manitoba lives with his second wife Mitzi Bamberger and their three border collies, Ruff, Scruff and Snuff, in a converted barn near Windermere in the English Lake District. They have an open house for their many visitors including their seven children and five grandchildren. Manitoba and Mitzi share interests in walking, cycling, tennis and astronomy, and they have recently converted part of the upper storey of their home into a well-equipped observatory.

Although he has authored many scientific papers, GOD KNOWS (or Sorbo Grundy) is Manitoba Heppingstal's first published novel.

The publisher

novum PUBLISHER FOR NEW AUTHORS

> *He who stops getting better stops being good.*

This is the motto of novum publishing, and our focus is on finding new manuscripts, publishing them and offering long-term support to the authors.
Our publishing house was founded in 1997, and since then it has become THE expert for new authors and has won numerous awards.

Our editorial team will peruse each manuscript within a few weeks free of charge and without obligation.

You will find more information about
novum publishing and our books on the internet:

w w w . n o v u m - p u b l i s h i n g . c o . u k